FINAL OUT

ALSO BY SHELDON SIEGEL

Mike Daley/Rosie Fernandez Novels

Special Circumstances
Incriminating Evidence
Criminal Intent
Final Verdict
The Confession
Judgment Day
Perfect Alibi
Felony Murder Rule
Serve and Protect
Hot Shot
The Dreamer
Final Out

David Gold/A.C. Battle Novels

The Terrorist Next Door

FINAL OUT

A Mike Daley/Rosie Fernandez Thriller

SHELDON SIEGEL

Sheldon M. Siegel, Inc.

Cover Design by Alan Siegel

ISBN: 978-1-952612-01-5 E-Book
ISBN: 978-1-952612-02-2 Paperback
ISBN: 978-1-952612-03-9 Hardcover

For Joe, Jan & Julia Garber

1
"THAT WASN'T AN ESPECIALLY WISE CHOICE"

The Honorable Robert J. Stumpf, Jr. scanned the empty gallery in his airless courtroom on the second floor of San Francisco's crumbling Hall of Justice. He arched a bushy gray eyebrow over his aviator-style glasses, flashed a charismatic smile, and spoke to me in a melodious baritone. "Nice to see you, Mr. Daley. You haven't appeared before me in several years."

"Thank you, Your Honor. It's good to be back."

At ten a.m. on Wednesday, June third, Judge Stumpf's courtroom smelled of mildew. The Hall of Justice had been declared unsafe in an earthquake, and the fifties-era warhorse was being mothballed department by department at a snail's pace. The Southern Police Station had moved to the new headquarters near the ballpark. The Public Defender's Office was around the corner on Seventh. The D.A. had relocated to a refurbished building at the foot of Potrero Hill. The Medical Examiner was now housed in a state-of-the art facility in India Basin.

On the other hand, some things hadn't changed since I had first entered the Hall as a rookie Public Defender more than a quarter of a century earlier. You could still pay your parking tickets at the window in the lobby. The Homicide Detail was still ensconced on the third floor. The two dozen courtrooms and judges' chambers were on the second and third floors. And the top two floors still housed the dingy County Jail Number 4, although most of the inmates were now located in the newer jail facility that was jammed between the Hall and the freeway in the nineties, or at County Jail Number 5, the Costco-like building fifteen miles south of here in the hills of San Bruno.

Judge Stumpf's smile broadened. "Please give my best to our distinguished Public Defender."

"I will, Your Honor." My boss, Rosita Carmela Fernandez, was San Francisco's first Latina Public Defender. She had recently won re-election for a second term. She was also my ex-wife and former law partner.

"Thank you, Mr. Daley."

The lanky native of Southern Indiana and one-time backup center on the USF basketball team had been a Superior Court judge longer than I had been a lawyer. He was appointed to the bench by Jerry Brown during his first stint as governor. Judge Stumpf worked his way up to presiding judge where he remained entrenched even though he had turned seventy-five a few months earlier. Along the way, he earned a reputation as smart, thoughtful, and practical. His gregarious manner and acerbic wit complemented a keen intellect and a thoroughness that wasn't always the norm among some of his colleagues. He still maintained a robust docket that put many of his younger associates to shame.

He rested his chin in his palm. "I didn't expect to see the co-head of the Felony Division of the Public Defender's Office here to argue a pre-trial motion."

"I'm pinch-hitting for my colleague, Ms. Nikonova, who is returning from her honeymoon later today."

His eyes lit up. "Nady and Max finally got married?"

"They did."

"Splendid news. Please extend my best wishes."

"I will."

Nadezhda "Nady" Nikonova was a whip-smart fellow alum of the law school at UC-Berkeley. Her tenacity and work ethic were matched by her husband, Max, a partner at one of the big firms downtown. After a decade-long engagement, they had postponed their wedding twice. The first time, Nady was in the middle of a murder trial. The second time, Max was called in to handle a securities fraud case after one of his partners was unceremoniously fired for engaging in Harvey Weinstein-style behavior. The third time was the charm, and I had promised to keep an eye on Nady's cases until she and Max got back from Maui.

Judge Stumpf's expression turned serious. "I see that we're here to discuss a motion to dismiss a grand theft charge against Rudolph Coleman."

"That's correct, Your Honor."

"Is Rudy here?"

"He is."

I nodded at the burly sheriff's deputy, who escorted my client from the holding tank to the defense table. Rudy Coleman was an army vet and a decent guy who lived in a single-room occupancy hotel, or "SRO," on Sixth Street, about a half mile north of the Hall. Now pushing fifty, the native of Hunters Point had completed two tours in Afghanistan. He returned depressed, disillusioned, and impulsive. He worked as a night clerk at a hotel in the Tenderloin for a couple of years until he began drinking heavily. Unable to hold a job, he started stealing to pay for the booze. Rudy wasn't the brightest guy in the world, but he'd never hurt anyone. He was a regular customer at the P.D.'s Office.

He took the seat next to mine. He was sporting a standard-issue orange jumpsuit. His salt-and-pepper hair was buzzed short.

I leaned over and whispered, "You good to go?"

His eyes fluttered as he answered in a smoky rasp. "Yeah, Mike."

"Judge Stumpf is a stickler for decorum. I need you to be respectful."

"I know. I've been here before."

The judge looked over at the prosecution table. "Good morning, Mr. Erickson."

"Good morning, Your Honor."

Andy Erickson had just turned forty. The alum of St. Ignatius High School (also my alma mater), USF, and USF Law School had spent fifteen years working the internal politics of the D.A's Office until he was rewarded with a promotion to the head of the Felony Unit. Smart, meticulous, and, above all, patient, Andy was now angling for the Chief Assistant job with an eye toward an eventual run for D.A. While he wasn't above throwing an occasional sharp elbow in court, he was generally a straight shooter, so I gave him a little more deference than some of the other hardworking public servants at the D.A.'s Office. In return, he let me use his dad's tickets behind the Giants dugout once or twice a season.

The judge pointed his glasses at Erickson. "I take it that you and Mr. Daley have been unable to reach a resolution of Rudy's case?"

"Correct, Your Honor."

The judge turned to me. "What's the issue, Mr. Daley?"

"Mr. Erickson has charged Rudy with felony grand theft under California Penal Code Section 487. However, Section 459.5 states that a person can be charged with grand theft only if he steals merchandise with a value greater than nine hundred and fifty dollars. Rudy did not."

The judge shifted his gaze to Erickson. "I take it that you disagree with Mr. Daley?"

"I do, Your Honor."

"Perhaps you could fill us in on the details?"

"Of course. At approximately ten-fifteen a.m. on Friday, May twenty-first, the defendant entered Liberal Jewelry and Loan on Sixth Street with intent to steal merchandise."

I stopped him. "You don't know what was going on inside Rudy's head, Mr. Erickson."

"Gimme a break, Mr. Daley."

The judge mimicked a basketball referee by forming the letter T with his hands. "Time out, gentlemen. Let's keep this professional." He looked at Erickson. "Am I correct that Liberal Jewelry and Loan is a pawn shop?"

"It is."

Located between a liquor store and the XXX Arcade and Adult Superstore, Liberal Jewelry and Loan was a landmark on skid row.

The judge looked at me. "Are you disputing that Rudy went inside the store?"

"No, Your Honor. But I am disputing Mr. Erickson's contention that he did so for the purpose of stealing."

Judge Stumpf had an excellent poker face, but his expression suggested skepticism. "Mr. Daley, why did your client go inside the pawn shop?"

"To buy bait."

"Excuse me?"

"Worms, Your Honor. Rudy was going fishing."

The judge looked at Rudy. "True?"

"Yes, Your Honor. I like to fish at the pier behind the Ferry Building. It's relaxing."

"You buy bait at a pawn shop?"

"Yes, Your Honor. The bait shop is connected to the pawn shop."

"Really?"

"Really."

Really. "Your Honor," I said, "in a rather unusual example of business integration, the owner of Liberal Jewelry and Loan also owns its next-door neighbor, Liberal Fishing Tackle and Supply. To get into the fishing store, you enter through the pawn shop and turn left."

"Seriously?"

"Seriously. The fishing store has been there almost a hundred years. The pawn shop came along a little later. The former owner of the fishing store sold both storefronts to the current owners of the pawn shop, who decided to keep the fishing store. Incidentally, the pawn shop also has a location in Santa Rosa, but it isn't connected to a fishing store."

"Uh, right." He turned to Erickson. "Putting aside the issue of why Rudy entered the store, did he actually take anything?"

"Yes, Your Honor. The defendant entered the pawn shop while the manager was assisting a customer." Erickson held up a clear plastic evidence bag. "When the manager's back was turned, the defendant took this Omega Speedmaster Racing Automatic Chronograph watch from the counter and left the store. Retail value: thirty-five hundred dollars."

"It's a used watch," I said. "As a result, its value was substantially lower."

"It'll be your turn in a minute, Mr. Daley." Judge Stumpf was still looking at Erickson. "Did the manager see the defendant take the watch?"

"No, Your Honor. Neither did the customer."

"So there's security video?"

"No, Your Honor. The camera was broken."

"How do you know that the defendant took the watch?"

Erickson smirked. "He came back a couple of days later and tried to pawn it."

Judge Stumpf couldn't help himself and cracked a smile. "Rudy tried to pawn the watch at the very same store from which he had stolen it?"

"That's correct, Your Honor."

"You're absolutely sure that it's the same watch?"

"Yes, Your Honor. It still had the tag from Liberal Jewelry and Loan when he brought it back to the store."

The judge spun around in his swivel chair, faced the Seal of California on the wall behind him, and stifled a laugh by pretending to cough. He took a moment to regain his composure before he turned around and spoke to me. "Are any of these facts in dispute, Mr. Daley?"

"No, Your Honor." Unfortunately, the Public Defender's Office is not allowed to administer an intelligence test to a potential client before we take on their representation.

Judge Stumpf's expression turned sympathetic as he looked at Rudy and opted for understatement. "That wasn't an especially wise choice, Rudy."

"I know, Your Honor."

I had also gently pointed out to Rudy that as a matter of good criminal practice, it's generally a bad idea to try to pawn a watch at the store from which you've stolen it.

The judge folded his arms. "Why are we here, Mr. Daley?"

Here goes. "We are not disagreeing with the fact that Rudy took the watch. However, we are disputing Mr. Erickson's decision to charge him with felony grand larceny. This case is a 'wobbler.' At most, Rudy should have been charged with misdemeanor shoplifting."

In legal lingo, a "wobbler" refers to a case where the D.A. has discretion to charge the defendant with a felony or a misdemeanor depending upon the severity of the crime and the attendant circumstances. While this may seem like lawyerly hair splitting, there were real-world consequences for Rudy. The maximum sentence for misdemeanor shoplifting is six months. The maximum for felony grand larceny is a year. When you're in jail, an extra six months is a long time.

"How do you figure, Mr. Daley?" the judge asked.

"Section 459.5 of the Penal Code says that shoplifting has three elements. First, you need to enter a commercial establishment. Second, it has to be during normal business hours. And third, you have to take something valued at nine hundred and fifty dollars or less."

"Mr. Erickson just told us that the watch is worth thirty-five hundred dollars."

"That's if you buy it new at a jewelry store. The value of a second-hand watch is substantially less. It's like buying a new car—it loses much of its value when you drive it out of the showroom."

"You're saying that it was worth less than nine hundred and fifty dollars?"

"Yes, Your Honor."

"We disagree," Erickson said. "We have provided the court with an independent appraisal stating that the watch is valued at approximately twelve hundred dollars."

"We dispute the appraisal," I said.

The judge shook his head. "You didn't submit one of your own."

"We didn't need to. We already had one."

"From whom?"

"The manager of Liberal Jewelry and Loan. He offered Rudy five hundred dollars."

The judge looked at Erickson. "True?"

"Uh, true."

I held up my hand triumphantly. "There you have it."

Erickson feigned indignation. "Your Honor, everybody knows that when you pawn something, the store offers you substantially less than its ultimate sale value. The pawn shop makes a profit by selling the merchandise for more than it paid. In this case, the manager offered the defendant five hundred dollars for a watch that he believed he could have resold for at least twelve hundred dollars."

"You're saying that the value was twelve hundred dollars?"

"Correct."

Incorrect. "Your Honor," I said, "the value was the amount that the manager offered to Rudy: five hundred dollars."

Erickson was adamant. "That's not how I read the statute, Mr. Daley."

"That's how I read it, Mr. Erickson." I turned back to the judge. "An item's value is what a person can get for it in an arms-length transaction when neither party is under duress. In this case, the manager offered Rudy five hundred dollars. That was its value."

Erickson wasn't buying. "But the *intrinsic* value of the watch was substantially higher."

"The statute doesn't say anything about *intrinsic* value. If I offer you a thousand dollars for your tie, that's its value even though there isn't another person on Planet Earth who would pay you so much. The fact that I might be able to sell it to somebody else for two grand doesn't change its value to you."

"That's ridiculous, Mr. Daley."

"No, it's not." *Well, maybe.* "A one-bedroom condo here in the City costs more than a million dollars. The same unit would sell for a tenth of that amount in many places. I don't know what its *intrinsic* value is under your definition, but I know that the value to the seller is whatever somebody is willing to pay."

"You're playing word games."

"No, I'm not." *Yes, I am.* "Value means whatever a person is willing to pay—period."

An expression of bemusement crossed Judge Stumpf's face as he sat back and listened to us argue for the next five minutes. He knew that Erickson and I were just making stuff up on the fly. Finally, he put on his glasses, cleared his throat, and made the call.

"Mr. Erickson, I understand that the manager believed that he could have gotten more than nine hundred and fifty dollars for the watch."

Erickson looked up hopefully.

"However, I am inclined to agree with Mr. Daley that 'value' means what it means: the amount to be paid by one party to another in a negotiated transaction. In this case, it would be the sum that the pawn shop offered to pay Rudy. I am therefore ruling that the value of the watch is five hundred dollars."

Ta-da!

"I am further ruling that it is inappropriate to charge Rudy with felony grand larceny. This does not preclude you from re-filing charges for shoplifting. I would encourage you and Mr. Daley to discuss an appropriate resolution on that charge."

"Yes, Your Honor." Erickson looked at me. "In the interest of expediency, would your client be willing to plead guilty to misdemeanor shoplifting in exchange for a three-month sentence with credit for time served?"

I looked over at Rudy, who nodded. "Yes, Mr. Erickson."

"I think we're in agreement."

Judge Stumpf smiled triumphantly. "It's a good day for justice. As always, Mr. Erickson, the court thanks you for your courtesy and professionalism. Mr. Daley, it has been a while since I have had the privilege of listening to one of your imaginative arguments. You bring a certain amount of creativity to our otherwise mundane proceedings."

"Thank you, Your Honor."

"We're adjourned."

* * *

A few minutes later, I was collecting my belongings at the defense table in the otherwise empty courtroom when the door opened, and the Public Defender of the City and County of San Francisco marched down the center aisle toward me. At fifty-four,

Rosie Fernandez brought a commanding presence. Twenty-six years after we'd met upstairs in the file room of the old Public Defender's Office, she was still the most beautiful woman and the best lawyer I had ever known.

"How did things go for Rudy?" she asked.

"I cut a deal for misdemeanor shoplifting. Three months with credit for time served."

"Not bad."

"I didn't expect to see you here this morning."

Her mouth turned up. "I like to keep an eye on my subordinates."

"Why are you really here?"

"I have a status conference." She tugged at the sleeve of her Hermes blouse, which was more elegant than the jeans and denim shirts that she used to wear when we were rookie Public Defenders. She had upgraded her wardrobe when she ran for her first term as P.D. five years earlier. "We have a new client upstairs. I want you to handle the intake interview."

"Sure. What's going on?"

"They pulled a body out of the bay behind the ballpark yesterday. Turns out that he was one of your former law partners."

Rosie and I left the P.D.'s Office after we got divorced. She started her own practice, and I went to work for a megafirm at the top of the Bank of America Building to pay child support for our daughter, Grace, who was two at the time. I was fired after the partners decided that they didn't like rubbing elbows with my clients who were technically, uh, criminals. Rosie took me in, and we'd been working together ever since. Eventually, we returned to the P.D.'s Office as the co-heads of the Felony Division. After our former boss retired, Rosie was elected as P.D.

Things had worked out reasonably well. Rosie and I have maintained a "divorcees-with-benefits" relationship which has lasted substantially longer than our marriage. Grace was now a college grad who worked as a production assistant at Pixar. Our son, Tommy, arrived a few years after Rosie and I got divorced. He had just graduated from high school and was heading to college at Cal in the fall.

"Which former partner?" I asked.

"Robert Blum."

Robbie Blum had the good fortune of being born into a well-connected San Francisco family. His father was a federal judge. His mother was a legislative analyst for Senator Dianne Feinstein. He grew up in the tony Sea Cliff neighborhood near the Golden Gate Bridge, attended the exclusive University High School, and later graduated from Harvard and Stanford Law School. He inherited the house in Sea Cliff and a rather substantial fortune when his parents died. He developed a lucrative practice representing media conglomerates, entertainment companies, and sports teams. He was also the subject of several multi-million-dollar settlements for sexual harassment. After he negotiated a nine-figure merger between two sports agencies, he got the bug to represent athletes himself, and he set up his own agency. Ten years later, his clients included a half dozen NFL quarterbacks, two NBA MVPs, and several members of the Giants.

"You knew him?" Rosie asked.

"I met him once. Power guys like Blum didn't talk to peons like me. I left the firm shortly after he arrived. Even in a big law firm filled with egos, he was a super-nova jerk." I looked my ex-wife in the eye. "What happened?"

"His skull was crushed."

Ouch. "Who do they think crushed it?"

"Our new client."

2
"I WAS MEETING SOMEBODY"

The wiry African-American man with the closely cropped hair, boyish features, and expressive brown eyes looked at me through scuffed Plexiglas. He adjusted his orange jumpsuit and spoke in a high-pitched voice. "Are you my lawyer?"

"Yes." At eleven-fifteen a.m., the heavy air smelled of disinfectant as I leaned on the dented metal ledge on the visitor side of the partition in the consultation area next to the raucous intake center of the jail on the seventh floor of the Hall. I pressed the phone to my ear. "Mike Daley. I'm with the Public Defender's Office."

"Jaylen Jenkins." His eyes locked onto mine. "I didn't kill Robbie Blum."

"Good to know."

Well, maybe not so good. We defense lawyers never ask our clients if they're guilty. The California Rules of Professional Conduct prohibit us from letting them lie on the stand, so I try to avoid putting myself into situations where I may be tempted to do so. In this case, if I found out that Jaylen did, in fact, kill Blum, I couldn't let him testify that he didn't. In all honesty, I've found ways to dance around this rule from time to time.

I held up a hand. "We'll talk about what happened in a minute. How old are you?"

"Twenty-five."

"You grew up around here?"

"Oakland—before it was woke."

"You still live there?"

"Yes."

"Ever been arrested?"

"Once for auto theft. A couple of times for shoplifting. No convictions."

"Good. Before we get started, I need to explain a few ground rules. First, don't talk to anybody but me. Not the guards, not the cops, not the prosecutors, and, most important, not the other inmates. Second, you need to assume that they're taping us now, and they may be taping you in your cell. So, you need to be careful about what you say."

"Got it."

"Third, you need to tell me the complete, absolute, and unvarnished truth, and you can't leave anything out. I will be very unhappy if you lie to me and the truth comes out in court. Any questions so far?"

"How soon can you get me out of here?"

That's always at the top of the list. "There will be an arraignment tomorrow where they'll read the charges. You will plead not guilty in a respectful voice. The San Francisco D.A. recently adopted a policy against asking for money bail in most cases, so I'll try to convince the judge that you aren't a flight risk. Even if you agree to wear an ankle bracelet, it will be very difficult to get you out if they charge you with murder. Do you have any family in the area?"

"Just my mother."

"Does she know that you're here?"

"I left a message on her phone, but she doesn't always pick up."

"When was the last time that you talked to her?"

"A couple of weeks ago. She's in a halfway house in Oakland. She's in rehab—again." He gave me an address and phone number.

"Did you live with her before she went into rehab?"

"Yes. We had an apartment near the West Oakland BART Station."

"We'll find her. Who else should we call?"

He shrugged.

"Are you married?"

"No."

"Girlfriend?"

"No."

"Boyfriend?"

"No."

"Kids?"

"No."

"Brothers or sisters?"

"Two older brothers. One is at Pelican Bay for armed robbery. The other died in a gang shootout a couple of years ago."

"I'm sorry. Anybody else?"

"No."

How sad. "Tell me a little more about yourself, Jaylen."

He took a deep breath and filled in some details. Born and raised in Oakland. Lived in the projects west of downtown with his mother and brothers. Never knew his father. His mother was in and out of rehab. His oldest brother was in and out of prison. His other brother got caught up with the gangs. Jaylen played baseball at McClymonds High School, where he showed enough potential to generate some interest from colleges, but he didn't have the grades or the money to attend. Worked at McDonald's and KFC. More recently, he drove for Uber and Lyft.

"You still driving?" I asked.

"No."

"What are you doing now?"

The corner of his mouth turned up. "I'm an entrepreneur."

Uh-huh. "What do you sell?"

"T-shirts and caps outside the Giants, A's, and Warriors games. I sell stuff online, too."

"Were you buying the stuff legally?"

"Most of the time."

Right. "Were you selling anything else?"

"Every once in a while, I was able to get my hands on some iPhones and laptops. I made some real money there."

"Stolen?"

"Not by me."

We have more pressing issues at the moment. "You were working at the ballpark on Monday night?"

"Yeah." He said that he set up a table on the sidewalk on King Street near the players' parking lot behind the left field wall. "The Giants won't let me sell on the stadium property."

"How was business?"

"Not great. The crowds are smaller when the team is losing."

"What time did you go home?"

"It was close to midnight."

"The game ended around ten. Why did you stay so late?"

His eyes darted over my shoulder. "I was meeting somebody."

"Who?"

"Robbie Blum."

3
"I RAN ERRANDS FOR HIM"

"You knew him?" I asked.

"Yeah."

"How well?"

"Not that well."

How do I say this? "How did a guy who sells T-shirts outside the ballpark meet a high-powered lawyer and sports agent?"

"He liked to stop at my stand after games and buy stuff for his son."

Not convincing. Blum could have gotten anything he wanted inside the ballpark or from one of his clients. "Anything else?"

He waited a beat. "I ran errands for him."

Uh-huh. "He didn't have an assistant?"

"Yes, he did."

"But he hired you to pick up his laundry?"

"Other kinds of errands."

"What kind?"

He lowered his voice. "I picked up Molly for him."

"Molly" is a purer form of Ecstasy. The designer drug induces feelings of euphoria. It can also cause hypertension, cardiac issues, and hypothermia. In severe cases, it can be fatal.

I leaned closer to the Plexiglas. "You sold it to him?"

"No, I picked it up from his supplier."

"You got a name?"

"If he finds out that I gave him up, he's going to be unhappy."

"It will be of interest to the D.A. If it comes down to a choice between the supplier and you, we'll give up the supplier."

"Brian Holton. He works the door at the Gold Club."

It was an upscale strip club near Moscone Center that was popular among the tech crowd. It's walking distance from the ballpark.

"Blum came to see you after the game to ask you to pick up drugs from Holton?"

"Yeah."

"How much did he pay you?"

"A thousand for Holton and five hundred for me. He also gave me some Giants swag to sell on eBay."

"Let's start at the beginning. How did you know that Blum wanted to see you?"

"He texted me." He said that they always communicated with burner phones. Jaylen also had an iPhone. "The cops took my burner and my iPhone."

"Did you give them your passwords?"

"I thought I had to."

"You didn't, but we'll assume that they have access to everything on your phones. Are they going to find anything damaging other than the fact that Blum contacted you?"

"No."

I hope so. "How often did you run errands for Blum?"

"Once or twice a month. He texted me when he needed something. We usually met by the ballpark."

"Was anybody else around?"

"No. The crowd had cleared out."

"Were you supposed to pick up the Molly from Holton that night?"

"The next night, but I never got there. They arrested me at my apartment the next day."

"Did you have the cash on you when you were arrested?"

"Yeah."

"The cops are going to say that it was robbery."

"It wasn't."

"How long did you talk to Blum?"

"A couple of minutes."

"I take it that you didn't see anybody hit Blum?"

"No."

"What aren't you telling me, Jaylen?"

"Nothing."

"Did Blum owe Holton a lot of money?"

"I don't know."

"Was Holton mad at Blum?"

"I don't know."

"Was anybody else mad at Blum?"

"I don't know."

Not helpful. "You talked to the cops?"

"Inspector Lee."

Ken Lee was a no-nonsense homicide inspector who wouldn't have arrested Jaylen unless he had something substantial.

"What did you tell him?" I asked.

"That I didn't kill Robbie."

"Seems he didn't believe you. Did you tell him that you knew Blum?"

"Yes. I said that Robbie used to buy stuff at my stand."

"Did you tell him about Holton?"

"No."

"What did he tell you?"

"He said that they have evidence that I killed Robbie."

"Did he mention what that evidence was?"

"No."

"I'll try to pay him a visit to see what I can find out."

4
"NO COMMENT"

"Got a sec?" I asked.

Inspector Ken Lee looked up from the sports section of the *Chronicle*. "I'm busy."

"This won't take long."

"One minute."

At two-fifteen p.m., Lee was sitting in a rickety swivel chair with his feet up on his gunmetal gray desk in the airless bullpen housing the Homicide Detail on the third floor of the Hall. The fluorescent lights buzzed. The chipped walls were a faded off-white. Since the building had been condemned, the City wasn't going to pay for a paint job. It reminded me of the last season at Candlestick Park—if an escalator broke, the City wasn't going to fix it.

Lee was the only one of San Francisco's two dozen homicide inspectors in the office. Presumably, his colleagues were out chasing bad guys and interviewing witnesses. "How'd you get inside?" he asked.

"I asked Lucy *very* nicely."

He feigned annoyance as he lowered his feet to the floor. "I need to talk to her—again."

It wasn't the first time that I had sweet-talked the longtime receptionist—a classmate of Rosie's at Mercy High School. "She's a good soul."

"She is."

For the most part, so was Lee. At forty-seven, the Chinatown native had been an inspector for a dozen years. He began his distinguished career working undercover in the crowded neighborhood where his parents owned a spice shop. He was promoted to homicide after he brought down one of Chinatown's deadliest gangs. He was trained by my father's first partner, the legendary Roosevelt Johnson, who took a promotion to homicide while Pop elected to stay on the street. Since Roosevelt retired, Lee had worked alone.

He didn't have to talk to me, so I decided to start with sugar. If that failed, I would move on to groveling. "Kids okay?"

He adjusted the sleeve of the charcoal suit that he bought off the rack at the Men's Wearhouse. "Fine. My older daughter is starting at Cal in the fall. The younger one will be a senior in high school. Life is going to get really expensive when I have two kids in college along with alimony and child support."

"Think of it as an investment. We'll be empty nesters in the fall. It goes by fast."

"It does." He put down the paper and stroked the scar that ran along his chin line—a memento from his undercover days. "To what do I owe the pleasure of a personal visit from the co-head of the Felony Division this fine afternoon?"

"Jaylen Jenkins."

"I didn't think you were doing cases anymore."

"We needed somebody on short notice. Nady is on her honeymoon. I was available."

"You going to pass it to somebody else?"

"Haven't decided."

"The arraignment is at ten-thirty tomorrow morning. I presume that your client will plead not guilty?"

"Correct. He told me that he didn't kill Robbie Blum."

"He lied. I would also remind you that I'm under no obligation to talk to you."

"Please, Ken. Just the basics."

"No comment."

"You arrested him for a reason."

"It was a righteous arrest."

"Evidence?"

"No comment."

"You're obligated to provide evidence that would tend to exonerate my client."

"I will—in due course."

"Cause of death?"

"Cracked skull."

"You believe that Jaylen hit him?"

"That's why we arrested him."

"Witnesses?"

"No comment."

"Video?"

"No comment."

"Motive?"

"Ask your client."

"He had none."

"He's lying about that, too."

"Evidence of premeditation?"

"In due course." He glanced at his watch. "Your minute is up."

"Charge?"

"You'll need to talk to the Assistant D.A. handling this case."

"Who is that?"

"Andy Erickson."

5
"FIRST-DEGREE MURDER"

Erickson rolled his eyes as I approached him in the empty corridor outside Judge Stumpf's courtroom at three o'clock on Wednesday afternoon. "I hope you aren't going to ask me to renegotiate Rudy Coleman's deal."

"I'm not."

"Good."

"I wanted to ask you about Jaylen Jenkins."

"Protocol requires you to set up an appointment through my assistant."

"I wanted to talk to you before the arraignment tomorrow morning."

"There's nothing to discuss, Mike. You know the drill. We show up in court. The judge reads the charges. Your client pleads not guilty. You ask for him to be released pending trial. We oppose it. The judge rules in our favor. You ask for a preliminary hearing within ten court days. And off we go."

Yup, that covers it. "Just a few highlights?"

"I need to get back to the office."

"I'll walk you to your car."

"I took an Uber."

"I'll walk you to your Uber."

"I can't stop you." He picked up his trial bag and headed down the hall.

I felt like a golden retriever as I walked alongside him. "What's the charge?"

"First-degree murder."

"Seriously?"

"Seriously."

"How did Blum die?"

"Your client crushed his skull."

"Witnesses?"

"No comment."

"Murder weapon?"

"No comment."

We reached the end of the corridor where Erickson opened the door to the stairway. We knew better than to take the sixty-year-old elevators.

"Motive?" I asked.

"I don't need to prove one."

"It'll help with a jury."

"In that case, no comment."

I followed him down the stairs and into the lobby. He waved at the security guards by the metal detectors, headed out the door, and walked down the steps past the smokers on the sidewalk. He pulled out his phone, summoned an Uber, and pretended to ignore me.

"You need premeditation for first-degree murder," I said.

"Thanks for bringing it to my attention."

"You have evidence?"

"We have video of your client following Blum."

Uh-oh. "It doesn't prove that he killed him."

"He was carrying a baseball bat."

6
"HE THANKED ME"

"I didn't kill Robbie," Jaylen insisted again, agitated.

"Keep your voice down," I said.

His voice was louder when he repeated, "I didn't kill Robbie."

An hour later, we were meeting in an attorney-client consultation room on the seventh floor of the Hall. It was better than talking through Plexiglas.

I tried to project calm. "The D.A. says that he has video of you following Blum."

"That's a lie."

"We're going to get a copy of it, Jaylen."

"It's still a lie."

"He said that you were carrying a bat."

No answer.

"If you have something to tell me, this would be a good time."

Still no answer.

"Let's take it from the top again, Jaylen. Tell me exactly what happened that night."

His story didn't change. He waited for Blum in his usual spot. Blum asked him to pick up Molly from his supplier the next day. Blum gave him fifteen hundred dollars along with a couple of Giants game jerseys. Blum went to his car. Jaylen went home.

I folded my arms. "I'm going to be really pissed off if the D.A. sends over video showing you chasing Blum with a bat in your hand."

A look of recognition crossed his face. "Robbie had a David Archer autographed bat that he was going to give to his son."

Archer was the Giants All-Star left fielder and cleanup hitter. He was also Blum's client.

Jaylen was still talking. "Robbie accidentally left the bat at my stand. I grabbed it and took it over to him as he was walking back to his car."

"You were running with a bat?"

"Jogging."

"How far?"

"About a hundred feet."

"Where did you catch up to him?"

"On the walking path between the players' lot and the marina."

"You gave him the bat?"

"Yeah." His eyes showed anger. "I didn't hit him."

"Did he say anything?"

"He thanked me." He added, "He said that his son would be happy."

"Then what?"

"I went back and collected my stuff and left."

"How long did you talk to him?"

"Just a minute."

"Was anybody else there?"

"No."

"Did he mention whether he was meeting somebody else?"

"He didn't say."

I paused to digest the new information. "If Erickson was telling the truth, a security camera must have caught you as you were jogging to catch up with Blum."

"Wouldn't surprise me. There are security cameras everywhere around the ballpark."

7
"WE HAVE A LOT OF WORK TO DO"

At six-thirty that evening, I knocked on the open door of the office next to mine. "Rosie said that you had contractions last night."

The co-head of the Felony Division looked up from her laptop. "False alarm, Mike. Zach and I spent some quality time at Saint Francis Hospital. Turns out that it was a combination of indigestion and cramps."

"So you're good?"

"I'm fine."

Rolanda Fernandez's straight black hair matched her eyes and nail polish. At thirty-five, Rosie's niece (and, technically, my ex-niece) could have passed for Rosie's younger sister. Her father, Tony, was Rosie's older brother. He ran a produce market in the Mission. The woman that Rosie and I had once babysat was now one of our best attorneys. She also had the unenviable job of riding herd on her ex-uncle to make sure that he completed his administrative duties. At the moment, she was also eight months pregnant with a baby girl.

I pointed at her stomach. "She okay?"

"Fine."

"Have you decided on a name?"

"Yes."

"You going to tell me?"

"No."

Okay. "What set off your stomach?"

"Enchiladas from Gracias Madre."

"An excellent choice." It was an upscale organic-vegan restaurant on Mission Street. Even carnivores like me thought their food was other-worldly. "Their food is very light."

"You never know when you're pregnant." Her lips transformed

into a radiant smile that was identical to Rosie's. "I heard you cut a deal for Rudy Coleman."

"Misdemeanor shoplifting."

"Not bad. I heard you picked up the Jaylen Jenkins case. You gonna do it yourself?"

"I think so. I talked to Andy Erickson. He claimed that Jaylen clocked Robbie Blum with a Louisville Slugger. Jaylen said he didn't."

"That gives you the deciding vote."

"I'll give Jaylen the benefit of the doubt until I have reason to believe otherwise."

"Anything I can do to help?"

"Yes. You were supposed to take off on Friday. I want you to go home, rest up, and have a healthy baby. We have your cases covered, and you have the rest of your life to be a lawyer."

"Thanks, Mike."

"It's the least that I can do. If you weren't here to help me with the admin stuff, Rosie would have fired me years ago."

"I doubt that."

I lowered my voice. "I know that Rosie and I got divorced a long time ago, but I'm always going to think of you as my niece."

"You're always going to be my uncle, Mike."

"Is it okay if I think of your daughter as my great-niece?"

"Absolutely."

"Good to hear. You'll let us know when the contractions start again?"

"Yes. Anything else?"

"Go home. And stay away from enchiladas."

* * *

"Is Rosie here?" I asked.

Our secretary, paralegal, process server, and, on occasion, bodyguard, looked up from his computer and pointed at the door to Rosie's office. "She's inside with Nady."

"Thanks, T."

Terrence "The Terminator" Love was a former heavyweight

boxer who lost more fights than he won. The recovering alcoholic and one-time semi-professional shoplifter had been my very first client. Over the years, I had cut countless deals and lost more trials than I won for the gentle giant who looked like Shaquille O'Neal. A decade earlier, I hired him as the receptionist at the law firm that Rosie and I were running at the time as part of a plea bargain that I had negotiated with a sympathetic judge. It was the best deal that I ever cut for him—and us. Terrence hadn't missed a day of work or taken a drink ever since.

He scratched his bald dome. "Did you finish your time report?"

"Working on it."

"What about the office supplies budget?"

"Working on that, too."

"Work faster." His broad smile revealed a gold front tooth as he let out a throaty laugh. "I can't cover for you forever, Mike."

"I'll take care of it, T."

I headed inside where Rosie was sitting behind the mahogany desk that she had bought on her own dime. Twenty years earlier, the P.D.'s Office had moved into a remodeled building on Seventh Street that once housed an auto repair shop. Except for the desk, Rosie's office was furnished in what she called "Twenty-first Century Bureaucrat." A bookcase from Scandinavian Design. A credenza that she inherited from her predecessor. A conference table that was a repurposed dinette set from IKEA.

"You good?" I asked.

"Fine."

"Kids okay?"

"Yes."

"Your mother?"

"Fine."

All accounted for. We had reached the point in our lives where every conversation began with a status report on family members. Rosie's mother, Sylvia, had just turned eighty-five, and she still lived in the bungalow in the Mission where Rosie had grown up. Sylvia was still as sharp as ever and her mobility had improved after her second knee replacement, but there was always the possibility that we would get a phone call about a medical issue.

Nadezhda "Nady" Nikonova sat in the chair on the opposite side of Rosie's desk. A couple of years earlier, I had liberated her from a high-end downtown firm. Smart, intense, and driven, she was one of our most promising attorneys. She was also a true believer that the disenfranchised were entitled to representation—traits that were useful in our line of work.

"When did you get in?" I asked.

Nady twirled her shoulder-length dirty blonde hair. "Earlier this afternoon."

"You could have stayed home for a couple of days."

"I wanted to see what was going on at the office."

"Good honeymoon?"

"Excellent."

"Max is back at work, too, isn't he?"

"You know the drill."

Her husband was a partner at Story, Short & Thompson, the mega-firm in Embarcadero Center that was the successor to Simpson & Gates, the mega-firm at the top of the Bank of America Building where I worked for five miserable years after Rosie and I split up.

I grinned. "Did either of you consider doing re-entry into the real world more gradually?"

"That isn't the way we're drawn, Mike."

True. "Where's Luna?"

Nady pointed at the gray Keeshond sleeping peacefully in the corner. "She missed you."

"I missed her, too."

Two years earlier, I had declared—by fiat—that the P.D.'s Office would be dog-friendly. That decision was well-received by our employees but was met with less enthusiasm by the bureaucrats at the Mayor's Office who pointed out—correctly—that this was a technical violation of the City Code. After a couple of weeks of negotiations, the powers-that-be relented after I graciously agreed to indemnify the City for any damage caused by our canine companions and any judgments in the unlikely event that one of our four-legged friends bit somebody. It was a small price to pay to keep Nady happy. Besides, everybody enjoyed Luna's company.

I walked over to the sleeping dog, who looked like a short, fluffy German Shepherd. I pulled a treat out of my pocket and held it under her nose. "How are you, Luna?"

Her nose wiggled. Her eyes fluttered open. She yawned. She stretched. Then she lifted herself up into the sitting position, wagged her tail, and extended a paw.

"Good girl." I gave her the treat, which she devoured. She looked up hopefully and her tail pounded the floor. "Sorry. That's all that I have."

Her eyes filled with disappointment and she lowered herself down to the floor. I scratched her behind her ears, walked across the room, and took a seat next to Nady.

Rosie took a sip of Diet Coke. She allowed herself one can on the days where she attended Pilates class. In a show of support and at the recommendation of our doctor, I was now limiting myself to one can of Diet Dr Pepper a week.

"Jaylen Jenkins qualifies for our services," she said.

"Good. He told me that he didn't kill Robbie Blum."

"Then you should be able to get the charges dropped at the arraignment tomorrow."

"Right." I smiled at Nady, and then I turned back to Rosie. "In the unlikely event that the judge doesn't rule in our favor, how do you want to staff this case?"

"It would have been perfect for Rolanda, but she's not available at the moment."

"Or for the next six months."

"Correct. As a result, we'll go to Plan B: you."

Excellent. "I'd like Nady to sit second chair."

"We were just discussing her availability. The good news is that she has time."

Nady spoke up. "Happy to help."

"Perfect." She took notes on her laptop as I filled her in on my conversations with Jaylen, Erickson, and Lee. "I want you to find out everything you can about Robbie Blum. He was good at his job, but he wasn't well-liked in the sports or legal communities. He had two acrimonious divorces and a drug problem. It wouldn't surprise me if there were alcohol or other issues."

Nady responded with a sardonic grin. "Sounds like some people may not be heartbroken about his untimely demise."

"Let's just say that it may provide us with some intriguing options. Do you know anything about Blum?"

"Just what I've read in the papers. I can call Jen Foster. We were housemates at UCLA."

Foster was an All-America softball player at UCLA who went into broadcasting. She had spent the last three years interviewing players and fans during the Giants broadcasts.

"What makes you think she knows anything about Blum?" I asked.

"She knows everything about everybody connected to baseball." She arched an eyebrow. "And she went out with him a couple of times."

"He was old enough to be her father."

"Let's just say that Jen hasn't always made wise choices about men."

"Was she still seeing him when he died?"

"No."

"I want you to reach out to her. In addition, I need you to put together the usual requests for police reports, the autopsy report, surveillance video, other forensic evidence, and witnesses."

"I'll get started right away."

"I want you to come to the arraignment tomorrow to meet Jaylen." I turned back to Rosie. "We'll need an investigator."

"Phil Dito is on vacation. Jane Gorsi just got her hip replaced. Bob Puts is busy with a gang shooting in the Mission."

"Let's use Pete."

My younger brother was a former cop who became a P.I. twenty years earlier after he was fired by SFPD when he and his partner broke up a gang fight too enthusiastically.

Rosie scowled. "It's better to use somebody here in the office."

"You just said that everybody is busy or unavailable."

She considered her limited options. "Fine."

"Do we have budget to pay him?"

"I'll find it."

"Great." I turned to Nady. "I'm glad you're well-rested. We have a lot of work to do."

8
"HE WAS A BLOWHARD"

The gregarious bartender put a massive hand on my shoulder and spoke to me in a practiced Irish brogue. "Guinness, lad?"

"Yes, please, Big John."

"Coming up."

My uncle, Big John Dunleavy, had celebrated his eighty-sixth birthday in December. The longtime proprietor of Dunleavy's Bar and Grill on Irving Street, around the corner from the house where I had grown up, had never set foot in the Emerald Isle, but he could turn on a faux Irish accent at will. At six-three and two-forty, the one-time all-city tight end at St. Ignatius looked as if he could still flatten a linebacker. While the few strands of hair on his bald dome were now pure white and his jowls wiggled when he talked, his mind was as quick as ever. He had handed over the day-to-day operations to his grandson, Joey, but he still showed up four days a week to chat with his customers and make the batter for his fish and chips.

He stood behind the pine bar that my dad, Tom Daley, Sr., had helped him build sixty years earlier. "You okay, Mikey?"

"All good."

"Our Public Defender?"

"Rosie's fine, too."

"My beautiful great-niece still making movies at Pixar? Little Tommy still going to Cal in the fall?"

"Yes."

His pasty face transformed into a broad grin. "Excellent."

Two of his sons and four of his grandchildren (and yours truly) were Cal alums.

At nine-fifteen on Wednesday night, he scanned the homey pub that he had run for more than a half-century. Except for the big-screen TVs and the ATM, the paneled room looked the same as it did when I was a kid. The pool table and dart board had decades of wear. You could smell cigarette smoke baked into the walls even though smoking had been prohibited for years. The regulars included cops, fire fighters, PG&E workers, and MUNI drivers. Over the years, many of the Irish and Italian residents of the Sunset had moved to the suburbs. During the daytime, Dunleavy's had become a gathering place for seniors in the Chinese community. At night, he attracted a younger crowd of tech workers who had moved into the neighborhood.

He filled a mug with Guinness and slid it over to me. "On the house, lad."

It always is. "You ever going to let me pay for a drink?"

"I never make a profit on family, Mikey. Besides, I still owe you tips from years ago."

I had started tending bar for Big John when I was seventeen. This was, of course, illegal, but the neighborhood cops—including my dad and several assistant chiefs—weren't inclined to blow the whistle. I continued working shifts when I was in college and law school. Looking back, it was the best job that I ever had.

I turned to the gray-haired African-American man sitting next to me. "You okay, Roosevelt?"

"Fine, Mike." Roosevelt Johnson's baritone was raspier than it was when he and my dad were walking the beat in the Tenderloin a half-century earlier.

"Janet?"

"So-so."

His wife lived in an assisted living facility near Stonestown Mall.

At eighty-three, Roosevelt Johnson was SFPD's most decorated homicide inspector. Until his retirement ten years earlier, he had handled countless high-profile cases. He and my father were San Francisco's first integrated team. Pop was thrilled when Roosevelt became SFPD's first African-American homicide inspector. My dad stayed on the beat and died of lung cancer when Grace was two. He and Roosevelt used to come into Big John's pub after work to wind down in a booth near the back door. My mom, who was Big John's sister, wasn't crazy about it, but she knew that my uncle would make sure that Pop made it home.

"What brings you here tonight?" Roosevelt asked.

"I came to see my favorite uncle."

Big John grinned. "I'm your only uncle, Mikey."

"You're still my favorite."

Roosevelt was nursing a cup of coffee. "I heard you picked up the Jaylen Jenkins case."

"You're retired, Roosevelt."

"I still hear things."

"Did Ken Lee tell you about it?"

"Yes. He was one of my better students." He finished his coffee. "Ken said your new client beat Robbie Blum to death with a bat."

"My client said he didn't."

"That's why we have lawyers. I knew Blum's parents. Ed was a fine judge and a solid citizen who was on the board of Temple Emanu-El. He and Cathy were married for forty years."

"Did you know Robbie?"

"I met him a few times. Smart, but arrogant. Successful in his law practice and business, but his life was a mess. Divorced twice. Drugs. Booze. It drove his parents crazy."

"Do you know if anybody was mad at him?"

"Afraid not."

The back door swung open and my younger brother, Pete, came inside. He closed the door behind him and sat down on the stool next to mine. He was a little stockier than I was, and his full head of gray hair was once a half-shade darker than mine. He took off his ever-present bomber jacket and nodded at Big John, who placed a cup of black coffee on the bar in front of him. He exchanged greetings with Roosevelt, played with his silver mustache, and turned to me.

"Donna's pissed off because I've been working late," he said.

"Comes with the territory, Pete."

"I know."

His wife was a patient soul who was the chief financial officer of a big law firm. She understood that Pete's job required him to work long and irregular hours. She was somewhat less understanding when he couldn't make it to their daughter's softball games.

Roosevelt spoke up. "Your mom was the same way when your dad came home late."

Pete nodded. "I know."

We chatted for a few minutes before Roosevelt excused himself and headed to the door.

Big John leaned across the bar and spoke to my brother. "Is my great-niece still seeing that boy?"

"No."

"Good."

Pete's daughter, Margaret (named after our mother), recently turned sixteen. As the father of a twenty-four-year-old daughter, I have advised Pete that nobody makes it through the teenage years unscathed.

Big John's gentle tone embodied the wisdom of a man who was the father of four and the grandfather of twelve. "Did Margaret get her driver's license?"

"Not yet," Pete said. "Kids don't need to drive anymore. They take Uber."

"I couldn't wait to get my license."

"Neither could I." My brother smiled. "Maybe it isn't such a bad thing. Our insurance will go through the roof. Besides, I'm not sure that I'm ready for her to be driving on her own."

"You gonna buy her a car?" I asked.

"Absolutely not."

"Stay strong, Pete."

"We will, Mick." His eyes narrowed. "Why'd you want to talk to me?"

"Our office is representing the guy accused of killing Robbie Blum."

"I heard. You gonna do it yourself?"

"Yeah."

"You don't do cases."

"We're shorthanded. Rolanda is about to have a baby. A couple of other lawyers are in trial."

"Rosie's cool with it?"

"It was her idea. I want to hire you to help with the investigation."

"Rosie's okay with that, too?"

"Yes."

"Standard rates?"

"Yes. You got time?"

"I'll make time."

"I don't want you to get in any deeper with Donna."

"She's already mad at me." He took a sip of coffee. "Did your guy do it?"

"He said that he didn't."

"They all do. What do you think?"

I answered him honestly. "I don't know."

"Where do you want me to start?"

"I need to know everything about Blum. I want you to find people who were mad at him. He wasn't a popular guy."

"I know. I met him a couple of times."

"You tailed him?"

"No, I played against him in lawyers' league softball. I was on the team for the D.A.'s Office."

"You played for the enemy?"

"They asked me."

"You aren't a lawyer, Pete."

"You think lawyers play by the rules? I didn't think it was my place to question the chief law enforcement officer of the City and County of San Francisco. They needed a third baseman. I was available."

"What did you think of Blum?"

"He was a blowhard. He was always talking crap to some poor park district ump making twelve bucks an hour. Every game was played under protest."

Sounds about right. "He was successful."

"He made a lot of money, but a prick is still a prick."

The wisdom of Peter Daley. "Anybody mad at him?"

"His two ex-wives don't like him."

"He cheated?"

"Even worse: he hit them."

That's horrific. "How do you know?"

"One of my pals at Richmond Station was called to his house by his second ex-wife. Blum was able to keep it quiet. He paid off the ex not to press charges."

"I hope she got a lot of money."

His brown eyes gleamed. "She did."

"Would your pal be willing to talk to us about it?"

"No."

Didn't think so. "Are the ex-wives still in town?"

"Nope. Number one lives in New York. Number two is in L.A. along with their kid."

"You think they had anything to do with his death?"

"Doubtful, Mick."

"We heard that Blum was buying Molly from a guy named Brian Holton, who works at the Gold Club."

"Wouldn't surprise me."

"Can you track him down?"

"Of course." He finished his coffee, stood up, and put on his bomber jacket. "When's the arraignment?"

"Tomorrow morning."

"I'll be in touch."

9
"NOT GUILTY"

Judge Elizabeth McDaniel glanced at her computer, took off her reading glasses, and spoke in an authoritative voice bearing a hint of her native Alabama. "Who's next?"

Her clerk answered her. "Jaylen Jenkins."

At eleven-thirty the following morning, a Thursday, the gallery in Judge McDaniel's courtroom was filled with lawyers waiting their respective turns for a few minutes of assembly-line justice. Nady and I were told to show up at ten-thirty, but the proceedings were running late. It was like standing in line for a sandwich at Subway.

Judge McDaniel spoke to a brawny sheriff's deputy. "Please bring the defendant inside."

"Yes, Your Honor."

Betsy McDaniel was a thoughtful jurist who dispensed justice evenly and with ruthless efficiency. When she turned seventy a couple of years earlier, the former A.D.A. had gone on senior status to spend more time with her grandchildren, take pre-dawn Pilates classes with Rosie, teach criminal procedure at Hastings Law School, and travel the world. On occasion, she sat in for her colleagues and handled arraignments, motions, and preliminary hearings.

The deputy returned with Jaylen, who joined Nady and me at the defense table. In his orange jumpsuit, he looked like a criminal.

I leaned over and whispered into his ear. "When the judge asks for your plea, I want you to say 'Not guilty' in a firm but respectful tone."

He was on edge. "Okay."

Erickson was standing at the prosecution table next to an A.D.A named Vanessa Turner. The African-American woman was an Oakland native and Hastings Law alum who was developing a reputation for legal acumen, thoughtfulness, precision, and relentlessness. Inspector Lee was sitting behind them in the gallery next to our D.A., DeSean Harper, who had moved into the top slot after his predecessor, Nicole Ward, was elected mayor in a bitter election battle resembling the final season of *Game of Thrones*. Politics in my hometown has always been a contact sport.

Judge McDaniel tapped her microphone. "Counsel will state their names for the record."

"Andrew Erickson and Vanessa Turner for the People."

"Good to see both of you. Will you or Ms. Turner be speaking for the People?"

Turner answered her. "I will, Your Honor."

"Very good." The judge turned our way. "And for the defense?"

"Michael Daley and Nadezhda Nikonova," I said. "Our office has been appointed. We will file the documentation with the court. Ms. Nikonova will be speaking for the defense."

"Fine." The judge's eyes shifted to Nady. "Congratulations on your nuptials."

"Thank you, Your Honor."

The judge spoke to Jaylen. "You lack the resources to hire a private attorney?"

"Yes, Your Honor."

"Okay." She read the customary admonition that if it was later determined that Jaylen had sufficient funds to hire a private attorney, he would have to reimburse the City for the cost of his representation. The chance of this happening was nil.

Judge McDaniel spoke rapidly as if reading from a script. "This is an arraignment. We will have a recitation of the charge and the defendant will enter a plea." She spoke to Jaylen again. "Do you understand why we are here, Mr. Jenkins?"

"Yes."

She turned to Turner. "Charge?"

"First-degree murder under California Penal Code Section 187."

It carried a minimum sentence of twenty-five years.

Nady spoke up. "The facts do not warrant a murder charge, Your

Honor."

"That's up to Ms. Turner and Mr. Erickson." The judge speed-read the complaint aloud—a required part of the process. Then she addressed Jaylen. "Do you understand the charge?"

"Yes."

"How do you wish to plead?"

"Not guilty, Your Honor."

"Thank you."

That takes care of today's substantive business.

The judge looked at Nady. "I presume that you'll want to schedule a prelim?"

"Yes, Your Honor."

A preliminary hearing, or "prelim," is a mini-trial where the D.A. must present enough evidence to demonstrate that there is a reasonable likelihood that the defendant committed a crime. It's frequently a one-sided affair where the D.A. holds the cards. By law, the judge is required to give the D.A. the benefit of the doubt on all evidentiary issues.

"I trust that you're willing to waive time?" the judge said.

Nady was standing at the defense table. "No, Your Honor."

"You're sure?"

"Yes, Your Honor."

The defense can request a prelim within ten court days after the arraignment. We frequently "waive time," which means that we agree to proceed after the ten-day window. It gives us more time to interview witnesses and look for exculpatory evidence. In this case, Jaylen was anxious to move forward, and Nady and I wanted to see the prosecution's evidence as soon as possible.

The judge shifted her gaze to Turner. "How many court days for the prelim?"

"One."

She studied her calendar. "I can fit you in on Thursday, June eleventh."

"Works for us."

It was a tight schedule—only a week away.

The judge turned to Nady. "That will work for you, right, Ms. Nikonova?"

Since we weren't waiving time, we couldn't complain about the expedited schedule.

"Yes, Your Honor," Nady said.

"Very good. I want to see motions no later than Monday." She glanced at her computer. "If there's nothing else—,"

"We have a couple items, Your Honor."

"I'm listening, Ms. Nikonova."

"First, given the tight timeframe, we ask you to order Mr. Erickson and Ms. Turner to provide copies of police reports, autopsy report, security videos, witness lists, and other evidence on an expedited basis."

"So ordered."

"Second, we request that you issue a gag order on all parties and lawyers and prohibit the media from taking pictures or video of these proceedings."

"So ordered."

"Third, we ask you to release Mr. Jenkins pending trial subject to the condition that he will wear an ankle bracelet and have regular check-ins."

The San Francisco D.A.'s policy eliminating money bail has been a mixed bag. On the positive side, it means that many smalltime offenders aren't incarcerated pending trial, and defendants are no longer required to come up with cash or buy a bail bond from the entrepreneurs across the street. On the other hand, it is frequently more difficult to obtain a client's release pending trial—especially in felony cases. It also makes life more complicated for the judges, who must decide whether the accused is likely to flee, taking into account the severity of the crime, the defendant's employment status, and his community ties. It's more of an art than a science, and judges frequently have to rely on their gut and err on the side of caution. The chances of negotiating a pre-trial release in a murder case are slim.

Turner spoke from her seat. "We've submitted our motion for

detention, Your Honor. Given the gravity of the crime, we oppose release."

"Alleged crime," Nady said. "Mr. Jenkins isn't a flight risk. He has lived in Oakland his entire life and has substantial community ties."

"Does he have any family in the area?" the judge asked.

"His mother."

"Is she present today?"

"She's unavailable." Nady left out the fact that she was in rehab and wasn't returning our calls.

Turner shot back. "Mr. Jenkins has an automobile and the ability to leave town. It would be highly unusual to allow release in a first-degree murder case."

"Your Honor has discretion," Nady said.

Judge McDaniel listened intently as Turner and Nady volleyed for another five minutes. Finally, she made the call. "I am not going to authorize the release of the defendant at this time. Mr. Jenkins is remanded to custody." The judge raised a hand. "We're finished."

I saw fear in Jaylen's eyes as the deputy came over to escort him from the courtroom. "What happens next?" he asked.

"We'll meet you upstairs in a few minutes. We can talk about it then."

10
"WHO SHOULD WE TALK TO?"

An hour later, Jaylen was agitated as he sat across the metal table from Nady and me in the consultation room on the seventh floor of the Hall. "What happens next?" he asked.

"There will be a preliminary hearing a week from today," I said.

"Can you get the charges dropped?"

I answered honestly. "Doubtful." I explained the nature of a prelim. "The burden of proof on the prosecution is low. The D.A. will show just enough evidence to move forward to trial."

"We'll put on a defense, right?"

"We'll challenge the D.A.'s evidence, but we won't show all of our cards."

He leaned back. "How soon can we go to trial?"

"You have a legal right to a trial within sixty days after the prelim."

"That's what I want to do."

"It's usually better to ask for a delay so that we have more time to prepare."

"You aren't rotting in this hellhole.

True. "We'll talk about it again after the prelim."

"Great."

"We'll get you through this, Jaylen. We need you to stay calm and help us."

"Easy for you to say."

"Who else was mad at Blum?" I asked.

"I didn't kill him."

"We need you to help us find the person who did."

He pushed out a sigh. "Talk to Brian Holton."

"We will. Who else?"

"I don't know."

"Help us, Jaylen. Please."

"I don't know."

* * *

"That didn't go well," Nady observed.

"True," I said.

It was quiet in the lobby of the Hall at one-fifteen the same afternoon. A couple of people were in line at the metal detectors. I looked out the window and saw only one person smoking next to the planter box.

"Have you heard from your friend the broadcaster?" I asked.

"She said that she would talk to us."

"Sooner rather than later."

"I'll set it up."

"Great. Pete is looking for people who were around the ballpark on Monday night."

She grinned. "Sooner rather than later."

"Right."

"You going back to the office?" she asked.

"I'll meet you there later. I'm going to see the Chief Medical Examiner."

11
"FRACTURED SKULL"

The Chief Medical Examiner of the City and County of San Francisco adjusted the sleeve of her white lab coat. "Good afternoon, Mr. Daley."

"Good afternoon, Dr. Siu. Thank you for seeing me."

"You're quite welcome."

There were no personal photos in Dr. Joy Siu's spacious office on the second floor of the new Medical Examiner's facility in a warehouse-like building in the grimy India Basin neighborhood, about halfway between downtown and Candlestick Point. The state-of-the-art examination rooms and expanded morgue were a substantial upgrade from her outdated quarters in the basement of the Hall of Justice and compensated for the less-than-ideal location and the less-than-stellar view of the recycling facility across the street on Pier 96.

"How can I help you?" she asked.

"I understand that you performed the autopsy on Robert Blum."

"I did."

She was sitting behind a glass-topped desk covered with file folders in orderly piles. From her pressed lab coat to her meticulously applied makeup to her precisely cut black hair, she exuded exactness. Now pushing fifty, the Princeton and Johns Hopkins Medical School alum and former research scientist at UCSF was a world-class academic and an internationally recognized expert in anatomic pathology. The one-time Olympic figure skating hopeful spent about a quarter of her time writing academic papers and consulting on complex autopsies around the world.

"I'm surprised that you didn't hand it off to one of your colleagues," I said.

"The Giants wanted this matter to be handled on an expedited basis."

"Is your report complete?"

"Still awaiting toxicology results."

"Any sign of alcohol or drugs in his system?"

"Too soon to tell."

"Do you have a preliminary cause of death?"

"Fractured skull."

Ouch.

She folded her hands. "I cannot tell you anything more at this time, Mr. Daley. You understand that the information that I just provided to you is preliminary, confidential, and subject to change."

"Of course." I held up a hand. "Can you give me a few more details?"

"Mr. Blum died of a crushed skull. That's all that I can tell you."

"You have reason to believe that my client crushed it?"

"That's a conversation you'll need to have with Inspector Lee and the D.A.'s Office."

"You're absolutely sure about the crushed skull?"

"How much tolerance do you have for autopsy photos?"

"I can handle it."

She invited me to stand behind her and look over her shoulder at her laptop. She typed a few keystrokes and a grisly image of a mangled skull appeared.

"Convinced?" she asked.

"Yes." I swallowed. "They found the body floating in the bay?"

"Correct."

"Any chance that Mr. Blum accidentally tripped and banged his head against a railing?"

"No." She pointed at the photo. "This is what is commonly known as a 'depressed skull fracture,' which results from substantial blunt-force trauma, such as being struck by a hammer or a tire iron. More specifically, it's a 'comminuted fracture' in which the broken bones displaced inward. In this case, it crushed the brain tissue. The decedent had no chance."

"You're saying this wound was caused by a blunt instrument?"

"Yes."

"Has the instrument been identified?"

"That's another question for Inspector Lee."

"Time of death?"

"Based on the state of digestion of food in his stomach, somewhere between midnight and four a.m. in the early morning of Tuesday, June second. He was pronounced at the scene at seven-twenty a.m."

"Any forensic evidence that my client struck Mr. Blum?"

"That's another question for Inspector Lee."

"Were you able to identify any physical characteristics of the alleged killer?"

"The wound was inflicted at a slight angle going from right to left. This suggests that the killer may have been right-handed, but it's impossible to know for sure."

Jaylen was right-handed. "Defensive wounds?"

"None."

"Blood spatter?"

"None."

"Did the evidence techs find any bloody clothing in my client's possession?"

"That's a question for Inspector Lee."

12
"I DON'T WANT ANY MORE EXCITEMENT"

Sylvia Fernandez's nimble fingers raced across the blanket that she was knitting for her first great-granddaughter. "Any word from Rolanda?"

"All quiet, Mama," Rosie said. She folded her hands and placed them on the table in the cramped dining room of the two-bedroom bungalow in the Mission where she had grown up. "Tony promised to call as soon as Rolanda goes into labor."

My ex-mother-in-law's lips formed a satisfied smile. "That's good, Rosita."

Sylvia Fernandez was born eighty-five years earlier on the outskirts of Monterrey, Mexico, and was an older, stockier, and equally intense version of Rosie. At twenty-four, Sylvia and her late husband, Eduardo, a carpenter, made their way to San Francisco, along with Rosie's older brother, Tony, who was a baby. Rosie was born a couple of years later. Her younger sister, Teresa, came along three years after Rosie's arrival. Sylvia and Eduardo saved their pennies for a down payment on the little house that cost the princely sum of twenty-four thousand dollars. Nowadays, Sylvia could sell it to a tech entrepreneur for almost two million, but she's made it abundantly clear that she has no intention of ever doing so.

She touched Rosie's hand. "I don't want any more excitement until Rolanda has the baby."

"Neither do I, Mama."

At twelve-thirty in the afternoon on Sunday, June seventh, the aroma of Sylvia's chicken enchiladas wafted in from the tiny kitchen which hadn't been remodeled since Rosie was a kid. The plaster walls were covered with photos of four generations of the Fernandez clan. Rosie and I had joined Sylvia for our customary post-mass lunch in the stucco house across the street from Garfield Square Park. Grace and Tommy frequently joined us, but Grace was working overtime, and Tommy was helping his high school football coach run a summer camp.

Rosie smiled at her mother. "Are you playing mahjong with Ann-Helen tonight?"

"Of course, dear. Every Sunday."

"You still smoking weed while you play?"

"It takes the edge off." Sylvia's eyes danced. "Besides, it's legal now."

Sylvia and a rotating cast of her neighbors had been playing mahjong on Sunday nights since Rosie was in grammar school. A few years ago, at the suggestion of her longtime friend, Ann-Helen Leff, a ninety-year-old hippie, great-grandmother, and inveterate rabble rouser, they switched the refreshments from sherry to marijuana.

"Does Ann-Helen buy the weed?" Rosie asked.

"No, dear. Her granddaughter gets it for us at that new place on Mission Street where the tech kids go. It's expensive, but it's very good."

The Mission has changed since I was a kid.

Sylvia took a sip of tea and looked at me. "Father Lopez led a beautiful mass this morning. Your mother would have enjoyed it."

"Yes, she would have."

My mom had been gone almost twenty years, my dad twenty-six. They had grown up on opposite sides of the park across the street when the Mission was still home to working-class Irish and Italian families. We lived in a two-bedroom apartment until I was seven, when we moved to a three-bedroom house two blocks from Big John's saloon. Around the same time, many of the Irish and Italian families moved out, and the Latino families (including Rosie's) moved in. The neighborhood was changing again as tech workers were squeezing out the Latino community. The only constant was St. Peter's Catholic Church at Twenty-fourth and Alabama, where my parents and later Rosie and I were married. Nowadays, four of the five Sunday masses were celebrated in Spanish.

Sylvia's expression turned thoughtful. "Do you ever miss being a priest?"

"Occasionally." I decided to become a priest when I was looking for answers after my older brother, Tommy, died in Vietnam. After a couple of years at St. Anne's in the Sunset, I didn't feel qualified to save other people's souls, so I went to law school. "We've talked about it, Sylvia. It wasn't a good fit for me."

"You still come to mass every Sunday."

"I still like going to church."

"You like being a lawyer better?"

I shot a playful glance at Rosie, then turned back to Sylvia. "Lawyers get to do stuff that priests can't."

"That's for sure. I heard that you're representing the man who killed the sports agent."

"*Allegedly*," I said out of habit.

"Allegedly," she repeated, sarcastic. "You're going to handle it yourself?"

"Yes."

Sylvia's eyes turned to Rosie. "I thought Michael wasn't doing cases."

"We're a little shorthanded with Rolanda on maternity leave."

"I trust that she will have no involvement in this matter?"

"Correct. We sent her home, Mama."

"You were supposed to send her home a week ago."

"We did. She came into the office without telling us."

"She ended up in the emergency room, Rosita."

"I made it absolutely clear to her that she needs to stay home until the baby is born."

"I hope you remember this when Grace is expecting."

"Let's not get ahead of ourselves, Mama. Grace is only twenty-four."

"It's never too early to plan, Rosita." Sylvia resumed knitting as she turned back to me. "Is your client guilty?"

"No."

"You always say that."

"You know the drill, Sylvia. Innocent until proven guilty."

"They said on the news that your client hit the agent with a bat and dumped his body into the bay."

"Our client said that he didn't."

"You believe him?"

"For now."

Rosie asked, "Did you find out anything useful from Dr. Siu?"

"Blum had a fractured skull."

"Maybe he fell and hit his head."

"Doubtful. The injury was likely caused by somebody hitting him with a heavy object."

"Like a bat?'

"Uh, yes."

Sylvia flashed a wry grin. "Still think your client is innocent?"

* * *

"Your mom was in a feisty mood this afternoon," I observed.

Rosie took a sip of Cab Franc. "She's been in a feisty mood for eighty-five years."

At ten-thirty on Sunday night, we were sitting on opposite ends of the sofa in the living room of Rosie's post-earthquake bungalow on Alexander Avenue in Larkspur, a leafy suburb about ten miles north of the Golden Gate Bridge. Since the Public Defender was technically required to reside within the San Francisco city limits, Rosie's official residence was a studio apartment down the block from her mother's house. Rosie and I spent most of our time in the little house that we had rented after Grace was born. After we got divorced, Rosie kept the house, and I moved into a one-bedroom apartment a few blocks away behind the Larkspur fire station and across the street from the Silver Peso, one of the last dive bars in Marin County. After we got a death penalty conviction overturned for a one-time mob lawyer, our client expressed his gratitude by buying us the house. Rosie and I still found it helpful to have separate spaces, so I spent a couple of nights a week at the apartment. This arrangement had lasted longer and worked out better than our marriage.

"Did you hear from Tommy?" I asked.

"He's staying at Jake's house tonight. He said that he's helping us prepare to become empty nesters in the fall."

"Very thoughtful. Grace was the same way during the summer after she graduated from high school."

Rosie took another sip of wine. "Are you going to file your motions for Jaylen's prelim tomorrow?"

"Yes. Nady has it under control."

"Did Erickson send over any evidence?"

"He promised to provide video tomorrow."

"Have they identified the murder weapon?"

"Not yet."

"It would be nice to see it."

"It would."

She finished her wine and set the glass down on the table. "You okay, Mike?"

"Fine."

She reached over and touched my cheek. "You look tired."

"Maybe a little."

"What is it?"

"We have one kid who's a college grad and self-sufficient. The other is going off to Cal in a couple of months."

"That's good."

"It is, but it makes me feel like a grown-up."

She leaned forward and kissed me. "Being a grown-up isn't so bad."

"I guess not."

"Are you planning to go over to the apartment tonight?"

"Do you want me to go?"

She flashed the smile that I still found beautiful almost three decades after we'd met. "No, I want you to stay."

13
"YOU CAN SEE IT IN THE VIDEO"

"Did you get our motions filed?" I asked.

Nady looked up from her laptop. "Yes. Judge McDaniel's clerk said that she'd get back to us in the next day or two."

We were three days from Jaylen's prelim. Nady, Pete, and I were sitting at the table in our conference room at eight-thirty on Monday night. The aroma of leftover pizza and Caesar salad wafted through the heavy air.

I turned to Pete. "Any luck finding Jaylen's mother?"

"Not yet. She isn't returning phone calls. I went over to the halfway house in Oakland, but she wasn't there. Evidently, she took off after Jaylen was arrested and hasn't returned. I talked to her sister, but she hasn't seen her, either. She may be living on the street."

I looked at Nady. "Did Lee send anything over?"

"There was a text to Jaylen's burner phone from Blum on the night that Blum died. Nothing useful on Jaylen's iPhone."

"What about Blum's phones?"

"He used a new burner to text Jaylen. There was also a text to Brian Holton confirming that Jaylen would meet him the following night. I'm still going through texts and calls on his iPhone, but it looks like it's mostly business-related stuff."

I asked if there was anything else from Lee.

"Surveillance video from a camera mounted above the players' parking lot."

"Let's see it."

She pressed a button and the TV sprung to life. The high-def video was in color, but it was taken on a foggy night, so it looked like a black-and-white movie. There was no sound.

Nady glanced at her notes. "This was taken at eleven-fifty-five p.m." She pointed at a Tesla parked outside the closed gate to the players' lot. "That's Blum's car. The parking attendant left it outside the gate after everybody else had left."

We watched the footage in silence. A man walked down the pedestrian path between the ballpark and the marina toward the players' lot. He walked past the Tesla and disappeared out of camera view.

"Blum?" I asked.

Nady paused the video. "Yes."

"He walked by his own car."

"So it seems."

She started the video again and ran it in slow motion. A second man jogged past the Tesla. He was wearing a gray hoodie and a Giants cap. Nady stopped the video.

"That's Jaylen," she said. She pointed at his right hand. "There's the bat."

"You can't tell for sure."

Pete chimed in. "Come on, Mick. You can see it in the video."

He was always a voice of cold, hard reality. "Yeah."

Nady started the video again. Jaylen disappeared from view. A minute passed. Then another one. Then he reappeared. This time, he was running in the opposite direction.

"Run it again in slow motion," I said. "Stop it when Jaylen is running back."

Nady did as I asked.

I pointed at the screen. "Notice anything?"

Pete squinted. "He isn't carrying the bat."

"It doesn't mean that he hit Blum with the bat."

"A jury will connect the dots." Pete pulled on his bomber jacket. "We're in serious trouble, Mick."

So it seems. "Did you find out anything about Blum's two ex-wives?"

"The first lives in New York. The second is in L.A. Both were out of town when he died."

"Did you find out who attended the funeral?"

"Yeah. It was a small gathering at the gravesite. His second ex-wife, his son, a brother, an assistant, and a couple of friends. It seems unlikely that anybody at the funeral killed him."

"Anybody else we should talk to?"

"I'm working on connections to people in Giants management. We should talk to Blum's former business partner, Jeff Franklin, who was Blum's roommate at Stanford Law School. Franklin worked for one of the law firms in Palo Alto for a few years, then he started representing baseball and basketball players."

"He was Blum's *former* partner?"

"They had a falling out over money. Evidently, they ended up in litigation and had a big fight over who got to keep the clients."

Figures. "Anybody else?"

"David Archer was Blum's biggest client."

The Giants clean-up hitter won't be hard to find—if he'll talk to us. "You think there's a chance that he killed Blum?"

"Seems doubtful." Pete looked down at his phone. "I just got a text from my mole at the Gold Club. Holton just got to work. You up for a reconnaissance mission to a strip club?"

"It's required by our job, Pete."

He looked at Nady. "Care to join us?"

"I'll let you guys handle this one."

14
"YOU NEED TO GET OUT MORE"

A cool breeze whipped down Howard Street as Pete and I approached the nondescript two-story building housing the Gold Club. When I was a kid, the strip of Mission between New Montgomery and Third Street was skid row. Nowadays, the upscale strip club was on the same block as the swanky W Hotel and around the corner from the refurbished Museum of Modern Art, smack-dab in the middle of the South of Market tech hub. The Gold Club had become a popular destination for the tech bros who worked in the neighborhood. The buffet was cheap, the food filling. And, of course, there were dancers.

Nobody was waiting at the rope line at eight-thirty on Monday night, so Pete and I approached the muscular doorman with the shaved head and the black leather jacket, whose phone was pressed to his ear.

"Let me do the talking," Pete muttered.

"I always do."

The young man finished his call, nodded respectfully, and spoke in a raspy voice. "Welcome to the Gold Club."

"Thank you," Pete said.

"Been here before?"

"Several times."

"You should sign up for our app," he said without conviction. "We'll let you know when we have specials." He explained that Monday had half-priced VIP dances, and Tuesday was two-for-one night. "Bring some friends. Best deals in town."

I gave him points for trying, but his sales pitch needed a little work.

"We'll check it out," Pete said. "Busy tonight?"

"Nah."

Pete slipped him a couple of twenties. "Who's dancing?"

"Candy. If you want something special, ask for Crystal."

Pete slipped him another twenty. "Thanks, man."

This is getting expensive.

My brother extended a hand. "Pete." This is my brother, Mike. It's his birthday."

"Brian. Happy birthday."

"Thanks."

We headed inside, where the cavernous space was decorated in gray tones accented by stainless steel trim. Two dozen mostly empty tables were scattered between the bar and the stage, where an acrobatic woman bathed in purple light was working her magic at the dance pole while Michael Jackson's "Billy Jean" blared. The room smelled of perspiration and beer. The Gold Club catered to a more upscale crowd than similar establishments in the Tenderloin, but a high-end strip club is still a strip club.

Pete and I took seats at a table next to the wall and watched the dancer go through the motions. When the music stopped, Pete walked up and placed a couple of twenties on the stage.

The young woman smiled with appreciation. "Thanks, Sugar."

He nodded. He came back to the table, took his seat, and looked at his texts.

"Do you know her?" I asked.

"Yeah."

"Can she help us?"

"No."

"Was that Brian Holton outside?"

"Yeah. We'll talk to him when we leave."

I never question Pete when he's working.

A college-aged waitress sporting a halter top and short-shorts approached us, tossed her shoulder-length blonde hair to one side, and flashed a practiced smile. "How are you, Pete?"

"Fine, Darlene. You still seeing the cop from Oakland?"

"Not anymore."

"Sorry." Pete pointed at me. "This is my brother, Mike."

"Darlene Green. You're the Public Defender?"

"Yes."

"Pete's told me a lot about you."

Pete spoke up again. "Darlene is a junior at State. She's studying to become a dental hygienist. She works here to help pay tuition."

"Good for you."

"Thanks, hon. What can I get you?"

It's been a long time since somebody called me "hon." "Anchor Steam, please."

"Same for me," Pete said.

Darlene smiled at me. "You don't spend a lot of time in clubs like this, do you?"

"Uh, no."

"That's okay, hon." She headed to the bar.

Pete looked up. "When was the last time you were in a strip club, Mick?"

"A couple of years ago—with you. We were looking for a witness."

"You need to get out more."

"Not my style anymore, Pete."

"It was *never* your style, Mick."

The music started again, and the dancer took another turn. Darlene returned with our beers. I handed her two twenties. She said that she needed another ten. The Gold Club was pricier than Dunleavy's.

Pete gave her his best sincere smile and went to work. "Mike is representing the guy accused of killing Robbie Blum. We heard that Blum used to come here. You ever meet him?"

"Once or twice," Darlene said. "Outstanding tipper."

"I presume that he came here to do more than drink Cokes?"

"Uh, yeah." Her mouth turned up. "Bonnie was his favorite."

"Is she here?"

"She left town a couple of weeks ago."

"Any idea where she went?"

"No."

She turned and started to make her way to the bar, but Pete held up a hand.

"You know anybody who was mad at Blum?" he asked.

"I don't ask my customers a lot of questions, Pete."

"We heard that Blum was friends with Brian."

She glanced at the door. "They were engaged in business."

Pete slid five twenties under his drink. "What kind of business?"

"Pharmaceuticals."

"We heard that Brian was providing product to Blum."

"Maybe. I can't talk about it." She reached down to grab the money, but Pete covered it before she could. "Come on, Pete."

"Was Brian working on the night that Blum died?"

"Yes."

"Was he here the entire time?"

"As far as I know. I work inside. He works outside. He may have taken a break."

"Did you ever see Brian and Blum argue?"

"Maybe."

Pete picked up his drink, and Darlene grabbed the cash. Pete set his mug down. "When was the last time that you saw Blum?"

"About a week before he died."

"Did he talk to Brian?"

"You can't get in the door without talking to Brian."

"You'll let us know if you hear anything that might be helpful?"

"Sure, Pete."

"Thanks, Darlene."

* * *

Brian Holton ended a call and put his cell phone inside his pocket as Pete and I walked out the door of the Gold Club. "You guys weren't inside very long."

Pete answered him. "Something came up."

Holton looked at me. "I hope it didn't ruin your birthday."

"Nothing serious," I said. Especially since my birthday isn't for another month.

Pete smiled. "A friend of mine told me that Robbie Blum used to hang out here. Helluva thing."

"Yeah."

"Did you know him?"

"He came in a couple of times a week."

Pete feigned surprise. "To watch the show?"

"To see a dancer named Bonnie."

"I heard that he was a jerk."

"He treated our people like they were his personal property."

"Not cool. Did he crap on you?"

"Sometimes. He sucked up to his clients and dumped on everybody else."

"You know what happened to him?"

"No."

"I heard that he was doing smack."

"He was doing a lot of stuff."

Pete lowered his voice. "You know where he got it?"

"Nope."

"Did he come in on the night that he died?"

"Not that I recall."

"You were here?"

"I'm always here."

"Any idea where we might be able to get some Molly?"

Holton waited a beat. "I can ask around."

Pete wrote his phone number on a piece of paper and handed it to Holton, along with five twenties. "Thanks for your help, Brian."

* * *

"What did you think of Holton?" I asked.

Pete's hands were jammed inside his pockets as we walked down Howard. "For one, he's jumpy, which means that he won't make a strong witness. That could work to our advantage. For two, he took my number and my money, which means that he's interested in doing business. We'll see if he calls. For three, there were two undercover cops inside and one outside, which means they're watching him."

It's helpful to have a P.I. who is a former cop. "Can you have somebody watch Holton?"

He chuckled. "I already do."

* * *

I was jolted awake from a restless sleep by the sound of my phone. It took me a moment to get my bearings and read the numerals on the display. Five-forty a.m.

I pressed the green button. "Gimme a sec, Pete."

I sat up, turned on the light, and looked around the bedroom of my cramped apartment behind the Larkspur fire station. The platform bed rested on cinder blocks. The nightstand came from IKEA.

I reached over and scratched the head of the pearl white cat sleeping soundly at the foot of my bed. "Morning, Wilma."

Her right ear wiggled, but her eyes remained closed. Technically, Wilma lived next door. When my neighbors had twin boys, Wilma started coming over to my apartment for peace and quiet. The twins were now sleeping through the night, but Wilma preferred the relative tranquility of my place. She went home in the mornings when she got hungry.

"What's up, Pete?" I asked.

"How soon can you get down to the ballpark?"

"A half hour," I said. I scratched Wilma's ear. "What have you got?"

"Meet me by the players' parking lot. I located the guy who found Blum's body."

15
"THE FISHERMEN GO OUT EARLY"

At seven a.m., the fog was heavy behind the left field wall of the ballpark as I stood on the tree-lined pedestrian path between the players' parking lot and the South Beach Marina. I pulled up my collar and inhaled the moist air that smelled of bay water, leftover hot dogs, stale peanuts, and beer. I looked up at the seagulls sitting on the giant Coca-Cola bottle atop the bleachers. The dampness didn't seem to bother them.

Just another summer morning in my hometown.

I took a sip of coffee from a paper cup, looked at my watch, and waited. A moment later, Pete emerged from the parking lot of the upscale South Beach Yacht Club. He was accompanied by a stocky man sporting a navy windbreaker bearing the Club's logo.

Pete held out a hand. "Coffee?"

I handed him a cup. "Peet's. Black."

He pointed at his companion. "This is Jesus Martinez. He works for the Yacht Club."

"Mike Daley." I shook his calloused hand and handed him a cup of Peet's. "Two sugars, right?"

"Right." His pockmarked face transformed into an appreciative half-smile which quickly disappeared. "I need to get back to work."

"We need just a couple of minutes of your time. You live here in the City?"

"The Mission."

"I grew up on Garfield Square. St. Peter's Parish. You know Father Lopez?"

"Of course."

"Tell him Mike Daley says hi."

"I will."

For the moment, he didn't appear to be in such a hurry. "How long have you worked at the Yacht Club?"

"Eighteen years."

"You like it?"

"It's a job."

"What do you do?"

"I fuel the boats. I help the members carry stuff to and from their cars."

"What time do you get to work?"

"Four a.m. The fishermen go out early."

"You like to fish?"

"Bores me to death."

"Me, too." I looked over at the ballpark. "You like baseball?"

"Yeah."

"You ever go to the games?"

"Too expensive."

"I can get you tickets."

"Great."

Pete decided that it was time for business. "Jesus, can you show Mike what you showed me?"

"Okay."

Pete and I followed him down the footpath along the marina, where there were seven piers with sailboats and power craft lined up on either side. We stopped in the plaza behind the scoreboard next to a squat building housing a public restroom. The walkway was separated from the water by a fence made of cement pillars supporting horizontal iron strands.

Jesus pointed at the water between piers six and seven. "That's where I found the body."

"What time was that?"

"Six-fifteen in the morning."

"Was anybody else around?"

"A couple of members were having breakfast in the clubhouse."

"Anybody outside? Homeless people?"

He shook his head. "The Giants and the cops keep the homeless away from the park during baseball season."

I asked him how he reacted when he saw the body.

"I threw him a life preserver and called my boss. He called the cops." He said that the police and an ambulance arrived a few minutes later. "The EMTs pulled him out of the water. They tried to revive him, but he was dead."

"Did you know that it was Robbie Blum?"

"Not until I read about it in the paper."

"Did you ever meet him?"

"No."

I looked over at the public restroom. "Anybody ever sleep in there?"

"No. The Giants lock it up after the crowd goes home."

"Security cameras?"

"Not in the bathroom."

"What about on the piers?"

"A couple by the clubhouse and one at the entrance to each of the docks."

"I presume that your boss provided the videos to the cops?"

"Yeah."

"Any chance there's video of somebody hitting Blum?"

Jesus shrugged. "He told me that he didn't see anything."

We would ask the D.A. for a copy.

Pete made his presence felt again. "The D.A. thinks our client hit Blum with a bat."

Jesus nodded. "There was a bat in the water next to the body."

I asked if he gave a statement to the police.

"Yeah." Jesus tensed. "I told them the same thing that I told you."

"Did the D.A. ask you to testify at the preliminary hearing on Thursday?"

"They said that I should be available, but they didn't think they'd need me."

"Anybody else that we should talk to?"

"Nobody else was around."

We thanked Jesus for his time, and he headed to the clubhouse. When he was out of earshot, I inhaled the cool air and spoke to my brother. "What did you think?"

"He had no reason to lie."

I trusted Pete's instincts. My phone vibrated. The display indicated that I had a text.

"What is it, Mick?" Pete asked.

"Blum's former business partner agreed to see me later this morning."

"You want company?"

"I think it might be better if I go see him myself."

16
"HE DIDN'T TAKE IT WELL"

"Nice view," I said.

The lanky man with the slicked-back hair flashed a toothy smile and spoke in a voice oozing with sugar. "Thank you, Mr. Daley."

"It's Mike, Mr. Franklin."

"Mike. And it's Jeff."

Blum's former business partner leaned back in his ergonomic chair behind the inlaid wood desk in his expansive office on the northeast corner on the fifty-fifth floor of the Salesforce Tower. The white walls were lined with framed jerseys and photos of his clients—an All-Star lineup of NFL, NBA, and MLB players, including a couple of Giants. At ten-thirty a.m., the fog was lifting, and I admired his one-hundred-and-eighty-degree view extending from the Golden Gate past Alcatraz to the Bay Bridge.

I took a seat in the chair opposite his desk. "Thank you for seeing me."

"I want to find out what happened to Robbie as much as you do."

I doubt that. I declined his offer of coffee and pointed at a framed photo of a younger version of Franklin along with two smiling boys and a super-model-looking wife who appeared to be about twenty years younger than Franklin. "How old are your sons?"

"Connor is seven. Max is six."

"Handsome lads. You live here in town?"

"Belvedere."

"Nice." The tony island-suburb at the end of the Tiburon Peninsula had unobstructed views of the Golden Gate and downtown San Francisco. "I presume that you can see this building from your house?"

"Yes."

The Salesforce Tower dominated the San Francisco skyline and dwarfed the Transamerica Pyramid. It's impressive in its size and technology, but it looks like an enlarged phallic symbol to me. "Where do your kids go to school?"

"Marin Country Day."

Figures. Tuition at the selective prep school in San Rafael was north of fifty grand a year before the "suggested" five-figure "voluntary" contributions expected of all parents.

"Our daughter graduated from USC a couple of years ago," I said. "She's working at Pixar. Our son just graduated from Redwood. He's going to Cal in the fall."

"He didn't get into Stanford or an Ivy?"

"We're a Cal family."

"Good for you." His expression indicated that the fake pleasantries were over. "You have some questions about Robbie?"

"I do. How long did you know him?"

"Thirty years. We were classmates at Stanford Law School. He was the best man at my first and second weddings. I was the best man at both of his weddings. I worked at a law firm in Palo Alto that represented tech companies whose names you would recognize. Some of the Warriors and Giants invested in my clients. I got to know them pretty well, and they asked me to represent them. A couple of years later, I decided to become a full-time agent."

I looked at the framed jerseys hanging on the walls. "You've done well."

"I have." He name-dropped three All-Star pitchers, four starting quarterbacks, a wide-receiver who was better at catching passes than listening to his coach, and an All-Pro linebacker who was traded by the Raiders to the Bears before the Raiders moved to Las Vegas.

This calls for flattery. "I would give anything to have your job."

"A lot of people would." He switched to a self-satisfied expression. "It's harder than it looks. People think that I go from luxury boxes to limos to parties. In reality, I work eighteen-hour days keeping my clients out of trouble, monitoring their finances, and making their wives, girlfriends, and mistresses happy."

Your humble-brag needs work. "Sounds a bit thankless."

"At times. When I'm not babysitting my clients, I'm arguing with general managers, negotiating endorsement deals, and finding nannies for my clients' kids."

For which you receive five percent of your clients' salaries. "You must have help."

He pointed at the young woman sitting outside his office who looked as if she had been transported intact from a fashion magazine. "It's just Stacey and me. I like to run a lean operation. We have relationships with accountants, lawyers, and financial planners."

"It must be a wildly competitive business."

"It is. A lot of people never sign any clients. And just because you sign somebody doesn't mean that they'll make any real money, which means that the agent doesn't make any money."

"What percentage of professional baseball players make real money?" I asked.

"Less than one percent. There are fewer than a thousand major leaguers. Every organization has a half-dozen minor league teams with a total of about a hundred and fifty players. A handful get signing bonuses and have a shot at the majors. The rest are there to play catch with the prospects." He tossed a nerf ball through a mini-hoop attached to his trash can. "It's even harder to make money in basketball. There are only about three hundred and fifty players in the NBA."

"Doesn't sound like great odds for the players or the agents."

"It isn't. Being a partner at a law firm wasn't exciting, but the paychecks were reliable."

And you didn't have to spend time in high school gyms trying to persuade seven-foot-tall teenagers to turn pro. "Do other agents try to steal your clients?"

"All the time."

"Have you ever made a discreet inquiry to a ballplayer about changing agents?"

"I don't need to. Players call me. They talk to each other. They know how much everybody else is making. Players don't care how much teams pay guys like Curry and LeBron. They get angry when the guy sitting next to them on the bench is making fifty grand more than they are."

Sounds like my old law firm "I understand that you and Robbie Blum were partners."

"For a short time. I started the business. Robbie had connections in sports and entertainment, so we decided to become partners. It seemed like a good fit." His lips turned down. "It wasn't."

"Sometimes it's hard to work with your friends."

"It was. Robbie was very smart and ambitious. And he was fun to hang out with. We partied with our clients in Vegas. We went to the NBA Finals, the Super Bowl, and the World Series."

"Sounds pretty good to me."

"It was for a while. Then I realized that Robbie and I weren't on the same page on some important stuff." He glanced at the photo of his wife and kids. "I don't cheat on my wife."

"Very admirable."

"I don't drink much, and I don't do anything stronger than weed."

I played dumb. "Robbie had a drinking problem?"

"Yes."

"Drugs?"

"Yes."

"We've heard rumors that he was using Molly."

"Among other things."

"Did it impact your business?"

"It clouded his judgment."

"He never got arrested."

"He got in a couple of fights and was hauled in a few times. We were able to smooth things over and sweet talk the D.A. into not pressing charges."

"He wasn't the first sports personality to get into trouble."

"His erratic behavior and substance issues became a liability. In our business, your biggest asset is your reputation. Some teams refused to deal with him. The leagues are very protective of their images—legitimately so. They didn't want to be associated with somebody tied to drugs. As a result, they made life difficult for Robbie and his clients, and, by extension, me." He lowered his voice. "Robbie started skimming money from our clients to pay his expenses. I had no choice but to terminate our partnership. Not surprisingly, he didn't take it well."

"Litigation?"

"Yes. Settled. Before you ask, I can't tell you anything else about it. Around the same time, Robbie and his second wife split up. It got ugly. Leslie got custody of their son, Sam, and moved down to L.A., where she has family. Robbie was furious, and his behavior got worse."

"When was the last time that you talked to him?"

"About a year ago when we signed the papers to settle the litigation."

"Did he try to steal your clients?"

"Yes."

"Was he successful?"

"Just one: David Archer."

That's a big poach. "You going to try to get him back?"

"I'll take his call."

"Were you at the game on the night that Robbie died?"

"I go to all of the games. I have a luxury suite."

"Did you see Robbie?"

"Briefly. We were both in the clubhouse after the game."

"Did you talk to each other?"

"We stopped talking when we terminated our partnership."

"Do you know if anybody was mad at him?"

"Everybody was mad at him."

* * *

My phone vibrated as I was leaving the Salesforce Tower. Nady's name appeared.

"How did it go with Franklin?" she asked.

"He was at the game on the night that Blum died. They couldn't stand each other."

"Interesting. How soon can you meet me at Eighty-eight King Street?"

It was a condo complex across from the ballpark. "Give me a half hour. Why?"

"Jen Foster agreed to talk to us."

17
"IT WAS A MISTAKE"

"Thank you for seeing us, Ms. Foster," I said, extending a hand.

"Happy to help." The statuesque brunette with the chiseled features and broad shoulders showed us the familiar smile that Giants fans saw on TV every night. "It's Jen."

"Mike." Her grip was firm. "I enjoy your work."

"Thank you."

Nady, Jen, and I took seats around Jen's kitchen table in a sterile one-bedroom condo on the fourth floor of a mid-rise complex across King Street from the left field corner of the ballpark. It had the ambiance of a long-term rental for a corporate executive. The walls were white, and the sparse furnishings were black and chrome. Unlike some of her neighbors who had views of the marina, Jen's living room window looked into the building across the street. The complex was built about twenty years earlier—around the same time as the ballpark. Those of us of a certain age remember when South Beach was an industrial area. Nowadays, Jen lived in the middle of a gentrified "city-within-a-city" extending from Market Street past the ballpark to the new Warriors' arena and the UCSF medical campus.

"What time do you have to be at the ballpark?" I asked.

Jen looked at her watch. "In an hour."

I glanced into the living room, which was furnished with a sofa, a coffee table, a recliner, and a big-screen TV. "How long have you lived here?"

"A couple of months. It's an easy commute on game days."

"I understand that you and Nady were housemates at UCLA."

"Seems like a long time ago. After my softball career ended, I worked for a paper in Modesto and a TV station in Sacramento before I landed the job with Giants Vision. I'd like to do play-by-play someday."

We exchanged small talk for a few more minutes before I nodded at Nady, who picked up on my cue.

"We were hoping you might be able to help us with the Jaylen Jenkins case. Our client says that he didn't kill Robbie Blum. We're trying to figure out who did."

Foster shrugged. "I'm a reporter, not a detective. All I know is what I've read in the papers."

"You know a lot more about what's going on at the ballpark than we do. You were working that night?"

"Of course." Foster confirmed that she arrived at two o'clock, did her usual pre-game preparations, and went on the air at seven. She handled in-game interviews in the stands and post-game interviews in the clubhouse.

"Did you see Blum?"

"Briefly. He came down to the clubhouse after the game to congratulate David Archer on his walk-off homer."

"Did you talk to him?"

"I said hello."

"Did you notice anything unusual in his behavior?"

"No."

"A lot has been written about the fact that Archer wasn't happy with Blum's attempts to negotiate an extension."

"I've read the same stuff. If David was unhappy, he didn't say anything to me. As a broadcaster and a fan, I hope that he stays, but it usually comes down to money."

"Do you know if anybody was angry at Blum?"

"I didn't see anything. My producer and I went through our game footage and post-game interviews. We provided a copy of the video to the police."

"We'll ask them for a copy."

"Fine with me."

Nady lowered her voice. "You knew Blum, didn't you?"

"Everybody in the media knew him."

"Smart guy?"

"Yes."

"Nice guy?"

"No."

Nady took a breath. "You told me that you went out with him a few times."

"Twice. It was a mistake."

Nady let her answer hang, hoping that Foster would be inclined to elaborate.

A moment later, she did. "Robbie was too old for me. He could be charming, but he had too much baggage. He cheated on his ex-wives. He drank too much. And he did designer drugs."

"Is that why you broke up?" Nady asked.

"We didn't break up because we were never in a relationship. In addition to the drinking and drugs, there was also the gambling."

Trifecta.

"This is the first we've heard about gambling," Nady said.

"I think he was addicted. He would bet on anything. He went down to Vegas a couple of times a month to play blackjack and craps. He also bet on sports."

"Did he owe anybody money?"

"Wouldn't surprise me."

"Do you know who?"

"I'm afraid not."

Nady lowered her voice. "Was he ever physically abusive?"

A hesitation. "I've heard rumors that he hit his ex-wives."

"Did he ever hit you?"

"He pushed me once after he'd had too much to drink. That was the last time I went out with him."

"That's horrible."

"It was." Foster took a moment to measure her words. "Robbie was a talented lawyer and an effective agent who blew up his life. He had a falling out with Jeff Franklin that ended in litigation. Some of his clients hired other agents after his behavior became erratic. I felt bad for his ex-wives. I felt worse for his son."

"Is there anybody else who knew him pretty well?"

"Franklin."

"We talked to him," I said. "There were hard feelings."

"I'm not surprised. You should also talk to David Archer and Giants management. They knew him better than I did."

"We've heard that the Giants management didn't like dealing with him."

"Management never likes dealing with agents." She glanced at her watch. "I need to get to the ballpark."

* * *

Pete was waiting for us in the lobby of Foster's building. "Hi, guys."

"What are you doing here?" I asked.

"I was talking to people at the businesses in the neighborhood." He pointed at the security guard behind the console. "This is my friend, Heather, who's head of security. I stopped in to say hi. Heather said that you were upstairs with Jen Foster."

"We were." I nodded at the guard. "Mike Daley. Nice to meet you."

"Heather Stewart. Nice to meet you, sir."

She was four-foot-ten, no makeup, salt-and-pepper hair worn in a sensible bob. In her maroon jacket with a narrow black tie, she was dressed like a waiter in a fifties-era restaurant.

"I recognized your name when you signed in," she said, "and I noticed the resemblance. Pete always talks about you."

If I ever move into a condo in the City, I hope that Heather is at the security console.

* * *

"How long have you known Heather?" I asked Pete.

We were standing on the sidewalk outside Foster's building.

"Years," he said. "In my line of work, it's useful to know the security people at every upscale condo complex in the City."

"She's willing to provide information about the residents?"

"I can be very charming. And I give her a box of See's Candy at Christmas every year."

"Filled with Nuts and Chews?"

"Filled with twenty-dollar bills."

I should have known. "Why did you wait for us, Pete?"

He pointed across the street at the ballpark. "I persuaded the Giants Director of Security to talk to us."

18
"WE HEARD RUMORS"

"This is my brother, Mike," Pete said. "He's a Public Defender."

The Giants Director of Security extended a meaty hand. "Tom Eisenmann."

"Mike Daley. Nice to meet you."

He looked at Pete. "I remembered your name. You and your partner provided backup when my team shut down a heroin ring on Capp Street. You did good work."

"Thanks." Pete gave him a conspiratorial smile. "In those days, people didn't get excited if we used a little muscle to arrest drug dealers."

Eisenmann's mouth turned up. "And people didn't record everything on their phones."

"Times change," I said. "I take it that you weren't working for the Giants at the time?"

"Correct."

"DEA?"

"FBI."

Of course.

Built like a mini-fridge, Eisenmann was wearing a charcoal suit, blinding white shirt, and polka dot tie. From his leathery face and gray crew cut, I figured he was about my age.

"How long were you with the Bureau?" I asked.

"Twenty-four years."

"You from here?"

"Twenty-Fourth and Clement. My dad was a firefighter."

"Washington High?"

"Yup. And State."

"How long have you worked for the Giants?"

"Fifteen years."

"You like it?"

"I love it. Nobody gets killed at the ballpark."

Except for Robbie Blum. "It must be fun to watch the games."

"I haven't seen a single inning since I took this job." He pointed at the monitors mounted on the wall. "I watch everything *except* what's happening on the field."

We were sitting in his windowless office on the executive suite-level on the King Street side of the ballpark. The furnishings were sparse: a metal desk, a swivel chair, two guest chairs, and a credenza. He operated the monitors with a console on his desk.

"I can't talk for long," he said. "I gotta get ready for tonight's game."

It didn't start for another four hours. "We're representing Jaylen Jenkins. I presume you were here on the night that Robbie Blum died?"

"Of course." He said that he arrived at eight a.m. and left at twelve-thirty the following morning. "Except for a few security guards, I'm always first one in, last one out."

"Did you see Mr. Blum that night?"

"No."

"Or my client?"

"No."

"You knew that Jaylen sold caps and shirts on the sidewalk behind the left field wall?"

"Yes. For the record, we do not approve of people selling unlicensed merchandise."

"You could have stopped him."

"We have no authority over activities conducted off stadium property."

"Did Jaylen ever give you any trouble?"

"No."

"You knew Blum?"

"I met him a couple of times. He represented several of our players. He was here in the ballpark on most nights."

"Did he ever give you any trouble?"

"Nothing out of the ordinary. On a couple of occasions, he had too many guests in his firm's luxury suite, so we had to ask some of them to leave."

"Was he good about it?"

"He was fine."

"Inappropriate behavior? Excessive drinking?"

"No."

"Were you aware of any drug issues?"

The corner of his mouth turned up slightly. "We heard rumors."

"We heard that he also had a significant gambling issue."

His thin lips curled into a grimace. "We heard rumors that he was betting on Giants games. The league became concerned that he was getting inside information from his clients, so they investigated. As far as I know, they found no evidence."

"We heard that he got in over his head on a gambling debt." This was a bluff. In reality, I didn't know.

"I don't know," he said.

"Any other issues?"

Another pause. "He used to go down to the clubhouse after the games to see David Archer. Some of the players thought that it was an invasion of their space."

"How did you feel about it?"

"Ideally, non-players should stay out of the clubhouse. On the other hand, you need to keep your stars happy. If David wanted to talk to his agent, we usually complied."

"How were Archer and Blum getting along?"

"They ran hot and cold. If David thought Blum was going to get him a contract extension for a lot of money, they got along great. If not, they would snipe at each other."

"Was anybody else angry at Blum?"

"If you're asking me if anybody was mad enough to crack his skull, I wouldn't know."

Fair enough. I pointed at the monitors. "A lot of security cameras."

"Hundreds—inside and out. You can't walk down a corridor without being filmed. Every entrance is covered. So is the players' parking lot. And the walkways behind the outfield walls."

"I presume that you provided security video to the police?"

"We did."

"I trust you have no objection if we ask them for a copy?"

"Fine with me. I must warn you that we sent over hundreds of hours of video."

"We'll give it a look. We'd also like to talk to David Archer."

"I'll see what I can do." He stood up to signal that our conversation was coming to end.

Pete spoke up again. "I spoke to the assistant for Mr. Higgins. She said that he would talk to us for a few minutes."

Bill Higgins was a Silicon Valley venture capitalist and the managing partner of the Giants ownership group.

Eisenmann scowled. "I'm not sure if he's here."

"We'll wait here while you check," Pete said.

"I'll see what I can do."

19

"IT IS OUR POLICY TO COOPERATE WITH THE POLICE"

The venture-capitalist-turned-baseball-owner flashed a puckish smile, extended a hand, and spoke with the hint of a New York accent. "Nice to meet you, Mr. Daley."

"Mike. Nice to meet you, too, Mr. Higgins."

"Bill."

The diminutive financier and one-time coxswain on the Princeton rowing team had celebrated his eightieth birthday a few weeks earlier at the exclusive Burlingame Country Club. According to the *Chronicle*'s gossip columnist, everybody who was anybody in Silicon Valley showed up to pay their respects. Raised on the Upper East Side and educated at New York's most exclusive private schools, the son of a Goldman Sachs partner worked on Wall Street for a few years before he moved to the West Coast and became an analyst at Kleiner Perkins. In 1969, he started his own firm and was an early investor in Apple and Genentech. Leveraging gains from his initial investments and tapping into capital from Hong Kong, Singapore, and Kuwait, Higgins raised over a billion dollars, which he managed from an office in a nondescript business park on Sand Hill Road. When the Giants entered into a deal to move to Tampa in 1992, a group of local business leaders—led by Safeway's Peter Magowan—bought the team and kept it in San Francisco. The publicity-shy Higgins was one of the bigger investors.

I took a moment to look around his neatly appointed office overlooking Willie Mays Plaza. The walls were covered with photos of every Giants team since 1992—the year that Higgins made his initial investment. Behind his desk were framed copies of the front pages of the *Chronicle* after the Giants World Series championships in 2010, 2012, and 2014. His credenza was lined with photos of his wife, adult children, grandchildren, and great-grandchildren.

I pointed at the family pictures. "Beautiful family."

"Thank you."

"Do you enjoy running the Giants?"

The crow's feet at the corners of his blue eyes crinkled as he chuckled. "Best job I've ever had. I get to hold up the trophies while everybody else does the real work. We have an excellent organization and terrific players. I've always believed that you should hire the best people and give them the freedom and responsibility to do their jobs."

"That's excellent advice."

It was a lovely sentiment. It was also widely known that "Chainsaw Bill" fired thousands of employees at the companies that he funded in order to cut costs.

"The team has been playing well lately," I observed.

"We're hoping for a big second half."

The Giants were hovering around .500. Unless they had a hot streak, it was likely that they would trade some of their older (and more expensive) players.

Higgins glanced at Eisenmann, who was sitting next to Pete. Neither had said a word. Higgins turned back to me. "I understand that you are representing the young man accused of killing Robbie Blum."

"I am."

"Helluva thing." Another glance at Eisenmann. "I trust that Tom is helping you?"

"He is."

"Very good. We have worked very hard to create a safe and friendly environment for our fans. Anything that might suggest otherwise runs contrary to our mission."

It's bad for business if a body washes up in the marina behind the center field scoreboard. "I'm one of those fans."

"We thank you for your support. I want to make it clear that it is our policy to cooperate with the police."

"Good to hear. I hope that policy includes cooperation with defense attorneys."

"It does. I trust that you'll be discreet?"

"Of course." *We'll see.*

"Anything else, Mr. Daley?"

I guess we aren't going to be using first names. "You knew Robbie Blum pretty well, didn't you?"

"We met a few times. I leave contract negotiations to our management team."

"We understand that he was difficult."

"At times."

"He had alcohol, drug, and gambling issues."

"So I've been told."

"Among the people in the organization, who had the most interactions with Mr. Blum?"

"Eric."

Eric Chen was the Giants general manager. "We'd like to talk to him, too."

"He's very busy."

"You just said that your policy is to cooperate."

He scowled. "Tom will make the arrangements."

"We'd also like to talk to the manager."

"You think he had something to do with Mr. Blum's death?"

"No, but he may be able to provide information regarding Mr. Blum."

"I hope you aren't suggesting that somebody in our organization had anything to do with his death?"

"Absolutely not." *We'll see.*

"We're in the middle of the season, Mr. Daley."

"I'll just need a few minutes of his time."

He looked over at Eisenmann. "Set it up, Tom."

Eisenmann nodded.

Higgins's eyes showed their first sign of irritation. "Anything else, Mr. Daley?"

"We'd like to talk to David Archer. He was Mr. Blum's biggest client."

"David is busy preparing for tonight's game."

"I don't need to talk to him tonight, but I would like to meet him as soon as possible. We think Mr. Blum may have been heavily indebted to one or more gamblers. We'd like to ask Mr. Archer about it."

"He doesn't know anything about it."

How do you know? "Then it will be a short conversation."

"You'll need to do it when it's convenient for him."

"Of course."

"And I need your word that you won't reveal anything to the press."

"Absolutely." That's a white lie.

"Or in court."

"Agreed." That's a whopper.

His eyes narrowed. "We are very protective of our players, our organization, and our brand. In my view, I am not just the owner of a baseball team. I am the steward of a public trust, and I take my responsibilities seriously. If you embarrass any of our players, any member of our organization, or Major League Baseball, we will not hesitate to sue you."

I believed him. "Thank you for your cooperation, Mr. Higgins."

* * *

Pete's phone rang as we were walking across Willie Mays Plaza. He answered, said, "Yes," several times, grunted, and ended the call. He put his phone inside his pocket and turned to me. "You need to get back to the office right away."

"Why?"

"One of my operatives found Jaylen's mother in a homeless camp in Oakland. She's bringing her over to the P.D.'s Office."

20
"I HAVEN'T DONE A VERY GOOD JOB"

LaTanya Jenkins sat across the table from Nady and me, eyes looking down at her hands. "Thank you for seeing me," she whispered.

"You're welcome," I said.

She was a petite woman whose scarred face and prematurely gray hair made her appear older than forty-three. Jaylen had told us that she had been a single mother since she was nineteen and had been fighting drug and alcohol addictions for most of her life. She was wearing a gray Giants hoodie and faded jeans. Her worn backpack held essential belongings. Her demeanor was stoic.

"You must be hungry," I said.

"A little."

I asked Terrence to get her a sandwich and a water bottle.

"I need to see my son," she said.

"We'll take you over to see him in a few minutes. We've had trouble finding you." Pete's operative had found her in a homeless camp near the West Oakland BART Station.

"I had an argument with the woman who runs the house where I'm staying."

"Will she let you back in?"

"If I stay clean."

"We'll help you."

"Thank you." She took a sip of water. "I need to see my son," she repeated.

"Jaylen is worried about you."

"Jaylen worries about everybody."

"The next few weeks are going to be very stressful for him. It would be great if you could provide support."

"I'll do the best that I can." She took another drink of water. "I have trouble dealing with legal stuff. My oldest son is at Pelican Bay.

I haven't seen him in three years."

"Jaylen told us. That must be really hard."

"It is. My middle son died around the same time that my oldest one went to jail. He was on the autism spectrum. He got involved with a gang in our neighborhood. I should have kept a closer eye on him, but—," her voice trailed off.

"Jaylen told us about him, too."

She swallowed. "Jaylen is my baby. He's all that I have, Mr. Daley."

Nady finally spoke up. "You're all that Jaylen has, LaTanya. That's why it's so important for you to be here."

"I haven't done a very good job."

"You're doing the best that you can."

"I don't know if I can handle it. I've had a lot of trouble taking care of myself."

"We need you to take care of yourself and help us take care of Jaylen."

"I'll do the best that I can."

* * *

Rosie knocked on the open door to my office at eight o'clock the same night. "You ready to head home?"

"In a few minutes."

"Where's LaTanya?"

"Pete took her back to the halfway house."

"They let her back in?"

"Yes. She can stay as long as she's clean."

"What are the odds?"

"Fifty-fifty."

She grimaced. "Whenever I think my life is stressful, I try to remind myself that there are people like LaTanya and Jaylen who have it a lot worse than I do. How did it go between Jaylen and LaTanya?"

"Not great.

She listened attentively as I filled her in. Jaylen expressed frustration at LaTanya's continuing substance issues. LaTanya became defensive but promised to try to stay clean. Jaylen didn't believe her. "She started crying. You could tell that they'd had the same conversation many times."

Rosie shook her head. "You remember what heroin did to my sister."

"I do." Rosie's younger sister, Teresa, fought drug and alcohol addiction for much of her life until her liver finally gave out a few weeks after her fiftieth birthday.

"Is she going to be able to provide any support for Jaylen?"

"Hard to say. She had a bad experience when her oldest son was arrested. And then a few weeks after he was convicted and sent up to Pelican Bay, her middle son was shot and killed."

"It's unimaginable. Is that when she got hooked on heroin?"

"She was already using, but I think it tipped her into serious addiction."

"Can we do anything to help her?"

"We don't have the manpower, expertise, or budget to provide a place for her to live or get her some additional counseling. We'll have to rely on the halfway house."

Rosie frowned. "Do what you can, Mike. Unfortunately, we aren't equipped to fix everybody's problems."

21
"I RESPECTED HIM"

Higgins and Eisenmann were true to their word. At eleven o'clock the following morning, a Wednesday, I was sitting in the cluttered office of Eric Chen, the Giants wunderkind GM. I studied the floor-to-ceiling white board on his wall. From left to right, the rosters of the Giants Rookie League, Low-Single-A, High-Single-A, Double-A and Triple-A teams were printed in block letters. On the far right, I read the names of the major league roster.

"Seems like a low-tech system for keeping track of everybody," I observed.

Chen smiled. "I like to see every player in our organization. It helps me figure out the big picture."

"How often do you modify the chart?"

"Whenever anything changes. Usually it's every few days."

"I read that you developed proprietary software to evaluate players."

"I did." His voice filled with pride as he pointed at his laptop. "Every team has a custom-designed algorithm. We've come a long way from the days where scouts would shuttle between minor-league parks, smoke cigars, and record their observations in spiral notebooks."

"Simpler times."

"Indeed."

Chen was a wiry man of thirty-two with intense eyes. The son of Google executives was baseball's youngest GM. He had graduated at the top of his class at Michigan, spent a couple of years with JP Morgan in New York, then got an MBA at Wharton. He wrote his thesis on maximizing value on power-hitting shortstops and left-handed relief pitchers. Instead of returning to New York after graduation, he persuaded the Dodgers to hire him as an analyst. Based upon his algorithm, the Dodgers won the National League

West seven seasons in a row. The Giants paid dearly to hire him as GM. The results, thus far, had been mixed.

He sat down in a leather chair behind a nondescript desk matching the cubicles outside his office where a dozen young computer jockeys were crunching numbers. I took a seat opposite his desk. Except for an aerial photo of the ballpark and the autographed picture of David Archer on his credenza, Chen could have passed for a partner at a venture capital firm.

"Did you play ball in high school?" he asked.

"I was a mediocre left-handed pitcher and a backup first baseman at St. Ignatius. You?"

"I sat on the bench at Palo Alto High."

"My brother was the family jock. He quit baseball to focus on football. He played quarterback at Cal."

"You're Tommy Daley's brother?"

"Yes."

"I've seen footage. He was very good."

"Yes, he was." My older brother, Tommy, was an All-City quarterback at St. Ignatius and first-team All-Pac-Eight at Cal before he volunteered to go to Vietnam and never came back.

Chen lowered his voice. "I'm sorry."

"Thank you." I switched topics. "The Giants have been playing well lately. Those of us who live and die with the team are hoping that you'll make a run in the second half. Are you going to pick up a player or two before the trading deadline?"

"We're always looking for ways to improve our ballclub."

"I hope you sign David Archer to an extension."

He repeated his mantra. "We're always looking for ways to improve our ballclub."

I pointed at the board. "How does the master plan work?"

"The progression goes from left to right. Our goal is getting the right mix of skills and salary at the major league level to create a multiyear window to compete for championships. If you have too many inexperienced players, it's hard to win. If you have too many veterans, it's hard to stay within budget. Most of the players on the left never make it all the way across to the right. My job is to mix and match so that we have a core group of impact players who hit their prime at the same time while we still have control over their salaries. Then we try to fill any holes by signing free agents."

"Wouldn't it be simpler to fill the roster with free agents?"

"Only if you have unlimited resources like the Yankees. You also run up against the luxury tax." He explained that unlike other sports, baseball doesn't have a "hard" salary cap. However, if your aggregate salaries exceed a certain threshold—slightly above two hundred million dollars—you have to pay a "tax" of twenty-two percent of the excess payroll. "The tax goes up for multiple violations. A four-time offender would be dinged for fifty percent."

"It's complicated," I observed, hoping to keep him talking.

"It is. Salaries are the biggest line item in our budget. We have to manage our dollars carefully to stay competitive and keep our investors happy."

"And try to win the World Series."

"Of course. It's even more challenging when our most expensive assets have personalities and walk out the door every night."

I smiled. "Still happy you left investment banking?"

"I wouldn't trade jobs with anybody. You didn't come here to talk about the luxury tax."

"I'm representing Jaylen Jenkins. You must have known Robbie Blum pretty well."

"I did."

"Did you like him?"

"I respected him."

"Was he good at his job?"

"He represented his clients zealously, and he made a lot of money."

Not exactly the answer to my question. "Was he honest?"

"He represented his clients zealously, and he made a lot of money."

Got it. "What was he like in negotiations?"

"Aggressive. He would start with a ridiculous offer and pound the table until we settled on something slightly less ridiculous. It was effective up to a point. There are diminishing returns for screamers. Eventually, people get tired of the drama."

"Did you?"

"It was my job to deal with him. He represented several of our best players, including David Archer."

"Was he happy with Blum's representation?"

"They got along fine when Robbie got David a lot of money."

"Did you ever socialize with Blum?"

"It was mostly business. We had drinks at the winter meetings on occasion." He said that he had never been to Blum's house or met either of his ex-wives. He confirmed that Blum's two divorces were acrimonious.

"We heard the Blum had a drinking problem."

"I heard the same thing."

"And drugs."

"I heard rumors."

"Did you ever see him lose control?"

"Hard to tell. His normal tone of voice was set at a high volume."

"We've heard rumors about gambling issues, too."

"The league heard about it, too. They looked into it and didn't find any evidence."

"Were you here on the night that Blum died?"

"Of course. I was sitting in the team's box behind the dugout."

"Did you see Blum?"

"Briefly. He came down to the clubhouse to congratulate David on his walk-off homer."

"Did you talk to him?"

"I said hello."

"Was he with anybody?"

"Not that I recall."

"How long was he there?"

"Just a few minutes."

"Did he talk to anybody besides Archer?"

"Not that I recall."

"Where did you go after the game?"

"Home." He glanced at his watch. "I need to get to a meeting, Mr. Daley."

"Thanks for your time, Mr. Chen."

* * *

I was walking by the Willie Mays statue when I heard a familiar rasp behind me.

"Mike Daley?"

I turned around and looked into the glassy eyes of the dean of San Francisco sports columnists. "How are you, Harv?"

"Not bad."

Harvey Tate was seventy years old, but he had a ninety-year-old body. The son of a mailman had grown up near Stonestown Mall and graduated from Lowell High. A Cal alum, Tate had covered Tommy when Tate was a staff reporter for the *Daily Californian*. He started his professional career at the *Fresno Bee*. A few years later, he landed a job reporting on high school sports at the *Chronicle*. He was the Giants beat reporter for twenty years before becoming a columnist. He had won every major journalism award. His younger brother, Tim, was a classmate of mine at law school.

"Your brother okay?" I asked.

"For a lawyer."

"Give him my best." I started to walk away, but he stopped me.

"Got a sec?" he asked. He didn't wait for an answer. "I heard you're representing the kid who popped Robbie Blum."

"Allegedly," I said.

"Allegedly," he repeated. "Did he?"

"No."

"Says who?"

"My client."

"Right." He was wearing a stained brown sport coat that looked as if he'd bought it in the seventies. "I heard you talked to Bill Higgins and Eric Chen."

"How did you find out?"

"I've been a reporter for a long time."

"A good one," I said.

"I like to think so. You think one of them was involved in Blum's death?"

"I was just looking for information, Harv."

"Would you care to comment about your client's case?"

I went with the standard. "Jaylen Jenkins has been unjustly accused of a crime that he did not commit. We look forward to defending him in court."

He chuckled. "How many times have you used that line?"

"Hundreds. Did you know Blum?"

"Yeah."

"Well?"

"Pretty well."

"Well enough to know about any skeletons in his closet?"

"Maybe."

"Like what?"

"Off the record?"

There's a switch. "Sure."

"His agency was imploding, and he was drowning in gambling debts."

I looked the grizzled reporter in the eye. "Can I buy you lunch?"

22
"HE GOT IN OVER HIS HEAD"

"Do you think the Giants will make a run in the second half?" I asked.

"Nah." Tate took a bite of his steak sandwich. "They're going to be sellers at the trading deadline. If I were in Eric Chen's shoes, I would ship everybody out."

"They gonna fire the manager?"

"I hope so."

In his columns, Tate fired the Giants manager at least once a week. "You said that they should have fired him at the end of last season."

"Just a suggestion." He took a sip of cheap cabernet. "Surprisingly, the GM doesn't consult me on personnel decisions."

"The team might be more successful if he did."

At twelve-fifteen on Wednesday afternoon, we were sitting at a table in the corner of Bechelli's, a coffee shop adjacent to the San Francisco Flower Market at Sixth and Brannan, about halfway between the ballpark and the Hall of Justice. The aroma of cheeseburgers, pesto chicken, cheesesteaks, and Caesar salads filled the wood-paneled room with a view of an off-ramp from the 280 Freeway. Bechelli's was within walking distance of the Hall, so I recognized several judges, lawyers, bailiffs, and cops.

Tate put his wine glass down. "You gonna get your client off?"

"Yeah. He told me that he didn't do it."

"How many of your clients tell you the same thing?"

"All of them." I leaned forward and spoke softly. "What's the deal with Blum?"

He glanced at our waitress, who came over and refilled his wine. He ate his last French fry and wiped his lips with a cloth napkin. "What's in it for me?"

"You get the first exclusive interview with my client."

"When?"

"Soon."

"How soon?"

"As soon as he's acquitted."

"That could be months from now. Come on, Mike. Want something, give something."

"I promise that I won't let Jaylen talk to anybody else before he talks to you. Best that I can do, Harv."

His full lips turned down. "Fine."

"What's the deal with Blum?"

"Follow the money."

"What do you mean?"

"He got in over his head."

"How?"

"First, he had an ugly breakup with Jeff Franklin. They got into a monumental pissing match that took two years to resolve and cost him millions. Then Blum's second marriage blew up, which cost him more millions. Then his second-biggest client fired him."

"Let me guess: it cost him even more millions."

"Correct."

"Why did he get fired?"

"The client was unhappy when contract negotiations stalled. There were also rumors that Blum started skimming money from his clients."

"Was he?"

"I don't know."

"Anybody angry enough to take a pop at him with a Louisville Slugger?"

"You never know."

"We've heard that he had an expensive lifestyle."

"He did. Big houses. Maseratis. Ferraris."

"He got a five percent commission on every penny that his clients made. Archer's last contract was worth almost two hundred million."

"Blum pissed it away on booze and drugs. It started with coke.

He moved up to more serious stuff. Last year, he spent six weeks in rehab, but it didn't work."

"We think a guy named Brian Holton was supplying Blum."

"I don't know."

Our waitress came over with the check, which I grabbed. "We heard that Blum had gambling issues."

His eyes darted out the window then back to me. "I've heard unsubstantiated gossip."

That's the best kind. "Was he betting on his clients?"

"Could be."

"You got a name?"

"No, but I heard that Blum owed a lot of money to a big-time gambler."

"How big-time?"

"Big enough that he would break your legs if you didn't pay."

Or whack you with a Louisville Slugger.

23
"IT'S IN THE BEST INTERESTS OF OUR CLIENT"

Nady looked up from her laptop. "I thought you had tickets to the Giants game tonight."

"I gave them to Pete. We need to get ready for Jaylen's prelim tomorrow morning."

"Your dedication is admirable. Shouldn't Pete be looking for witnesses?"

"After the game. He works late and operates on his own timetable."

"Did you get inside the Giants clubhouse?"

"Briefly. It's even nicer in person than it looks on TV. I talked to the manager. He said that he had a few interactions with Blum, but Chen had most of the contact."

"Did you get any skinny on why the team has been playing like crap for the past week?"

"Afraid not."

We were in our conference room at eight-thirty on Wednesday night. The aroma of Nady's kale salad filled the room. Most of our colleagues had gone home.

I pointed at Luna, who was curled up in the corner. "How long has she been sleeping?"

"A couple of hours."

"Nice life. Did you get a witness list from Erickson and Turner?"

"Yes."

"How many names?"

"Just one: Ken Lee."

I wasn't surprised. The D.A. was going to show just enough evidence to move Jaylen's case forward to trial—and nothing more. In my long and infrequently illustrious career, I have gotten the charges dropped at a prelim just a handful of times.

"How do you want to play this?" Nady asked.

"We'll challenge everything Lee says and try to get the D.A. to reveal as much of his case as possible."

"Do you think we should call any witnesses?"

"Yes, but I may change my mind. Add Brian Holton and Jeff Franklin on our list. Holton was selling drugs to Blum. Franklin and Blum had a falling out."

"It won't be enough to get Judge McDaniel to drop the charges tomorrow."

"Probably not, but it'll give Erickson and Turner something to think about."

She arched an eyebrow. "You're thinking of a 'SODDI' defense?"

"For now."

"SODDI" was lawyer-speak for "Some other dude did it." It's a defense lawyer's best friend and last resort when you have nothing better. You offer the jury a couple of plausible suspects and hope for the best. It's more effective when you actually have some credible evidence that somebody else did, in fact, do it.

Nady closed her laptop. "I'll e-mail our witness list to Turner. Anything else?"

"I went over and saw Jaylen. He's pissed off. That's actually a positive sign. Guilty people change their stories and get defensive. Innocent people get mad."

"You think he's innocent?"

"Ask me again in a couple of weeks. Would you like to do the opening statement and handle Lee's cross tomorrow?"

"I'd love it. You don't want to do it yourself?"

"Yes, but it's in the best interests of our client. You're an excellent lawyer and it would be a good experience for you."

"And because Judge McDaniel is a woman?"

"In part. My sources at the D.A.'s Office informed me that Vanessa Turner has been rehearsing her opening. I think Erickson is going to let her handle the prelim."

"So you want a female defense attorney to go up against a female prosecutor in front of a female judge?"

Yes. "It's in the best interests of our client," I repeated.

The corner of her mouth turned up. "That's sexist, you know."

"I do."

"You're okay with it?"

"Absolutely. Good lawyers use all of the tools available to us."

"Is Rosie okay with it?"

I grinned. "It was her idea."

* * *

Rosie was behind the wheel of her Prius and I was in the passenger seat as we drove north on the Golden Gate Bridge at ten-thirty p.m. I could barely make out the Alcatraz beacon through the mist.

Her eyes were on the road. "Has Pete found anything useful?"

"Working on it. Still looking for some viable options."

She darted a glance my way. "You and Nady good to go tomorrow?"

"Yeah."

"This case is going to trial, isn't it?"

"Probably."

"You and Nady are good lawyers, Mike."

"Probably not good enough to get the charges dropped tomorrow."

She nodded. "You going to waive time?"

"Jaylen doesn't want to."

"It's going to be tight if you don't."

In California, the accused has the right to a jury trial within sixty days after the prelim. In most cases, defense attorneys "waive time," which means that we agree to move the trial beyond the sixty-day window. This gives us more time to prepare. The flip side is that it could take a year or longer to get a trial date.

"You should try to talk him out of it," she said.

"I will." My phone vibrated, and Pete's name appeared on the display. I pressed the green button. "Did the Giants win?"

"Yeah."

"You got something for me?"

"Not sure."

He loved playing cat-and-mouse. "Where are you?"

"The Gold Club."

I heard music blaring in the background. "Business?"

"Of course." He cleared his throat. "Darlene called. Brian Holton was arrested for selling Ecstasy to an undercover cop. I don't have any details."

"Is he still in the lockup?"

"Joe Petrillo already bailed him out."

Petrillo was a well-known defense lawyer who represented drug dealers and gang bangers.

"I'll see what I can find out. Thanks, Pete."

"You're welcome." He ended the call.

Rosie glanced at me. "You got something?"

"Holton was arrested for dealing drugs."

"Sounds like he just became a more viable option for your SODDI defense."

24
"LET'S GET STARTED"

The world-weary bailiff called the stuffy courtroom to order at ten o'clock the following morning. "All rise."

Nady, Jaylen, and I stood at the defense table. Erickson and Turner were at the prosecution table. So was Lee. As the lead investigator, he was the only witness allowed in court before his testimony.

I glanced at Erickson, who smiled with confidence. Then he refocused on the front of the courtroom, where Judge McDaniel was making her way to the bench.

Jaylen leaned toward me and whispered, "Where is she?"

"She must have been delayed."

Rosie was sitting behind us in the front row of the gallery next to the empty seat that she had saved for LaTanya.

Jaylen grimaced. "What's that smell?"

Sewage. "The plumbing doesn't always work very well."

I surveyed the half-full gallery. There were no members of Blum's family. Since LaTanya hadn't shown up, no family members or friends were present to provide moral support for Jaylen, either. Harvey Tate was in the second row. The *San Jose Mercury*, the *East Bay Times*, and the *Marin Independent Journal* had sent reporters. So had the local TV stations. The usual assortment of retirees, homeless people, and courtroom regulars were spread out in the gallery.

Judge McDaniel took her seat and held up a hand. "Please be seated."

We did as we were told.

She put on her reading glasses and pretended to study her docket. She looked at her clerk. "Please call our first case."

"The People versus Jaylen DeMarcus Jenkins. Preliminary hearing."

"Is the defendant present?"

"Yes."

"Counsel will state their names for the record."

"Vanessa Turner and Andrew Erickson for the People."

"Nadezhda Nikonova and Michael Daley for the defense."

"Thank you." Judge McDaniel tapped her microphone. "We are here to determine whether there is sufficient evidence to bind the defendant over for trial. I would remind everybody that a preliminary hearing is different from a trial. There is no jury. The burden of proof is lower. And by law, I am required to give the District Attorney the benefit of the doubt on evidentiary issues." She looked at Jaylen. "Do you understand why we're here, Mr. Jenkins?"

"Yes, Your Honor."

She turned to Turner. "Did you wish to make an opening statement?"

"Yes, Your Honor."

"Let's get started."

* * *

Twenty-five minutes later, Turner and Nady had completed their respective opening statements, neither of which appeared to have made a significant impression on Judge McDaniel. A good opener can win over a jury at trial. It's harder to dazzle a smart judge at a prelim.

Turner was positioned a respectful distance from the witness box, where Lee was sitting, arms at his sides. You never crowd a strong witness. "Inspector," she said, "were you called to the South Beach Marina behind the ballpark in the early morning of Tuesday, June second?"

"Yes."

He was wearing a charcoal suit from the Men's Wearhouse. Roosevelt always said that if you notice a homicide inspector's clothing, it's too flashy. Lee had poured himself a cup of water that he wouldn't touch. Drinking makes you look nervous.

"Could you please tell us why?" Turner asked.

"An employee of the Marina named Jesus Martinez had found a body in the bay. The decedent was pronounced at the scene at seven-twenty a.m. He was later identified as a sports agent named Robert Blum."

The first point went to Turner: to charge somebody with murder, you need a decedent.

She adjusted the sleeve of her navy pantsuit. "Was Mr. Martinez cooperative?"

"Yes. I took his statement and found no evidence that he was involved in Mr. Blum's death."

"Do you know how Mr. Blum died?"

"Our Medical Examiner determined that Mr. Blum died of brain damage associated with a fractured skull caused by being struck by a blunt object."

"Move to strike," Nady said. "Foundation. Either our Medical Examiner should address this issue herself, or her report should be introduced into evidence."

"Sustained."

It was a proper—albeit futile—objection. Turner quickly introduced the autopsy report into evidence. Lee confirmed its conclusion. Then Turner moved on.

"Inspector, did you find any evidence placing the defendant in the vicinity of the ballpark at approximately eleven-forty-five on the night of Monday, June first of this year?"

"Yes. The defendant appeared in a Giants surveillance video taken by a camera mounted above the exit to the players' parking lot behind the left field wall."

Turner introduced the video into evidence and cued it on the flatscreen TV which she had positioned so that the judge, the attorneys, and the people in the gallery could see it. "Could you please describe what's going on?"

"Yes, Ms. Turner." Lee moved in front of the TV and narrated as Turner ran the video in slow motion. "The decedent, Robert Blum, is walking along the path behind the players' parking lot. The defendant is following him."

Turner stopped the video. "There's an object in the defendant's hand, isn't there?"

"Yes." Lee pointed at the screen. "A baseball bat."

Turner started the video again, and Lee picked up his narrative when Jaylen reappeared.

"Here we see the defendant running in the opposite direction." Turner stopped the video, and Lee pointed at the screen. "He is no longer holding the bat."

Turner waited as Lee returned to the box. Then she walked to the evidence cart, picked up a soiled Louisville Slugger wrapped in plastic with an identifying tag, and handed it to him. "Are you familiar with this object, Inspector?"

"It's a professional-grade Louisville Slugger baseball bat, thirty-four-inch length, thirty-two-ounce weight, bearing the autograph of David Archer, the Giants left fielder. Mr. Archer confirmed that it was one of several bats that he used during batting practice. He provided the bat to Mr. Blum to take home as a souvenir for his son."

"How did you happen to come into possession of this bat?"

"Mr. Martinez found it floating in the bay a few feet from Mr. Blum's body."

"Do you know how the bat got into the water?"

"I believe that the defendant used this bat to hit Mr. Blum, whereupon he discarded it into the water."

"Move to strike," Nady said. "There is no foundation for Inspector Lee's testimony."

"Noted."

Turner didn't fluster. "You believe that the defendant used this bat to hit Mr. Blum in the head and crack his skull?"

"Objection," Nady said. "Speculation."

"Sustained."

"No further questions, Your Honor."

"Cross-exam, Ms. Nikonova?"

"Yes, Your Honor." Nady stood, buttoned her jacket, and moved in front of Lee. "Mr. Martinez told you that he found the decedent's body floating in the bay, didn't he?"

"Yes."

"It's your contention that he wasn't present when Mr. Blum fell into the bay?"

"Correct."

"How do you know?"

"I found no evidence that he was there."

"But you can't rule out the possibility that Mr. Martinez hit Mr. Blum with a heavy object and pushed him into the bay, can you?"

"I found no evidence that he did."

"Mr. Martinez didn't see Jaylen hit the decedent with a bat, did he?"

"No."

"And you have found no witnesses who saw Jaylen hit the decedent, correct?"

"Correct."

"So you have no physical evidence or witnesses proving that Jaylen hit Mr. Blum, right?"

"The video and the bat."

"Ah, yes. The video and the bat." Nady walked back to the defense table, pressed a button on her computer, and the video appeared on the TV. She ran it in slow motion, then stopped it as Blum walked by his car. "That's Mr. Blum's car?"

"Yes."

"Why did he walk by his own car?"

"I don't know."

"It must have seemed odd to you that he walked by his own car late at night, didn't it?"

"Maybe he wanted to get some air."

"Or maybe he was meeting somebody. And maybe somebody attacked him, right?"

"Objection," Turner said. "Speculation."

"Sustained."

Nady acted as if she hadn't heard it. "Inspector, it's possible that Mr. Blum ran into somebody on the pathway other than Jaylen, isn't it?"

"Anything's possible, but we have video of your client running after Mr. Blum with a bat. We have no evidence of anybody else in the vicinity at the time."

Nady walked to the evidence cart, picked up the bat, walked back to the box, and handed it to Lee. "This bat?"

"Yes."

"Did you find Jaylen's fingerprints on this bat?"

"No."

"His blood?"

"No."

"So you have no way of connecting this bat to Jaylen, do you?"

"You can see it in the video."

"But you don't know that it's the same bat, do you?"

"It's a logical conclusion."

"Logic is nice, Inspector, but we need evidence in court."

"Objection," Turner said. "Ms. Nikonova is testifying."

"Withdrawn." Nady retrieved the bat from Lee and put it back on the cart. "Inspector, are you aware that the decedent was a frequent customer of the Gold Club on Howard Street?"

"We heard rumors."

"Could you describe the nature of that business?"

"It's a strip club."

"Mr. Blum was acquainted with an employee named Brian Holton, wasn't he?"

"I believe so."

"Mr. Holton is the club's bouncer, isn't he?"

"He's the doorman."

"Mr. Holton was arrested last night for selling illegal drugs to an undercover officer, wasn't he?"

"Objection. Relevance."

"Overruled."

"Yes."

"Mr. Holton was also selling drugs to Mr. Blum, wasn't he?"

"Objection. Foundation."

"Overruled."

"I don't know," Lee said.

"But you found text messages from Mr. Blum to Mr. Holton, didn't you?"

"Yes."

"Mr. Blum owed Mr. Holton money, didn't he?"

"I don't know."

"Mr. Holton and the decedent didn't like each other, did they? In fact, Mr. Holton and the decedent had gotten into several altercations at the club, hadn't they?"

"I don't know."

"Did you consider the possibility that Mr. Holton came to the ballpark to collect on a debt from Mr. Blum?"

"Objection. Speculation."

Nady addressed the judge. "I'm not asking Inspector Lee to speculate. I'm inquiring about his thought process based upon his years of experience as a homicide inspector."

"Overruled."

I didn't think we'd get that one.

Lee sighed. "I found no evidence suggesting that Mr. Holton was involved."

"Did you consider the possibility that Mr. Holton got angry at Mr. Blum and struck him with the bat?"

"I found no evidence."

"No further questions, Your Honor."

"Redirect, Ms. Turner?"

"No, Your Honor."

"Do you wish to call any additional witnesses?"

"No, Your Honor. The prosecution rests."

"Ms. Nikonova, are you prepared to call your first witness?"

Nady looked my way, and I closed my eyes. She turned around and spoke to the judge. "We will not be calling any witnesses, Your Honor. We move that the charges be dropped as a matter of law. The prosecution has failed to meet its burden of proof."

"Denied. I am also ruling that the defendant shall be bound over for trial."

"But Your Honor—,"

"I've ruled, Ms. Nikonova." The judge darted a glance at Turner, then she turned back to Nady. "We'll need to discuss scheduling. I trust that your client will waive time?"

"No, Your Honor. California Penal Code Section 1382 provides that our client has a right to a trial within sixty days. Mr. Jenkins has instructed us to move forward within the statutorily mandated period."

"Fine." The judge's eyes moved to the prosecution table. "You'll be ready to go within sixty days, Ms. Turner?"

"Yes, Your Honor."

The courtroom went silent as the judge looked at her computer. "We have an opening on Thursday, August sixth, in front of Judge Ignatius Tsang."

Not an ideal draw. The former prosecutor was smart, thoughtful, and generally fair, but his rulings often tilted in favor of the D.A.

Judge McDaniel eyed Nady. "I trust you'll be ready, Ms. Nikonova?"

"Yes, Your Honor."

"Then it's settled. You'll get in touch with Judge Tsang's clerk to work out a schedule for pre-trial motions." She stood up. "We're adjourned."

Jaylen turned to me and said, "I'm glad that we're moving forward quickly."

"It's going to be tight, Jaylen. Nady and I will come see you later this afternoon to talk about what happens next."

"Why can't you come now?"

"I want to talk to Erickson."

25
"IN DUE COURSE"

Erickson feigned surprise as I approached him at the prosecution table in the otherwise empty courtroom. "You're really going to take this to trial in sixty days?"

"Yes."

"If I were in your shoes, I might have wanted a little more time to prepare."

"Our client isn't giving us the luxury."

"We'll be ready."

So will we. "We're going to ask for expedited discovery."

"We will provide everything you're entitled to as expeditiously as possible."

"Anything you'd care to share now?"

"No." He picked up his briefcase and made a move toward the door before he stopped abruptly. "Your client killed Blum."

"He says that he didn't."

"They all do."

"You don't have any witnesses and there was no evidence of premeditation."

"We have the video. Your client was holding a bat."

"Doesn't prove anything."

"A jury will tie it together."

"I can be very persuasive."

"So can I." He set his briefcase down. "I might be able to convince DeSean to authorize a deal for second-degree murder with a recommended sentence at the shorter end of the spectrum."

"How short?"

"Fifteen years."

Not bad. It was the minimum for second-degree in a case not involving a firearm. The minimum for first-degree was twenty-five years. "You won't get twelve jurors to convict on murder."

"I disagree."

Solid bluff. "If you want to discuss manslaughter, we may have something to consider."

"Can't do it, Mike."

"Sure you can."

"No, I can't."

Fine. "Just so we're clear, are you offering a deal for second-degree?"

He hesitated—a tipoff that he was trying to decide whether he could sell it to his boss. "Yes."

"I'll take it up with my client."

"The offer will remain open until close of business tomorrow."

"Fine." I held up a hand. "The police arrested Brian Holton for selling drugs."

"So I'm told. It isn't my case."

"There are texts between Holton and Blum. Holton was selling Molly to Blum. We have reason to believe that Blum owed money to Holton. You're obligated to provide evidence that may tend to exonerate my client."

"I have no evidence regarding financial issues between Holton and Blum. I will provide everything you're entitled to in due course."

* * *

Jaylen's response to Erickson's offer was succinct. "No deal."

"You sure?"

"Yeah." His voice filled with irritation. "You think I'm guilty?"

"I didn't say that."

"They why are we talking about a deal?"

"You need to understand your options. And I have a legal obligation to present it."

"It's rejected. I didn't kill Blum. I'm not going to plead guilty to a crime that I didn't commit."

"I'll inform the D.A."

Jaylen, Nady, and I were seated around the dented metal table in a windowless consultation room in the bowels of the newer jail adjacent to the Hall, which the cops had dubbed the "Glamour Slammer." Jaylen had been moved from his cell on the seventh floor of the Hall to more livable quarters on the fourth floor of the newer facility. He was trying to maintain his composure, but his expression revealed a combination of fear and desperation.

"You need to get me out of here," he snapped.

"We'll make another request for pre-trial release, but the odds are slim."

His full lips formed a tight ball, but he didn't respond.

I glanced at Nady, who tried to sound reassuring. "We're going to take care of you, Jaylen."

"You didn't even put on a defense at the prelim earlier today."

"The D.A. had enough to bind you over for trial. We didn't want to show our cards."

"From where I was sitting, we don't have any."

"Yes, we do. Brian Holton was selling drugs to Blum."

"It doesn't mean that he killed him."

"We don't have to prove it. We just need to suggest it persuasively enough to get one juror to reasonable doubt."

"Holton isn't going to confess."

"He won't be a sympathetic witness."

"You got anything else?"

I answered him. "We need your help in finding some other people who didn't like Blum—preferably people who won't be sympathetic witnesses."

"Like who?"

"Unhappy clients. Drug dealers. Gamblers."

"I don't know."

We stared at each other for a moment. Finally, I pushed my chair back, stood up, and knocked on the door. "We'll keep you posted."

* * *

"That didn't go well," Nady observed.

"It rarely does," I said.

A warm breeze hit my face as we were standing on the front

steps of the Hall at two o'clock on Thursday afternoon. The aroma of cigarette smoke lingered in the air. The smokers—including Harvey Tate—always congregated next to the planter adjacent to the stairs. Traffic was heavy on Bryant. A steady stream of humanity made its way into the Hall. Some were visiting incarcerated friends and relatives. Others were going to see their parole officers. A few were going to pay parking tickets.

"You going back to the office?" I asked Nady.

"Yes. You?"

"I'll meet you there later. I'm heading over to the Gold Club."

26
"I HAVE A LAWYER"

The Gold Club was quiet when I walked inside at four o'clock on Thursday afternoon. A bartender was preparing for the evening crowd. The music was off. The stage was empty.

I nodded at Darlene, who was chatting with a busboy. Then I walked over to a table near the stage, where Holton was staring at his phone.

"Got a sec?" I asked.

He looked up. "You're back."

"I am."

"Did you decide to leave the priesthood because you liked going to clubs?"

He had checked me out. "It wasn't a good fit for me, so I became a lawyer."

"At least you can go to clubs now and not have to explain it to your boss."

"My boss also happens to be my ex-wife and San Francisco's Public Defender. If somebody takes a picture of me in a compromising position in this club, there will be repercussions on a professional and a personal level."

"I take it that you aren't interested in a little private time with one of our hostesses?"

"Afraid not."

"You still need to buy a drink."

"Fair enough. I'll buy one for you, too. I motioned to Darlene, who came over and took our order for two Diet Cokes.

Holton's eyes narrowed. "I heard that one of your colleagues accused me of murder in court today."

"She didn't accuse you."

"She strongly suggested it. I didn't kill Robbie Blum."

"Then you should have no problem testifying at Jaylen's trial."

"I have nothing to hide. Why are you here?"

"I was hoping that you could help us find the person who killed Blum."

"From what I hear, your client did."

"He said that he didn't."

"Then you shouldn't have any trouble getting him off."

"Where were you on the night that he died?"

"Here."

"All night?"

"Until we closed at two a.m."

"You didn't take a break?"

"No."

"We understand that you and Blum were business associates."

"He was a customer of the Club."

"We heard that he was your customer, too."

"I don't know what you're talking about."

"Our client told us that Blum gave him money to deliver to you. In exchange, he was supposed to pick up some pharmaceuticals."

"I don't know what you're talking about."

"I heard you had a little excitement last night. My sources at the D.A.'s Office told me that you spent a little quality time at the intake center of County Jail Number 4."

"It was a misunderstanding."

"If you need a lawyer, I'm available."

"I have a lawyer—a good one."

"I take it that's why you're here at work today instead of sitting in an eight-by-six room over at the Hall of Justice?"

"My lawyer got the charges dropped." He glanced at his phone, then he looked up at me. "I don't know who killed Robbie Blum."

"Here's the deal, Brian. We have texts between you and Blum. We know that you were selling Molly to him. I'm guessing that he wasn't your only customer—hence your little visit to the Hall of Justice last night. If you can help us find the guy who popped Blum, I might be able to avoid putting you on the stand at Jaylen's trial to explain your 'business arrangements.'"

"I didn't kill him."

"I believe you. And you seem like a decent guy. On the other hand, it's my job to fill the jurors' heads with enough doubt to get one of them to vote to acquit. If that means that I need to throw a little shade your way, that's what I'm going to do."

"That's crap."

"That's how the legal system works."

Darlene reappeared with two Diet Cokes. Holton didn't say anything as she set them in front of us, smiled, presented me with the check, and returned to the bar.

He finally spoke up again. "Blum was having big-time financial issues."

"Drugs?"

"Gambling. He used to go down to Vegas, but the casinos kept him on a short leash. He owed somebody some real money."

"Who?"

"I don't know. If you find the answer, you may have found the killer—assuming that it isn't your client."

"Thanks for your help, Brian."

27
"HE WAS MY AGENT"

Whack.

The sound of a bat hitting a ball echoed in the batting cage beneath the left field stands.

Whack.

"Sounded good," I observed.

David Archer wiped the sweat from his brow and adjusted his batting gloves. "Not bad."

"Ted Williams said that when he hit one on the barrel, he could smell burning wood. You ever notice it?"

The Giants slugger smiled. "Every time."

The All-Star left fielder was listed as six-two, but he was under six feet. He carried a muscular two hundred and thirty pounds on his barrel-chested body. His massive torso was supported by spindly legs that propelled him around the bases at sprinter's speed. The forearms beneath his drenched warmup jersey were the same size as my thighs, and his round head appeared to be attached directly to his shoulders. He wasn't wearing a batting helmet, so his sandy blonde hair cascaded down to his shoulders.

"Thanks for taking the time to see me," I said.

"Give me a few more swings. Then we'll talk in the clubhouse."

He spent the next fifteen minutes pulverizing the lollipop fastballs served up by the Giants longtime batting practice pitcher—a onetime star at Redwood High School whose fastball had topped out at eighty-five miles per hour. Perfect for batting practice, but not enough for a spot on a major league roster.

Two weeks had passed since the prelim. The Giants had been on the road, so this was my first chance to talk to Archer. It was early afternoon on Thursday, June twenty-fifth. Tonight's game wouldn't start for six hours, but Archer was an hour into his pre-game routine. Baseball players are creatures of habit. They tune their swings the way that Itzhak Perlman tunes his violin.

He took another dozen swings before he helped the pitcher collect the balls. Many superstars are not so accommodating. He grabbed his two practice bats and motioned me to follow him to the clubhouse. Unlike the wood-paneled executive and club levels, the tunnel was lined with cement blocks.

"You live down on the peninsula?" I asked.

"San Mateo. It's a good place to raise kids. My parents live in Burlingame, so we have babysitters nearby."

He and his wife had two toddlers. Archer had grown up in Burlingame and played at Serra High, also the alma mater of Barry Bonds and Tom Brady. He spent three years crushing Pac-12 pitching at Stanford before the Giants took him with the fifth pick in the draft. He was promoted to the majors after only seventy-eight games in the minors. At twenty-seven, he had been to three All-Star games. If you believed Harvey Tate, Archer's next contract could command north of three hundred million dollars. Old-timers said that he looked like Mickey Mantle. Younger fans compared him to Mike Trout. Unlike many of his contemporaries, he seemed reasonably grounded, and he had no entourage of hangers-on.

I followed him into the spacious clubhouse where each player had a dressing stall with a pressed jersey hanging beneath his name and number. He took a seat on the recliner in front of his cubicle. He put one bat on the floor and kept one in his lap.

"Did you play?" he asked.

"I was a mediocre pitcher and a backup first baseman at S.I."

He gripped the bat. "They were always good when I played against them."

"My older brother was a lot better than I was. He played baseball, basketball, and football at S.I. He ended up playing quarterback at Cal."

He stopped fiddling with the bat. "Tommy Daley?"

"Yeah."

His eyes locked onto mine. "I'm so sorry, man." The red skin on his wide forehead wrinkled as his eyes narrowed. "People say that he would have been a first-round pick if he had stuck with baseball. How hard did he throw?"

"I'd guess mid-nineties. He was unhittable in high school— except for somebody like you. He's still tied for the city record for strikeouts in a single game: eighteen."

"That's almost impossible in a seven-inning game."

"A couple of guys bunted. He decided to play football and got a full ride to Cal."

"You do what you love, I guess."

"I guess." *Time for business.* "You know that I'm representing Jaylen Jenkins?"

"Yes."

"You ever meet him?"

"No."

"He's a good guy."

"I'll take your word for it."

"You knew Robbie Blum?"

"Of course. He was my agent."

"Was he good?"

"He made me a lot of money."

"You made yourself a lot of money."

"He was a good negotiator. He never left a penny on the table."

Sounds about right. "Was he a nice guy?"

"To me."

If I were getting a five percent commission on every penny you made, I would have been nice to you, too. "What about to others?"

"Sometimes."

"Eric Chen told us that he was hard to deal with."

"Every general manager thinks every agent is hard to deal with."

"How did you hook up with Blum?"

"My dad knew his former partner, Jeff Franklin. Jeff handled my rookie contract. Then he was out of the country when it was time to finalize my next deal, so Robbie handled it."

"You decided to stick with Robbie when he and Franklin split up?"

"Yes. Jeff wasn't happy about it."

Not surprising. "You gonna ask Franklin to represent you on your new contract?"

"We'll see."

"Were you friends with Blum?"

"I try to keep business and friendships separate. We didn't socialize. Robbie was a partier. I like to stay home. He was with a different woman every time I saw him—even when he was still married." He shrugged. "I know that this sounds old-fashioned, but the only woman I'm interested in is my wife. We've been together since college. It isn't very exciting for people on social media, but it's the way I'm drawn."

"And Blum?"

"He drank too much. He did drugs."

"I take it that you aren't into that stuff?"

"I'll have a post-game beer, but that's it. Baseball careers are short, so I take care of myself. We get tested regularly, so I'm extra careful."

"Wise choices. We heard he had a gambling issue."

"I heard rumors."

"Did he bet on games?"

"I don't know."

"Did he ever pump you for inside information?"

"On occasion." He squeezed the handle of the bat. "The league takes that stuff very seriously, so I stay away from it."

"Did he ever offer you drugs?"

"He knew better."

"Do you know who was supplying him?"

He waited a beat. "A guy at the Gold Club. Robbie said that he could get me anything."

"Brian Holton?"

"Could have been. He never mentioned his name."

"Did you see Blum the night that he died?"

"He came down to the clubhouse to say hi."

"The police found one of your bats near the body. Any idea how it got there?"

"I gave Robbie a bat to take home to his son. I presume it was the same one."

"Do you have any idea who hit him?"

"The police think it was your client."

"He says that he didn't. Was anybody mad at Blum?"

"He pissed off a lot of people."

"You think Holton was mad at him?"

"You'll have to ask him."

"When was the last time that you saw him?"

"When he left the clubhouse. He usually parked in the players' lot."

"When did you leave?"

"Around eleven-thirty."

"Did you see Blum outside?"

"No."

"Or my client?"

"No." He put the bat on the floor and stood up. "I need to get treatment on my shoulder."

"Understood." I tossed up a final flare. "Do you have any idea if Blum owed anybody some real money for gambling?"

"Wouldn't surprise me."

"Any idea who?"

"Afraid not."

* * *

My head was throbbing as I pulled into Rosie's driveway at eleven o'clock the same night. Pete's name appeared on my phone.

"Did you get anything useful from Archer?" he asked me.

"Not much."

"Meet me at Whiz Burgers at eleven-thirty tomorrow morning."

It was a drive-in at the corner of Eighteenth and South Van Ness in the ungentrified corner of the Mission. "May I ask why?"

"If you want to know what's going on with a baseball team, you don't talk to the players, the manager, or the GM. You talk to the clubhouse manager."

28

"WHAT HAPPENS IN THE CLUBHOUSE STAYS IN THE CLUBHOUSE"

The smell of cheeseburgers, greasy fries, and banana shakes wafted through the parking lot of the drive-in which looked the same as it did in 1955. Whiz Burgers had been operating on the corner of Eighteenth and Mission since I was a kid. The nondescript hamburger stand was painted dirty yellow accented by chipped blue trim. The vintage Coca-Cola sign was faded. The seating—such as it was—consisted of three wobbly stools at the counter next to the order window and three picnic tables beneath an awning that looked like it might collapse. Two delivery guys from the nearby UPS facility were sitting at the next table. A family of well-fed pigeons with high cholesterol was poised to collect any stray fries that dropped to the pavement.

The restaurant was also the unlikely site of an important event in LGBT history. In 1977, Robert Hillsborough and Jerry Taylor stopped at Whiz Burgers. Four men attacked them in the parking lot. Taylor escaped, but Hillsborough was killed. This tragedy brought the LGBT community together and bolstered its efforts to stand up to discrimination.

Pete took a bite of his Whiz Burger. The signature sandwich was a third of a pound of ground chuck served with two strips of bacon, avocado, lettuce, tomato, onion, pickles, mustard, and mayo on a French roll. He wiped his fingers with a handful of napkins and pointed at the gray-haired man whose jowly face resembled a bulldog's. "You remember Yosh?"

"I do." I set down my shake and extended a hand. "I'm Tom Daley's son. We met years ago when our dad picked up a few extra bucks working security at Candlestick."

"I remember him. Good cop. Good guy."

At seventy-five, Yosh Kawakami was the Giants longest-tenured employee. In an interview with Jen Foster, the clubhouse manager said that he wanted to keep working until he turned eighty. The native of Daly City and alum of Jefferson High had taken over the job from his father, who had survived the Japanese internment camp at Tule Lake near the Oregon border. When he returned to San Francisco, he found work as a clubhouse assistant for the old Seals and, later, the Giants.

"You live around here?" I asked.

He pointed up the street. "My wife and I bought a house on Potrero Hill when we got married. The neighborhood was pretty sketchy in those days, so we got a good deal, and it was close to the Stick. When the Giants moved to the new ballpark, it was even more convenient."

"You could make a fortune if you decide to sell."

"I get a couple of e-mails a week from real estate agents asking me if we'd like to move. It's tempting, but we like our house."

I smiled. "Our parents grew up here in the Mission. They bought a house in the Sunset in 1961 for twenty-seven thousand. We sold it a few years ago for seven figures."

"The City has changed a lot since we were kids."

"It has." I ate a couple of fries. "You come here often?"

"Once or twice a month. I'm trying to help John and Tony stay in business."

John and Tony Kim were the longtime owners of Whiz Burgers. "Are they going to be able to afford to stay open?"

"Hopefully. It isn't an easy time to run a business in the City."

We exchanged small talk as we ate our burgers. He said that the Giants treated their employees well. His all-time favorite players were Willie Mays and Willie McCovey, who were always gracious. Barry Bonds treated him respectfully but kept to himself. Bruce Bochy was the friendliest manager. Yosh demurred when I asked him who was the hardest player to deal with. When you work in a major league clubhouse for almost a half-century, you learn to be discreet.

His tone turned philosophical when I asked him about players on the current roster. "They're fine, but they spend a lot of time texting and tweeting. They're trying to build their social media platforms. I get it, but I liked the camaraderie in the old days. And then there's the money. The big stars make hundreds of millions. But even the lowest-paid guys pull down more than a half million a year. When I started, some of the players weren't making much more than I was, and most had jobs in the offseason. Everybody used to play cards and go out after the games. It doesn't happen very much anymore, and it never includes guys like me."

"It's too bad," I said. "You think these guys are worth what they're getting paid?"

"You're worth whatever somebody will pay you."

Pete finished his burger and tossed the wrapper into the trash. He leaned toward Yosh. "You heard that Mike's representing Jaylen Jenkins?"

"Yes."

"Do you know him?"

"I've seen him outside the park. Never gave me any trouble."

"Ever see him with Robbie Blum?"

"No."

Pete looked my way.

"Did you know Blum?" I asked Yosh.

"I knew who he was. He used to come down to the clubhouse after games. Our manager and the other players weren't happy about it. He treated me like I wasn't there." His tone turned sharp. "Blum sucked up to his clients and punched down to guys like me. He would have gotten more cooperation if he had been nicer."

"Was anybody pissed off at Blum?"

"Wouldn't surprise me."

I asked him how Blum and Archer were getting along.

"There's been some tension lately. David's contract is up at the end of the season. He wants to stay with the Giants, but Blum wanted him to test free agency. If the team falls out of contention, Eric Chen may trade him for prospects. Nothing personal—just business."

"Does Chen want to keep him?"

"At the right price. David's a great hitter and a super teammate. He's a local guy who's never gotten into trouble or embarrassed the team. Nowadays, that's important. On the other hand, there are only so many dollars in the budget."

"We heard that Blum was having financial issues."

"I don't know anything about it."

"And drug and alcohol issues."

"I don't know anything about it."

"And he had a gambling problem."

He paused. "You didn't hear this from me, but it was an open secret that he spent a lot of time at the casinos in Vegas. I heard rumors that he owed a lot of money."

"Did he also place bets privately?"

"I don't know."

I exchanged a glance with Pete. Then I turned back to Kawakami. "Were you in the clubhouse on the night that Blum died?"

"Of course."

"David Archer told us that Blum came down to see him."

"He did."

"He said that he gave Blum a batting practice bat."

"Actually, he asked me to give Blum a bat."

"Blum took it with him?"

"Yes."

"How were Archer and Blum getting along that night?"

"Nothing out of the ordinary."

"Did Blum get into it with anybody in the clubhouse?"

"Jen Foster said something to him after he interrupted her when she was setting up her live shot. And he got into an argument with A.B."

"A.B.?"

"Adam Bryant."

I recognized the name. Bryant was Archer's college teammate at Stanford and current personal trainer. He ran an upscale gym south of the ballpark near the new Warriors arena.

"Do you know what they were arguing about?" I asked.

"Blum invested in A.B.'s gym. A.B. is trying to raise money to open a second location. Blum had promised to make an investment. Evidently, he didn't come up with the money. A.B. seemed pretty unhappy about it."

"Do you recall anything that Bryant said to Blum?"

The baseball lifer responded with a knowing smile exposing his tobacco-stained teeth. "He suggested that Blum perform an unnatural sexual act upon himself."

Nice. "This conversation was very helpful, Yosh."

"This conversation never took place, Mike. What happens in the clubhouse stays in the clubhouse."

29
"WE WORK OUT TOGETHER"

The smell of sweat and the sound of hip-hop filled the high-tech workout facility on the ground floor of an upscale new apartment complex across the street from Pier 50, about halfway between the ballpark and the new Warriors arena. At six-thirty a.m. on Friday, June twenty-sixth, the three-dozen state-of-the-art workout stations were occupied by athletic, spandex-clad young people. Everyone had a personal trainer. Nobody was admiring the view of the bay through the picture windows.

Pete and I were out of place. He was wearing his bomber jacket and khakis. I was due in court later that morning, so I was wearing a suit and a tie. Ironically, we were both high school football players and gym rats—albeit in more earthy surroundings. I still worked out at the Embarcadero Y near the Ferry Building.

Pete admired the palatial health club. "I remember when this area was rusted rail yards."

It had taken three decades and billions of dollars to transform the wasteland south of the ballpark into a sparkling city within a city which housed a new UCSF medical campus, a biotech office park, the new Warriors arena, and countless upscale condos, apartments, restaurants, and gyms. The redevelopment was continuing to push south and west into the formerly working-class enclaves in Dogpatch, Potrero Hill, and the Mission.

"Where is he?" I asked.

Pete pointed at a young man doing squats with a barbell weighing more than I did. "Adam Bryant. A.B." He glanced at his watch. "He should be finished soon."

At six-six and two-sixty, Bryant looked like a human Pez dispenser. He carried the weight of an offensive lineman with the muscle tone of a power forward. He had played right field and batted cleanup for the Stanford baseball team that made it to the semi-finals of the College World Series. Bigger and stronger than his teammate, David Archer, Bryant was a first-round draft pick of the Chicago White Sox. A Google search had revealed that Bryant's baseball career flamed out in rookie league when he couldn't hit a curve ball. He had returned to the Bay Area and opened the high-end gym where we were standing.

Bryant put the weight on its stand, wiped the padded bench, and thanked his two spotters, whom I recognized as linemen for the Niners. He took a lap around his empire, stopping to encourage his customers and employees. He paused to consume three cups of filtered water and beckoned us to join him at the juice bar.

He wiped his glistening shaved head with a towel and extended a meaty hand. "A.B."

"Mike Daley. This is my brother, Pete. Thanks for taking the time to see us."

"My pleasure." His wide face had the leathery complexion of a someone who had spent the summers of his youth standing in the outfield. His trim goatee had a few flecks of gray. He escorted us into the café, where he offered each of us a twenty-dollar organic juice-and-kale-and-smoothie concoction, which we politely declined. "Let's go up to my office," he suggested.

He led us through an unmarked door next to the registration desk and then up a stairway to a suite of offices with picture windows overlooking the exercise floor. The walls were covered with framed photos of Bryant with local sports legends: Steph Curry, Joe Montana, Buster Posey, Madison Bumgarner, Barry Bonds, Willie Mays, Orlando Cepeda, and Juan Marichal. An enlarged photo of the Stanford baseball team was in the most prominent spot. I recognized Bryant and Archer in the back row.

I pointed at an elaborate architectural drawing on his credenza. "Are you opening a second location?"

"Hopefully. It's in Santa Clara near the Niners' workout facility. We're still trying to finalize plans and financing."

Bryant took a seat on a big exercise ball that he used instead of a chair. Pete and I sat down on the conventional armchairs opposite his desk.

Bryant pulled at his drenched Under Armour workout shirt. "If you can wait ten minutes, I can go take a quick shower."

"Not necessary," I said. "Pete and I played football at S.I. We know locker rooms."

We exchanged small talk for a few minutes before I tried to ease him into the matters at hand. "How long has this facility been open?"

"Three years in September."

"It's spectacular. Looks like you cater to an upscale clientele."

"We specialize in pro and college athletes. We have a few Olympic hopefuls. The tech people in the neighborhood also have money to pay for personalized programs."

The Public Defender's Office services a clientele with different demographics. "How much do you charge for a membership?"

"Basic memberships start at twenty thousand."

More than the Y.

He added, "There's also a monthly fee plus a daily charge for specialized services. Food and drinks are extra. And, of course, the amount you tip your trainer is up to you."

Of course. "I'll bet you have a waiting list."

"We do."

"How did you get started?"

"I got to know some of the Giants when I was at Stanford. They were interested in an upscale facility near the ballpark. It seemed like a good niche."

Any niche where your customers have money burning through their pockets is a good one. "This is high-end real estate."

"Our timing was fortuitous. We signed our lease when the neighborhood was still under construction. People were starting to move into the condos next to the new UC Medical Center. Then Chase Center opened. The Giants are working on a development near the ballpark. This is becoming one of the nicest areas in town."

"You live nearby?"

He pointed at the ceiling. "Upstairs."

"Easy commute." I pointed at the workout area. "Your operating costs must be astronomical."

"That's why we need to charge so much. Our policy is that every client gets an individual trainer and a personalized program."

"I take it that you have investors?"

"Names you would recognize."

I arched an eyebrow. "Any chance your list might include David Archer?"

The corner of his mouth turned up. "It might."

"And a few other Giants?"

"Possibly."

"Robbie Blum?"

"Maybe."

Not surprising. "I understand that you're David's personal trainer."

"I am. We work out together. And I put together a baseball-specific program for him. I help him stretch before and after games."

"The Giants are okay with it?"

"It's a collaboration. We're all on the same page."

"David told us that you spend a lot of time at the ballpark."

"I do."

I shot a glance at Pete, who took the cue.

"Mike is representing Jaylen Jenkins. Ever met him?"

"No."

"He sold T-shirts behind the players' parking lot. Did you ever stop to look at his merchandise?"

"Not that I recall."

"But you knew Robbie Blum?"

"Yes."

"Did you think about hiring him as your agent when you turned pro?"

"I used Jeff Franklin. I wish my career had lasted longer so that we could have continued to work together."

"We heard that Blum could be difficult."

A hesitation. "That's fair."

Pete pointed at the architectural plans. "Did you ask him to invest in the new facility?"

"We had some preliminary discussions. He wasn't interested."

Yosh said that Blum reneged on his financial commitment.

"When was the last time you saw him?" Pete asked.

"He was in the clubhouse on the night that he died."

"Did you talk to him?"

"I said a quick hello."

Yosh said that they argued.

"Was Blum a good agent?" Pete asked.

Bryant nodded. "He never left a penny on the table."

"That's the idea, right?"

"Most of the time. Sometimes I thought Robbie was more concerned about maximizing his fees than addressing his clients' needs."

Pete responded with an inquisitive expression. "Wouldn't maximizing his fees be the result of maximizing contract value for his players?"

"Depends on what's important to the client. David is a local guy who wants to stay with the Giants. His wife and kids like it here. His parents live nearby. He's willing to give the Giants a home-team discount to stay put. He asked Robbie to work out a deal with the Giants, but Robbie advised him to wait until the end of the season and test free agency. David won't admit it to the press, but he'll be very unhappy if the Giants trade him at the deadline."

"He could re-sign with the team as a free agent."

"There are no guarantees."

"It's hard to replace your cleanup hitter. David will get his money from somebody."

"True." He picked up a rubber ball and squeezed it. "David likes his teammates. He believes they're on the verge of competing for another World Series. He wants to be like Mickey Mantle or George Brett—he wants to see only one team listed on the back of his baseball card."

Pete held up a hand. "Did he consider the possibility of changing agents?"

"Maybe."

"Jeff Franklin?"

"I'm not at liberty to say."

"We heard that Blum had some serious issues with alcohol and drugs."

"He was out of control at times."

"He was never arrested."

"I heard that some stuff got covered up."

"Was that another reason why David was thinking about switching agents?"

"Possibly."

"We think that Blum may have owed one of his drug suppliers some money—a guy named Brian Holton."

"I don't know."

"We also heard that Blum had a gambling problem."

"He did."

"Any chance he got in sideways with somebody on a big gambling debt?"

"Wouldn't surprise me."

"You wouldn't happen to have a name?"

"He mentioned a guy named Kevin Killian. I don't know anything about him."

"Any idea where we might find him?"

"No."

"Thanks for your help, A.B."

"If you guys want to come back down to the club sometime, I'd be happy to have one of our trainers take you through personalized workouts."

30
"CAN YOU FIND HIM?"

"Did your people find out anything about Killian?" I asked.

Pete was staring at his phone. "He's a supervisor for Bayshore Moving and Storage."

"And?"

"Gimme a sec, Mick."

I tried to remain patient as we sat at a table in front of Farley's, a coffee shop on Eighteenth between Missouri and Texas Streets, on the downslope of Potrero Hill. We could have gone to the Starbucks across the street from Bryant's gym, but Pete knew the owners of Farley's, and he tried to stop in when he was in the neighborhood. The funky café was founded by Zen Master Roger Hillyard on St. Patrick's Day in 1989 as a coffee and tea paraphernalia store, which he named after his grandfather, Jack Farley. Roger started selling beverages as a community service after the 1989 Loma Prieta earthquake. The coffee and homemade pastries were some of the best in town.

"Pete?"

He finally put down his phone. "Yeah?"

"How is a supervisor on a moving van connected to Robbie Blum?"

"That's what we need to find out."

"You'll find him?"

"I already have somebody looking for him."

* * *

Nady was staring at her laptop as she reached down and gave Luna a treat. "Good puppy," she said.

I smiled. "Are you talking to me?"

"No."

The engaging Keeshond devoured the cookie and looked at me hopefully.

"Sorry, Luna. I don't have anything for you tonight."

She responded with a disappointed sigh.

Nady picked at her kale salad. "Did Pete find out anything else about Killian?"

"Still looking. We need to figure out his connection—if any—to Blum."

The conference room at the P.D.'s Office was quiet at eight-thirty on Friday night.

"Anything else come in from the D.A.?" I asked.

"More video from the night that Blum died."

"Anything useful?"

"Too soon to tell."

"I'll come in and help you look at the new video over the weekend."

"Much appreciated."

Nady and two of our paralegals had spent hours poring over security videos from the ballpark and the nearby businesses from the night that Blum had died.

"Did you find anything in the security videos so far?" I asked.

"Maybe." Her fingers flew over her keyboard and the flatscreen TV came to life. The footage showed the illuminated walkway between the exterior wall in right field and McCovey Cove. "This was taken at eleven-forty p.m."

The time stamp in the upper right corner of the soundless video confirmed the date and time. The sidewalk was empty.

"What am I looking for?" I asked.

"Be patient." She stopped the video and pointed at the screen. "There."

A man walked along the promenade from the right field corner toward center field.

"Who?" I asked.

"It's Brian Holton."

I studied the frozen frame. "Could be."

"It is." She enhanced the image. "You can see his face."

Yes, I can. "He told me that he was working that night."

"Maybe he took a break. Either way, he was there."

"Which means he lied to me." *And we have a viable suspect.* "Did you see Holton in any other video?"

"Not yet."

"You should also request security video from the Gold Club that night. Send them a subpoena if you have to."

"I did." Nady frowned. "It's gone. They save security videos for two weeks."

Dammit.

Her scowl became more pronounced. "We know that Holton was in the vicinity of the ballpark that night, but we have no hard evidence that he saw or confronted Blum."

"Keep looking. Anything else?"

"Maybe." Nady cued another video. "Turner sent over a copy of Jen Foster's footage from the clubhouse on the night that Blum died."

The video showed players milling around in their uniforms. The manager was talking to Harvey Tate. Archer was sitting behind a dozen microphones and cell phones, answering questions about his walk-off homer.

Nady paused the footage. "There's Blum."

Blum walked past Foster toward Archer. As he passed her, his elbow glanced her arm. She responded with a look of annoyance. Blum marched over to Archer and gave his client and meal ticket a two-handed high-five. Archer smiled and clasped a fist over his head. It was impossible to hear what they said. Blum moved behind Archer, who continued his interviews.

Nady fast-forwarded and then stopped the video again. "Watch this," she said.

She ran it in slow-motion. Archer sipped a beer as he continued to answer questions. She stopped it again. "Look behind Archer. Blum is talking to A.B."

I could see Blum and Bryant in the upper left corner of the screen. Bryant towered over Blum. I couldn't hear what they were saying as they spoke to each other. Blum's expression turned serious, then angry. Bryant's expression turned grim. They exchanged heated words. Then Blum shoved Bryant with two hands. Bryant glared at him as if to say, "Are you serious?" Bryant extended a long right arm and pushed Blum against the wall. Blum held up his hands in a defensive posture, and Bryant released him. Blum walked out of camera view.

"Run it again," I said.

Nady did as I asked.

We watched the video two more times before Nady stopped it.

"Looks like there were hard feelings between Blum and A.B.," I said.

"Looks like it was more than hard feelings. We might be able to use this."

"We'll definitely be able to use it."

She reached down and rubbed Luna's nose. "Are you going home?"

"I'm meeting Rosie at her mother's house."

31
"DO YOU THINK THAT'S WISE?"

Rosie looked across the table at her older brother, Tony. "Any update on Rolanda?"

"Status quo." He glanced at his watch. "The baby should arrive any day now."

"You getting excited?"

"Yes."

"Nervous?

"Very."

"Everything is going to be fine."

Tony was three years older than Rosie. The widower was anxiously awaiting the arrival of his first grandchild. The one-time Marine's muscular frame, pockmarked face, and bushy mustache gave off an intimidating vibe. In reality, the soft-spoken owner of a produce market on Twenty-fourth Street was a savvy businessman and as gentle as a cocker spaniel.

"You'll let us know as soon as anything happens?" Rosie said.

"Of course."

Rosie's mother, Rosie, Tony, and I were sitting around Sylvia's dining room table at nine-forty-five on Friday night. The windows were open, and a cool breeze flowed through the tight space. In the summer, the Mission was sunnier and warmer than much of the City. The fog had rolled in and cooled things down as I was driving over here from the office.

Sylvia poured hot water onto a tea bag in the ceramic cup in front of me. "Are you really going to trial for Jaylen Jenkins next month?"

"Yes."

"Do you think that's wise?"

"No."

"But?"

"Our client has a right to a trial within sixty days after his prelim. We have explained the risks of moving forward so quickly, but he has instructed us to proceed."

My ex-mother-in-law turned to my ex-wife. "Do *you* think that's wise?"

I no longer took it personally that Sylvia always asked Rosie for a second opinion on my strategic decisions.

"No, Mama," Rosie said. "You know how things work. It isn't uncommon for our clients to instruct us to move forward in a hurry—even against our advice and better judgment."

Sylvia scooped a couple of enchiladas into a Tupperware container. "You'll take these home for Tommy?"

"Thanks, Mama. He'll appreciate it."

"You want some ice cream?"

"The doctor wants me to avoid sugar. And I'm trying to watch my figure."

"You don't need to lose weight, Rosita."

"Just trying to maintain."

Rosie went to pre-dawn Pilates or spin classes at least three days a week.

Sylvia looked my way. "You?"

"No, thanks, Sylvia."

She arched an eyebrow. "It's from Mitchell's. Tony picked it up at the shop."

Tempting. Mitchell's had been selling hand-crafted ice cream from a hole-in-the-wall at Twenty-ninth and San Jose in the southern end of the Mission since 1953. For those of us who had grown up in the neighborhood, it was a religious experience. Nowadays, you could buy their ice cream at the supermarket, but purists believed that the ice cream at the store was better.

"What kind?" I asked.

Tony answered. "The summer specials are fresh peach and cantaloupe. They buy their fruit from me. I always sell them my best stuff."

Tony had been running his produce market for more than two

decades. Half of his store was filled with organic fruit and vegetables that he sold to the affluent tech kids who were gentrifying the Mission. He stocked the other half with non-organic, but nevertheless excellent produce, that he sold to the members of the community who couldn't afford the higher-end stuff.

I grinned at my ex-brother-in-law. "Any chance you also brought over something with a little less nutritional value?"

He returned my smile. "Peanut Butter Indulgence."

Excellent. It was a concoction of dark chocolate ice cream with peanut butter swirls and chocolate-covered peanut butter cups. I winked at Sylvia. "I'll have some of that. You interested?"

She smiled. "Yes, dear."

Rosie spoke up. "Dr. Yee wants you to lay off sugar, too, Mike."

"Just a taste, Rosie. I'll get up early tomorrow morning and walk the steps with Zvi."

"Fine."

My friend, neighbor, and hero, Zvi Danenberg, was a retired science teacher who had taught at Mission High School for forty years. He got up every morning at the crack of dawn and walked up and down the one hundred and thirty-nine steps connecting Magnolia Avenue in downtown Larkspur with the houses on the adjacent hill. He had started this ritual thirty years earlier when he retired at sixty-five. The ninety-five-year-old climbed more than a million steps a year. In my never-ending and generally futile quest to improve my conditioning and to justify my all-too-frequent indulgences in Mitchell's ice cream, I joined him a couple of days a week. On occasion, Zvi and I would have a post-workout cup of coffee and a chocolate old-fashioned at Donut Alley, just past St. Patrick's Catholic Church, where I confessed my sins to my seminary classmate, Father Andy Shanahan.

We exchanged small talk as we ate our ice cream. Tony kept a watchful eye on his phone. Finally, he looked up and spoke to me. "Did Jaylen Jenkins kill Robbie Blum?"

"He says he didn't."

"Does that mean that you've found the real murderer?" He made air-quotes as he said the word "real."

"We have some possibilities."

He grinned. "You're gonna do your usual song-and-dance and try to blame the forty thousand people who were at the game that night, aren't you?"

I smiled. "If I have to."

"Juries really buy it?"

"Sometimes. I can be very persuasive."

Rosie changed the subject. "Did Nady find anything in the first batch of security videos?"

"Brian Holton was walking along the promenade behind the right field wall about twenty minutes before Blum left the ballpark. It can't be just a coincidence."

"Was he carrying a bat?"

"No."

"I hope you aren't planning to base our entire defense on the fact that Holton went out for a walk."

"He lied to me. He said that he was at work that night."

"Which makes him a liar, but not necessarily a killer. Do you have any evidence that he killed Blum?"

"Uh, no."

"Then you'd better find some."

Tony looked up. "Are you talking about Brian Holton who works at the Gold Club?"

"Yes. Do you know him?"

"I've met him."

"At the Gold Club?"

"At the gym."

I winked at Sylvia, then turned back to Tony. "Have you ever been to the Gold Club?"

He glanced at his mother, then he turned back to me. "I went to a bachelor party once."

"Did you like it?"

"It was okay."

"How well do you know Holton?"

"Not that well."

"We heard that he was supplying Blum with Molly."

"Wouldn't surprise me. I think he supplied some people at the gym."

"Is he a good guy?"

"Most of the time. I've seen him go after a couple of guys during basketball games. I saw him break a guy's arm once."

"You think he's the kind of guy who might have taken a shot at Blum?"

"Wouldn't surprise me."

* * *

The call came in two nights later as I was driving north on 101 above Sausalito. Pete's name appeared on the display. I answered on the first ring.

"What have you got, Pete?"

"Did you and Nady find anything useful in the new video?"

"No."

Nady and I had spent Saturday and Sunday going through the latest round of security videos that the D.A. had sent over on Friday night. It was an excruciatingly tedious and time-consuming exercise. It was also profoundly frustrating—our efforts had come up empty.

"You got anything more on Holton?" I asked.

"Not yet."

"What about Killian?"

"I may have a line on something. Meet me at Tommaso's at six-thirty tomorrow night."

32
"HE'S AN ERRAND BOY"

The owlish man with the wisp of a mustache and wire-rimmed bifocals looked at us from behind the weathered podium. He greeted my brother with a warm smile. "How are you, Pete?"

"Fine, Augie. You got room for us?"

"Of course. I always have room for Tommy Daley's boys."

Agostino Crotti had been the manager of Tommaso's since the seventies. The hole-in-the-wall was located on the ground floor of a post-earthquake-era building on Kearney between the Transamerica Pyramid and the strip clubs on Broadway. Tommaso's was a longtime North Beach gathering spot, and Augie was the neighborhood's unofficial mayor.

The consummate host acknowledged his regulars as he led us through the inviting space that was opened in 1935 by the Cantalupo family, who brought pizza recipes from Naples. They commissioned a German craftsman to build a wood-burning pizza oven—the first on the West Coast. In 1971, the Cantalupos sold the restaurant to their chef, Tommy Chin, who renamed it after himself: Tommaso's. Two years later, he sold the restaurant and the Cantalupo family recipe book to the Crotti family. A half-century later, Augie's staff still went through a cord of oak every ten days to fire up the oven to eight-hundred degrees.

Augie directed us to a table in the back where our diminutive dinner companion was waiting for us. He touched the fresh red rose on the lapel of his three-piece Brioni suit, held out a hand, and flashed a charismatic smile. "How the hell are you boys?"

I shook his hand. "Couldn't be better, Nick. You?"

"Couldn't be better, Mike." He shook hands with Pete, adjusted his toupee, sat down, and pointed at the table laden with three large pizzas, a double order of meatballs, a plate of stuffed manicotti with marinara sauce, and a full antipasto consisting of prosciutto, rosemary ham, bresaola, and artichoke hearts. "I took the liberty of ordering for us. Enjoy."

"Much appreciated, Nick." I was pleased to see that he had ordered a Tommaso's Super Deluxe: mushrooms, anchovies, peppers, green onions, ham, sausage, and black olives.

Our host darted an appreciative glance at Agostino, who headed back to the podium. "I want to make sure that Augie and his family are still here thirty years from now."

"I trust that you plan to be here, too?"

"Indeed I do."

Nick "the Dick" Hanson had recently celebrated his ninety-fifth birthday with a pre-dawn swim in the bay at Aquatic Park, lunch at Scoma's at the Wharf, and a traditional North Beach banquet with four hundred of his friends at the Italian Athletic Club on Washington Square. At five feet tall and a wiry hundred and thirty pounds, Nick had opened the Hanson Investigative Agency seventy-five years earlier in a single room above the Condor Club on Broadway. Nowadays, he headed a high-tech operation employing dozens of his children, grandchildren, and great-grandchildren. A savvy businessman and astute investor, he had accumulated a portfolio of apartment buildings in North Beach rumored to be worth at least fifty million dollars. In his spare time, he wrote mystery novels that were thinly veiled embellishments of his more colorful cases. His books appeared regularly on best-seller lists, and Danny DeVito played Nick in a long-running Netflix series. He showed no signs of slowing down.

When you get together with Nick, you need to observe certain protocols. First, you have to eat a lot. Second, you need to sit through an update on his family. Third, you have to listen to him expound upon the marketing plans for his latest literary masterpiece. These formalities always lasted at least two hours, usually longer.

I started with his favorite topic—his TV show. "I saw that you got renewed for another season."

"Indeed we did." He took a sip of Tommaso's in-house red—a

hearty Syrah. "Negotiations got a little contentious, but we were able to work things out."

"I saw a report that you were asked to leave the set."

"Indeed I was." His rubbery face transformed into a crooked grin. "The director said that I was a distraction." He wiped his mouth with his starched napkin. "I offered a few friendly suggestions. He said that I overstepped by giving Danny notes about how to play his character."

"But *you're* his character."

"Indeed I am. The director said that I didn't fully understand the nuances between the fictional me and the real-life me."

"Is there any difference?"

"In my mind, no. When I politely expressed my views, the director had security remove me from the set. He told me that I couldn't come back until I wrote an apology to the cast and crew."

"He made you write a 'sorry letter'?"

"Yes, he did."

"You didn't do it, did you?"

The cagey old P.I.'s eyes twinkled. "Indeed I did."

This finally got Pete's attention. "You're kidding."

"We were in the middle of negotiations for another season. I figure that my little 'sorry letter' got me an extra two million."

"You planned the whole thing?"

"Indeed I did."

It got a smile from my brother—who almost never smiles.

Nick spent another thirty minutes regaling us with stories about his recent investigations, his trip to the Emmy Awards (nominated, but lost), the updated headcount at his agency (now the largest on the West Coast), and his plans for an updated headquarters in refurbished Gold Rush-era buildings around the corner on Pacific Avenue (the biggest remodel job in North Beach). Mercifully, Agostino brought out tiramisu, spumoni, and crème brûlée—all for Nick—and we finally turned to business.

"You heard that I'm representing Jaylen Jenkins?" I asked.

"Of course. Did he whack Robbie Blum?"

"He says he didn't. Did you know Blum?"

"I met him a couple of times at social events. He wasn't a nice guy. My grandson, Nick the third, followed him around town for a couple of months when his second wife was getting ready to file for divorce. It wasn't pretty."

"Cheating?"

"Check."

"Drinking?"

"Check."

"Drugs?"

"Check."

"Gambling?"

"Check."

"Anything else?"

The twinkle in his eye disappeared and his tone turned serious. "He hit her."

"Not good. We heard rumors."

"They're true. Blum was a first-class dick who paid off a lot of people to keep it quiet." He polished off his tiramisu and turned to the crème brûlée. "If your client didn't kill Blum, who did?"

"That's what we're trying to find out."

Nick poured himself more wine. "What have you got so far?"

He listened intently as I filled him in. "Got any other suspects?"

"You know a guy named Brian Holton who works at the Gold Club?"

"Of course."

"Good guy?"

"Bad guy."

"We think he was selling drugs to Blum."

"Wouldn't surprise me. He delivers high-end product to a high-end clientele. What makes you think he killed Blum?"

"We think Blum owed him money. And we saw Holton in security video outside the ballpark around the time that Blum was killed. Our sources tell us that Holton has a temper."

"As far as I know, he's never killed anybody. He's just a delivery boy."

"You heard that he got arrested a few weeks ago?"

"Indeed I did. Let me guess: somebody posted bail for him right away and he was back at the club in time for the late show. The next day, the D.A. dropped the charges."

"How did you know?"

"This isn't the first time. He's a little fish. The D.A. is looking for a big shark."

"Who's the shark?"

"I don't know."

"Any chance the shark killed Blum?"

"Doubtful. The heads of cartels don't soil their hands."

"Maybe he paid Holton to do it."

"Maybe. You're going to have a helluva time proving it. You don't get to be a shark unless you're careful."

"Ever heard of a guy named Kevin Killian?"

"Yes. He's a supervisor for Bayshore Moving and Storage."

"We think Blum owed him some gambling money."

"Doubtful. He's an errand boy. Blum may have owed Killian's boss some money."

"Who's he?"

"Benjamin Logan. He owns Bayshore. It's one of the bigger operations in the Bay Area. He's also a big gambler."

"How do you know?"

He arched a bushy eyebrow. "A few years ago, an individual with business interests in Las Vegas asked us to keep an eye on Logan."

"Does that mean that Killian a muscle guy?"

"Let's just say that he specializes in debt collection."

"Is Logan the kind of guy who would break somebody's legs if he didn't pay?"

"It's more likely that he would send Killian."

"Any idea where we can find him?"

"If you find his moving van, you'll find Killian."

33
"HUNCHES AREN'T ADMISSIBLE"

The light was on in Nady's office at ten-thirty the same night. "I didn't expect to see you here," I said.

"We've been going through more surveillance video from the ballpark."

"Anything we can use?"

"No." She pointed at Terrence "The Terminator," who was sitting at the desk of one of Nady's two officemates. "I called in reinforcements."

"Thanks for your help, T. Be sure to record every second you work on your timesheet."

"You can afford overtime for this case?"

"No, but I'll authorize it anyway."

"Thanks, Mike."

Manipulating our overtime budget was one of the few perks of my job.

Nady grinned. "Did you have fun with Nick 'the Dick'?"

"Indeed I did." I handed her photos of Kevin Killian and Benjamin Logan. "I need you to find out everything that you can about these guys. Pete is looking for them."

"You got anything on either of them?"

"Just hunches."

"Hunches aren't admissible in court."

I looked at Terrence. "You can play, too. Do you have any hunches?"

His wide face broke into a broad grin. "It usually comes down to money, love, or jealousy. Maybe Blum owed money to Holton, although it seems a bit extreme that Holton would have cracked Blum's skull unless it involved a lot of money."

"Maybe he was trying to send his other customers a not-too-subtle message."

"Not subtle at all. Maybe he owed Logan a big gambling debt. Maybe Logan decided to send a message. Or he sent Killian to handle it."

"Are you talking from personal experience?"

In his youth, Terrence had supplemented his meager purses from boxing by doing collections for a small-time bookmaker who took bets at a liquor store on Sixth Street.

"I never hurt anybody," he said.

"But you tried to scare them."

"It was in my job description. I look pretty intimidating to a lot of people."

Nady grinned. "You wouldn't hurt a fly, T."

"Let's just say that I wasn't always as nice as I am now."

I looked at Nady. "I need you to go through the security videos once more to see if you can find Killian or Logan. It would help if we can place one or both of them at the ballpark on the night that Blum died."

"There's hundreds of hours of video."

"You can use the fast-forward button judiciously."

She pointed at Terrence. "Can I enlist my faithful assistant to help?"

"Of course."

The Terminator looked up again. "Are you authorizing more overtime?"

"Whatever you need, T."

* * *

"Is Nick okay?" Rosie asked.

I couldn't resist. "Indeed he is. His Netflix series has been renewed, and he provided some useful information about Kevin Killian and Benjamin Logan."

"Were either of them anywhere near the ballpark on the night that Blum died?"

"Nady and Terrence are going through more security video to figure it out."

Her cobalt eyes reflected the light from the candle burning on the countertop in her kitchen. "So you've got nothing."

Technically, that's true. "Let's just say that we're working on some promising leads."

"Uh, yeah."

It was almost midnight. I had stopped at the house to eat leftover chicken, have a glass of cabernet that was smoother than the Syrah at Tommaso's, and update my boss on Jaylen's case.

I looked down the hallway at the closed door of Tommy's room, where I could see the light in the crack near the floor. "He okay?"

"Fine."

"Your mother?"

"Status quo." She took a sip of wine. "Your trial starts in less than a month."

"We may have enough to muddy the waters to get to reasonable doubt."

"In other words, you've got nothing."

This seems to be a recurring theme. "We have time, Rosie."

"Not much. You going to set up a SODDI defense?"

"Unless we find something better. We have plausible options for the jury: Brian Holton, Jeff Franklin, and Adam Bryant. With a little luck, we'll also be able to point a finger at Kevin Killian and Benjamin Logan."

"Any evidence directly connecting Killian or Logan to Blum?"

"Not yet."

Her eyes lit up as her full lips transformed into the perfect smile that looked the same as it did a quarter of a century earlier. "You'll figure it out, Mike. You always do."

* * *

The call came in as I was walking down the corridor of the Hall of Justice at ten-thirty the following Thursday morning. Pete's name appeared on the display.

"How soon can you get out to Ingleside?" he asked.

"Depending on traffic, I'll be there in a half hour. What's up?"

"I found Killian."

34
"I HAVE NO IDEA WHAT YOU'RE TALKING ABOUT"

"Where's Killian?" I asked.

Pete pointed over my shoulder. "Fourth in line. Let me handle it, Mick."

It was foggy at eleven-forty-five. We were sitting at a picnic table outside Beep's Burgers, a hamburger stand on the corner of Ocean and Lee that was similar in age, ambiance, and cuisine to Whiz Burgers. The drive-in across the street from City College was painted yellow and had a half-dozen mismatched stools at the counter. When I was a kid, Ingleside was a working-class neighborhood. A dive bar called Randy's Place was on the southwest corner of Ocean and Lee. Randy's was still open, but there was a Whole Foods on the ground floor of a new upscale apartment building across Ocean Avenue.

"When was the last time you were here?" I asked.

"It's been a while." Pete took a bite of his Beep's Burger—a half-pound slab with lettuce, tomato, pickles, onions, and Beep's sauce. "When I was working at Mission Station."

The ground shook as a semi barreled down Ocean Avenue.

My brother's lips turned up into a wry grin. "Are we ever going to work on a case where we eat someplace better than Beep's and Whiz?"

A legitimate question. "When you're a Public Defender, your clients and witnesses generally don't eat at The French Laundry. If we get an acquittal for Jaylen, I'll buy you and Donna dinner anyplace you'd like."

"If?"

"I meant 'when.'"

"Right, Mick. I need to get to work."

He walked over and got in line behind Killian. My brother—who barely spoke to anybody when he wasn't working—struck up a conversation. Five minutes later, he and his new BFF joined me at the picnic table. Pete started eating his second Beep's Burger, Killian his first. My brother's metabolism was remarkably fast.

Pete handled introductions between French fries. "This is my brother, Mike."

"Kevin Killian. Nice to meet you."

"Same here."

Killian looked as if he could have been our cousin. A few years younger than I am, he had a wide pasty face, a flat nose, and a full head of neatly combed hair that was more gray than red. He wore a windbreaker bearing the Bayshore Moving and Storage logo.

Pete took a bite of his burger. "Kevin played defensive line at Riordan. We probably banged on each other forty years ago."

Archbishop Riordan High School was a few blocks from us on the north side of City College. The Crusaders were S.I.'s big rival.

I smiled. "No hard feelings."

"None here." Killian grabbed a couple of fries and spoke in a raspy voice. "Don't tell my girlfriend that I'm here. She thinks I eat salad for lunch."

Pete gave him a conspiratorial nod. "Your secret is safe with us. You live around here?"

"I inherited my parents' house around the corner. It's the only way that I can afford to live here."

"You don't want to cash out and move someplace cheaper?"

"I like it here. Besides, it's paid for."

"You got kids?"

"One. He just turned twenty-two. He's at the police academy."

"Our dad was a cop. You must be very proud of your son."

"I am."

Pete pointed at the Bayshore Moving van blocking two driveways across the street. "You been working for Bayshore for a while?"

"About ten years. My dad started a moving company back in the sixties. Then he got sick and passed away, so I inherited the company along with the house. I didn't like running the business, so I sold it to Bayshore. Life is expensive when you have alimony and child support, so I stayed on as a supervisor."

"Does Bayshore treat you okay?"

"Not bad most of the time."

"You like your boss?"

"He's okay."

"What's his name?"

"Ben Logan."

Pete and I chatted him up for a few more minutes. Killian struck me as a solid guy who showed up for work on time, did his job, and went home and watched sports on TV.

When Killian finished his burger, Pete finally turned to business. "I need to be honest with you, Kevin. Mike is representing Jaylen Jenkins."

Killian wiped his lips with a paper napkin. "The guy who killed the sports agent?"

"Allegedly."

"I don't know anything about it."

"It turns out that your number came up on Robbie Blum's cell phone." This was a bluff. "I take it that you knew him?"

A hesitation. "I delivered some documents to his office for my boss."

Pete looked my way, and I picked up the cue.

"Kevin," I said, "we've learned that Mr. Blum had serious drinking and drug problems."

"I have no idea what you're talking about."

"And a bigger gambling problem."

"I don't know anything about it."

"We believe that Blum was placing bets with Mr. Logan."

Another hesitation. "I don't know anything about it."

"We think that Blum may have gotten in over his head."

"Blum had plenty of money to pay his debts."

"Were you at the game on the night that Blum died?"

"I was at home watching the game on TV with my girlfriend."

Who would undoubtedly provide an alibi. "Any idea where we might find Mr. Logan?"

"Bayshore's headquarters is in the China Basin Building."

Which is across the street from the ballpark.

* * *

Pete finished his last French fry. "He's hiding something, Mick."

"What makes you think so?" I asked.

"Never trust a Riordan guy."

"Agreed. Keep an eye on him. And Logan."

"I will. You going back to the office?"

"I'm going to see Jaylen first."

35
"I DON'T KNOW"

"How's my mother?" Jaylen asked. His face looked thinner than it did a week earlier.

"Trying to be strong," I said. "She's at the halfway house. She's working hard to stay clean."

"That's good."

"It is. You look tired."

"I am."

"Looks like you've lost weight. You eating?"

"A little."

"We need you to stay strong, Jaylen."

"Right."

Later the same day, the windowless consultation room in the Glamour Slammer smelled of disinfectant and perspiration as Nady and I sat across from Jaylen. He had been in jail for a month, but he looked as if he had aged a year. His face was drawn, eyes hollow, demeanor subdued, if not defeated. His orange jumpsuit looked a size too big for him.

"Trial starts in a month," I said. "We need you to stay dialed in."

"Right."

"We may need you to testify."

"I'm not sure that I'm up to it."

"We have a few weeks to make a final decision. We talked to Kevin Killian. We haven't been able to place him at the ballpark, but he admitted that he had made some deliveries to Blum."

"It doesn't prove that he killed him."

"It's a direct connection. We think that Blum may have been into Killian's boss for a substantial gambling debt. You know anything about it?"

"No."

"Help us, Jaylen—please."

His voice filled with resignation. "I don't know."

* * *

"He's giving up," Nady said.

"He'll rally by the time the trial starts," I said half-heartedly.

"We'll see."

We were sitting in my office at seven-thirty the same night. The corridors were quiet.

"You're still thinking a SODDI defense?" she asked.

"Yes."

"It's better if we have some solid evidence that somebody else actually did it."

Indeed. "We can place Holton, Franklin, and Bryant at the ballpark."

"Not within a hundred feet of Blum's body."

"They all had issues with Blum. Bryant argued with Blum in the clubhouse."

"We can't place Bryant on the walkway by the marina."

"We can also tee up Killian and maybe Logan."

"We have no evidence that either of them was at the ballpark."

"Then we'll have to find some."

She pushed out a frustrated sigh. "We've been through hundreds of hours of video."

"Then we'll need to go through it again."

"We need to start being realistic, Mike."

I pointed at my computer. "I'll help you go through the video again—especially from the cameras outside the park. Maybe we'll find something."

Her expression indicated that she wasn't convinced. "Maybe."

* * *

Rosie knocked on my open door. "Didn't think you'd still be here."

"I didn't expect to see you at this hour, either." I was sitting at my desk at ten-thirty the same night. "How was the dinner?"

"The food was awful, but we raised a lot of money for the mock-trial program at public high schools. It was one of the rare occasions where the mayor, the D.A., and I sat at the same table and made nice."

"No sniping?"

"None."

"Impressive self-control."

"Thank you. Why are you still here?"

"Looking for something we can count on for Jaylen's defense. We have some possibilities, but nothing really solid."

"You going to ask for a continuance?"

"No. Jaylen doesn't want to wait."

"Maybe you should ask for a change of venue."

"I'll rather take my chances with a San Francisco jury."

"You going to put Jaylen on the stand?"

"Not in his current frame of mind."

"Now I understand why you're still here. What do you have?"

She listened as I filled her in. Good lawyers are good talkers. Great lawyers like Rosie are world-class listeners.

She took it all in, synthesized the information, and issued her analysis. "Make the prosecution prove its case. Unless you can find a witness or a video showing somebody other than Jaylen hitting Blum, you'll need to focus on alternate suspects that you can place at the ballpark that night—preferably ones with motive, means, and opportunity. Ideally, somebody who detested Blum."

"We have options. Holton was at the ballpark. So was Franklin. And Bryant. Maybe we'll be able to place Killian there, too. We've been trying to chase down Benjamin Logan, who has been out of town."

"You should ask for security videos from the condos and businesses near the ballpark. You never know what might turn up."

"Pete's working on it."

"Trial starts soon, Mike."

36
"ALL OF THEM"

Two weeks later, at ten-thirty a.m. on Thursday, July sixteenth, Benjamin Logan sat down in his over-sized leather chair, took a swig of Coke Classic from a can, and spoke to me in a nasal voice. "Nice to meet you, Mr. Daley."

"Mike. Thank you for seeing me, Mr. Logan."

"Ben. You're welcome."

There was no reason to be disingenuous. "I'm representing Jaylen Jenkins."

"I know. I have no idea why you think I may have any relevant information regarding your case, but I'm happy to do whatever I can to help."

"Thank you."

Everything about the owner of Bayshore Moving and Storage was super-sized. His desk was as big as a pool table. His expansive office was on the fourth floor of the China Basin Building, a block west of the ballpark. At six-four, two-seventy, he could have lined up toe-to-toe with Terrence "The Terminator." I figured that he was somewhere north of sixty, but it was hard to tell. His full head of salt-and-pepper hair matched a trim goatee covering an elongated face sitting directly on his round shoulders. A navy polo shirt struggled to contain his girth.

"I've been trying to see you for a couple of weeks," I said. "Your assistant said that you were out of town. Vacation, I hope?"

"Mostly. A little business, too."

I wanted to keep him talking. "Where?"

"Vegas."

"I hope that you came out ahead."

He smiled triumphantly. "I always do."

I admired the enlarged photo of a 40s-era moving van bearing the Bayshore insignia that was mounted on the wall behind his desk. To its left was a black-and-white portrait of a man who bore a noticeable resemblance to Logan. "Is that your father?"

"My grandfather," he said. "He started our company in 1944 with one truck and a warehouse near the Cow Palace. Now we have almost a hundred trucks and hundreds of employees." He pointed at a color photo of a man who could have been Logan's brother. "That's my dad. He died about twenty years ago."

"I'm sorry."

"Thank you."

The wall to his right was filled with photos of a beaming Logan along with politicians and local celebrities. The wall to his left was lined with pictures of Logan with a Hall of Fame lineup of players from the Giants, Niners, and Warriors. The most prominent was a poster-sized shot of Logan standing between Steph Curry and Kevin Durant after the Warriors had won their third championship in four years in 2018.

I admired the photos of four generations of Logans displayed on his otherwise empty credenza. "Beautiful family," I said. "How many kids do you have?"

"Five. And eight grandchildren—so far. You?"

"Two kids. No grandkids yet. Our daughter graduated from USC and is working for Pixar. Our son starts at Cal next month."

"Go Bears."

"Thanks. I like your office. How long have you been here?"

"Almost forty years. My grandfather rented the space when this was an industrial wasteland, and the rent was cheap." He pointed at the picture window looking directly into a mid-rise residential building across the creek, with the new UCSF campus in the background. "When we moved in, there was nothing but rail yards. We could see Potrero Hill."

He's warming up. "I take it that you grew up here in the City?"

"Cole Valley." His jowls wiggled as he grinned. "Before it was trendy."

"I grew up in the Sunset, which still isn't trendy. St. Anne's Parish."

"St. Ignatius Parish."

"Did you go to S.I.?"

"Sacred Heart."

"We might have met on the football field a long time ago." I grinned. "You okay talking to an S.I. guy?"

"Absolutely."

He appeared to be in no hurry as he filled in a few more biographical details. Graduated near the top of his class at Sacred Heart. Earned a football scholarship to Santa Clara—back in the days when they still had a football team. He applied to grad school, but his plans changed when he was conscripted to work in the family business after his father had a heart attack. He had been working for the company for thirty-seven years.

"Do you still live in Cole Valley?" I asked.

"Sea Cliff."

The moving business was lucrative. The whitewashed mansions in the neighborhood between the Golden Gate Bridge and Land's End started at about five million dollars.

"It's nice that you were able to keep the business in the family," I said.

He scowled. "Family businesses are complicated. I have three brothers and a sister who are involved in the company. We haven't always seen eye-to-eye on everything, but they've agreed that I would make the big decisions."

There's undoubtedly more to the story. "My dad wanted me to go into the family business, too."

"Was he a lawyer?"

"No, he was a cop. He wasn't ecstatic when I became a Public Defender." I pointed at the family portrait on the credenza. "Are any of your kids working here?"

"Two. They're excellent employees." His expression turned serious. "Why did you want to talk to me, Mr. Daley?"

So much for first names. "We're trying to figure out who killed Robbie Blum."

"From what I've read in the papers, your client did."

"He said that he didn't."

"SFPD didn't pull his name out of a hat."

"I understand that you knew Mr. Blum."

"I saw him at Giants and Warriors games. His luxury suite at the ballpark was next to ours. We socialized a little. We went to Vegas a couple of times."

"So you were friends?"

"Acquaintances. I tried to persuade him to recommend us to his clients. Professional athletes move a lot. Sooner or later, everybody needs moving and storage."

"Did you know that he had a drinking problem?"

"Yes. I was told that he was dealing with it. I never saw him behave inappropriately."

"Did you know that he also had a drug problem?"

"I had suspicions." His expression turned stern. "It was never an issue when we were together."

Fair enough. "Did you know that he had a gambling issue?"

"No."

"He must have gambled when you were in Las Vegas."

"He did."

"Large amounts?"

"He was rich, Mr. Daley."

"Do you think he was a compulsive gambler?"

"I don't know."

"Did you ever see him place bets outside the casinos?"

"No."

"Do you have any idea where he might have been placing those bets?"

"I'm afraid not, Mr. Daley."

You're a smooth liar, but you're still a liar. "When was the last time that you saw him?"

"On the night that he died. I said hello to him on the suite level at the ballpark."

"Do you go to many games?"

"All of them." He said that he chatted with Blum about whether the Giants would extend David Archer's contract. "Robbie didn't offer any predictions or inside information."

"Did you stay to the end of the game?"

"I always do. Then I came back here to get my car, which I parked in the garage."

"Did you see him after the game?"

"No."

"Do you know if anybody was angry at Mr. Blum?"

"I'm afraid not, Mr. Daley."

"We understand that your employee, Kevin Killian, made several deliveries on your behalf to and from Mr. Blum's office."

His eyes narrowed. "As I told you, I was trying to persuade Robbie to recommend our company to his clients. I sent over some information about our services and rates."

"You couldn't e-mail it to him?"

"This is a relationship business, Mr. Daley. I wanted to have it delivered personally."

Right. "Is it your practice to use your movers to deliver such information?"

"I use Kevin for special assignments from time to time. He's very reliable."

"Kevin told us that he had made several deliveries to Mr. Blum."

"In addition to pricing information, I sent over some company swag—shirts, caps, etc. I sent him a case of wine at Christmas."

Because it's a relationship business. I handed him a card. "If you have any additional information about Mr. Blum, I would appreciate it if you would give me a call."

"Of course, Mr. Daley."

* * *

Nady's voice was tense. "Did you get anything from Logan?"

I pressed my phone to my ear. A brisk wind hit my face as I walked past the CalTrain station. "No."

"How did he explain Killian's deliveries?"

"He said that he was trying to get Blum to hire his moving company."

"Sounds like B.S. to me. Will he be a strong witness?"

"He isn't going to lose his cool."

"Swell." She waited a beat. "Are you coming back to the office?"

"I'll be there later this afternoon. I'm taking Harvey Tate out for lunch. I want to see if he's found out anything more about Blum's gambling."

37
"STRANGER THINGS HAVE HAPPENED"

Harvey Tate tossed his food-stained tie over his shoulder. He picked up his cheeseburger, took a bite, set it down, and washed it down with a drink of Cabernet. "Not bad," he proclaimed.

Eleven-thirty a.m. was too early for wine, so I sipped iced tea and picked at a cobb salad. Tate and I were sitting at a table in the back of Mars Bar, a block south of our office. Housed in a nondescript building erected after the 1906 Earthquake, the hangout for P.D.s and the tech crowd had opened two decades earlier as the then-sketchy neighborhood was starting to gentrify. The timing was fortuitous, and the watering hole was now situated a few blocks from Airbnb, Zynga, and Stripe. The vibe was friendly, the food plentiful.

Tate pulled out a leather notebook and opened it to a fresh page. "You wanted to talk?"

"Yes."

"We're on the record. You really going to trial in three weeks?"

"Yes."

"You going to get your client off?"

"Yes."

"You going to ask for a change of venue?"

"No. We have great confidence in San Francisco jurors." I took another bite of salad. "Heard any gossip about our case?"

He ate a couple of fries. "Your client is guilty."

"We have reason to believe that Blum owed a big gambling debt to Benjamin Logan of Bayshore Moving and Storage."

He stopped eating his fries. "How confident are you in this information?"

"Ninety percent," I lied.

"Proof?"

"Working on it. I'll share any relevant information as soon as I can confirm it."

"You mean as soon as your brother confirms it."

"Did you find any additional information on Blum's gambling?"

"No." He tapped his pen on his notebook. "What do you want from me?"

"Look into Logan's gambling. See what you can find about his relationship with Blum."

"Isn't that your job?"

"You'll win a Pulitzer if you crack this case."

His rubbery face rearranged itself into a skeptical expression. "You think Logan went after him to settle a debt?"

"Maybe. He was at the ballgame on the night that Blum died."

"So were forty thousand other people. Can you place him in the area where Blum died?"

"We're still looking into it."

"You really think the owner of one of the biggest moving companies in the Bay Area whacked Blum in a public place over a gambling debt?"

"Stranger things have happened, Harvey. Maybe he wanted to deliver a message to Blum and things got out of hand. Or maybe he paid somebody else to do it. Either way, it's plausible."

"For a defense attorney who is desperate to blame his client's crime on somebody else."

That, too. "He had motive, means, and opportunity."

"Then you should be able to prove it."

That may be harder. "We were hoping that you would be able to bring the resources of a major daily newspaper to the investigation."

"Right." He slid the check over to my side of the table. "You think I'll be able to find something that you haven't"

"You're very resourceful. You heard that the charges against Brian Holton were dropped?"

"I did."

"My sources at the D.A.'s Office told me that they let Holton go because he may have provided information about a bigger target."

"Wouldn't surprise me. What does it have to do with your case?"

Maybe nothing. "Holton was selling drugs to Blum. We have video showing Holton walking along the waterfront behind the right field wall on the night that Blum died."

"You think Holton killed Blum in a dispute over an unpaid debt for drugs?"

"Stranger things have happened," I repeated.

* * *

Nady smirked. "How was your lunch with Tate?"

"Fine. He tried to fire the manager in today's column. Third time this week."

"Evidently, the Giants aren't listening."

We were sitting in my office at two o'clock in the afternoon. The air conditioner had gone out again, so it was ninety degrees. Just another day at the P.D.'s Office.

Nady closed her laptop. "Did you get anything useful from him?"

"No, but I tried to plant the seed that Logan or Killian killed Blum because of a gambling debt."

"We have no evidence."

"Tate said that he would look into it. He's as tenacious as Pete. And if he doesn't find anything, we're no worse off than we are now. Did you file our pre-trial motions?"

"Yes. No response yet. We asked for the usual. A gag order on the press. No cameras in court. Exchange of evidence and final witness lists by the end of next week."

"Did you get an updated witness list from Turner?"

"Yes. It's short: Inspector Lee. Dr. Siu. Yosh Kawakami. Jesus Martinez. The first officer at the scene. My guess is that their case will be brief. Jesus will describe the discovery of the body. The first officer will say that he processed the scene properly. Dr. Siu will testify as to cause of death. Yosh will confirm that Blum took a bat when he left the clubhouse. Lee will show the security video with Jaylen carrying the bat and tie their case together."

"Who's on our list so far?"

"Holton. Yosh. Archer. Franklin. Bryant. Eisenmann. Chen. Killian. Logan. We may not need to call all of them, but it's better to be inclusive—especially if we're planning to use a SODDI defense."

"It would be better if we can narrow the jury's options."

She grinned. "If you can't go to trial with the evidence you'd like, you go to trial with the evidence that you have. Who do you like the best?"

"Holton. We can place him at the ballpark that night. He was selling drugs to Blum. He's a bouncer at a strip club. He was recently arrested. We should be able to convince at least one juror that there's a reasonably good chance that Holton killed Blum over a drug debt."

"Has Pete come up with any evidence that somebody else did it?"

"Still looking."

She glanced at her watch. "Trial starts in three weeks."

I studied our witness list. "Add Jen Foster. We may need her to testify that Blum was a jerk who was detested by a lot of people."

"Will do. Do we have resources to hire a jury consultant?"

"Afraid not. We'll have to go with our instincts."

"Should we follow your usual advice that we should pick simpletons who can be easily manipulated?"

"Not this time. We should try to seat educated women and men of color. We need people who are smart enough to understand the concept of reasonable doubt and might be sympathetic to an African American defendant." I waited a beat. "And I want you to take the lead."

Her eyes lit up. "Great. You don't want to sit first chair?"

"Of course, but I think it would be in the best interests of our client if you do. Turner is going to sit first chair for the D.A. I think a jury would be more receptive to you."

"Because I'm a woman?"

"Because you're an excellent lawyer who also happens to be a woman."

"Did you and Rosie decide to put me on this case just because

I'm female?"

"No, we put you on this case because you're an excellent lawyer. The fact that you also happen to be a woman makes you even more valuable to our client."

"That's still sexist."

"You pointed it out to me before the prelim."

"It's still true."

"It's still in the best interests of our client. Are you in?"

"Yes."

Rosie appeared in my doorway. "We gotta go to Saint Francis Hospital right away."

Uh-oh. "Is your mother okay?"

"Fine. Rolanda is in labor. I promised Tony that we would pick up Mama on our way. I'd like to be there when our first great-niece arrives."

38
"YOU'RE A BEAUTY"

"You're a beauty," I whispered.

Maria Sylvia Teresa Fernandez Epstein responded with a yawn.

I smiled at Rolanda, who was holding her baby daughter. "My great-niece is barely two hours old, and I'm already boring her."

Her eyes sparkled. "She just met you, Mike. She'll appreciate you more after she gets to know you a little better."

Maria Sylvia Teresa Fernandez Epstein was born at 7:20 p.m. on Thursday, July sixteenth, at Saint Francis Hospital in San Francisco. The delivery was uneventful after four hours of labor. My punctual great-niece arrived within an hour after Rolanda had requested an epidural. She clocked in at twenty-one inches in length and a robust eight pounds and four ounces. She had a full head of jet-black hair and matching cobalt eyes. It brought back memories of Grace's arrival twenty-four years earlier at the same hospital.

"You feeling okay?" I asked Rolanda.

"A little tired, but otherwise fine."

She was sitting up in bed at nine-fifteen on Thursday night. Her husband, Zach, sat to her right. The partner at a big downtown law firm couldn't stop smiling. Rolanda's father, Tony, sat next to Zach, eyes beaming at his first grandchild. Sylvia was to Rolanda's left, eyes locked onto her first great-grandchild. Rosie was sitting next to her mother and clutching her hand.

"You weren't in labor for very long," I said to Rolanda.

"Maria is impatient."

"Just like her mother."

Rolanda looked at Sylvia and then Rosie. "And her grandmother and her aunt." She turned to Sylvia. "Would you like to hold her, Grandma?"

"I thought you'd never ask."

I thought about my mom, who had died twenty years earlier, and my dad, who had been gone twenty-six years. Mama got to meet Grace, but not Tommy. Pop died of lung cancer a few days after Grace's second birthday. They never met Pete's daughter. And they never met the daughter of my older brother Tommy, whose Vietnamese wife gave birth to a baby in Vietnam.

Rolanda gingerly handed the baby to Sylvia, who held her great-granddaughter with the confidence of a woman who had raised three children and had five grandchildren.

"I like her names," I said to Rolanda.

She shot a knowing glance at her father, then she turned back to me. "We like them, too."

Rolanda and Zach had chosen the names with care. Maria was the name of Rolanda's mother and Tony's wife, who had died of cancer when Rolanda was in high school. Sylvia was, of course, her grandmother. Teresa was Rosie and Tony's younger sister, who had died a few years earlier.

Sylvia passed the baby over to Rosie.

"She reminds me of Grace," Rosie said.

Sylvia smiled. "She reminds me of you, Rosita."

We sat in silence for a few minutes. Then we resumed taking photos and texting the good news to the extended Fernandez clan. Zach's parents arrived from Chicago. Teresa's daughter, Angelina, joined us from L.A. on Facetime. Pete phoned in to offer his congratulations. Big John sent over a bouquet of roses with a balloon and a teddy bear.

A nurse entered the room and spoke in a gentle tone. "We need Rolanda and the baby for a few minutes."

Rosie handed the sleeping baby to our niece. We exchanged hugs and good wishes. Then Rosie, Sylvia, and I made our way to the door.

As we walked down the corridor, Sylvia turned to Rosie. "I wouldn't mind having another great-grandchild. Are you ready to be a grandma, Rosita?"

"Pretty soon, Mama." She squeezed her mother's hand. "It isn't up to me, you know."

"Is Grace still seeing that boy?"

"Yes. His name is Chuck."

"Right. Chuck. I like him."

"So do I." Rosie smiled. "What about the tattoos?"

"I'll learn to live with them."

"You told me that you would disown me if I ever went out with a boy with tattoos."

"I've become more flexible as I've gotten older, Rosita."

Grace's boyfriend was a fellow production assistant at Pixar. Technically, they weren't supposed to be dating each other, but things happen. He was a graduate of UCLA film school and a promising filmmaker. His latest animated short was going to have its premiere at the Sundance Film Festival. More important, he was very nice to Grace.

Sylvia flashed a sly grin. "You think this might be the one?"

Rosie shrugged. "They've been seeing each other for only six months."

"Grace told me that they were thinking about moving in together."

"So, I've heard. You're okay with it?"

"Of course, dear."

Rosie smiled at her mother. "When I was Grace's age, you told me that you would disown me if I ever moved in with a boy that wasn't my husband."

Sylvia's eyes twinkled. "I've become more flexible as I've gotten older," she repeated. "Besides, it would be nice for little Maria to have a playmate."

* * *

Big John placed a pint of Guinness in front of Rosie. "Congratulations on the arrival of your new great-niece."

"Thank you, Big John."

"You're welcome, darlin'."

He was the only person on Planet Earth who could get away with calling Rosie "darlin'."

Dunleavy's was quiet at eleven-thirty on Thursday night. We had dropped off Rosie's mom at her house and stopped for a celebratory nightcap on our way home. We would resume our legal battles in the morning.

"It was nice of you to send over the flowers and the teddy bear," Rosie said.

"My pleasure." Big John's wide face transformed into his real smile—not the phony one that he reserved for his customers when he was spewing blarney from behind the bar. "You're looking as beautiful as ever."

"You're sweet, Big John."

"Don't let the politicians get to you."

"I never do."

He put a Guinness down in front of me. "And congratulations to my favorite nephew. Everything going smoothly over at Saint Francis Hospital?"

"All good. Rolanda and Maria will be going home tomorrow."

"Excellent. I remember when you were born, Mikey. Your dad went through two packs of Camels in the waiting room."

"Mama appreciated your efforts to keep him calm."

"My pleasure, lad."

I took a sip of my beer. "Somebody broke into our car in the parking lot at St. Francis."

"Part of the joy of living in San Francisco."

"We didn't leave anything inside worth stealing." There are almost a hundred auto break-ins in my hometown every day. "We aren't going to let it dampen our spirits tonight."

"Attaboy. It's also nice that you can take a little break from the Jenkins case."

"Just for tonight."

"My darlin' great-niece and great-nephew okay?"

"Fine, Big John."

"Is Grace still seeing Chuck?"

"Yes."

He winked. "No pressure, Mikey, but I wouldn't mind having a great-great niece or great-great nephew to spoil while I'm still able to enjoy their company."

"Sylvia made a similar request. We have limited influence with our daughter."

"I'll talk to her the next time she comes in." He tossed his ever-present dishtowel over his shoulder. "You really going to trial in a couple of weeks?"

"Yes."

"You feeling good about it?"

I exchanged a glance with Rosie. "Pretty good."

"If I was on the jury, I'd vote to acquit."

"You don't know anything about the evidence."

"I trust you."

"Any chance you have jury duty on August sixth?"

"Afraid not, Mikey." He excused himself to make last call and to tote up the day's receipts.

Rosie took a draw of her Guinness. "Rolanda looked very happy. And Maria is a keeper."

"Yes, she is. I was a little surprised that your mother was so enthusiastic about Grace moving in with Chuck."

"She's evolving." Her expression turned thoughtful. "When you have more yesterdays than tomorrows, you develop a sense of pragmatism." Her expression turned serious. "Are you ready to be a grandparent?"

"I think so." I quickly added, "I'd prefer that Grace do it in an orderly way—you know—when she's sure that she's in love with the guy, they get married, and then have a kid."

"We weren't very good role models."

"No, we weren't." Grace was born eight months after Rosie and I got married. Tommy was born after we got divorced. "Does that mean that you're ready to be a grandparent?"

"Whenever Grace is ready."

"Very mature." I reached over and touched her hand. Then my phone rang. Pete's name appeared on the display.

"Rolanda and the baby okay?" he asked.

"Perfect."

"Good. You still at Dunleavy's?"

"Yes."

"How soon can you come over to the Gold Club?"

"It's late, Pete."

"I still think you should come over here now, Mick. Brian Holton is dead."

39
"THAT CHANGES THINGS"

Rosie was driving home from Dunleavy's, so I took a Lyft to the Gold Club, where I found Pete standing outside the yellow crime scene tape. I pointed at the six police cars and the Medical Examiner's van parked haphazardly on Howard Street. "Were you here when it happened?"

"No, but one of my operatives was sitting in his car across the street. He didn't see anything, but we talked to one of the cops. Holton was stabbed in the alley behind the club. He bled out before the ambulance got here."

I thought back to our earlier visit to the Gold Club. "Was Darlene here?"

"She's off tonight."

"Did you get anything else from the cop?"

"A kid bought some crystal meth from Holton. Evidently, they had a disagreement, and the kid stabbed Holton."

"Did they catch him?"

"He's dead. Holton shot him."

"Holton was packing while working at a crowded club?"

"You gotta protect yourself, Mick."

It didn't protect Holton. "What are the chances that somebody sent the kid to kill Holton?"

"Doubtful. The cops knew him. He was a small-time addict who lived on Sixth Street. He was probably getting a fix."

"Has anybody from Homicide shown up?"

"Ken Lee. He wouldn't talk to me."

"We just lost an important witness and our best alternate suspect."

"He's still our best alternate suspect, Mick. Now he can't defend himself."

* * *

Rosie was sitting at her kitchen table at two-twenty a.m. "That changes things."

I took a sip of Diet Dr Pepper from a can. "It does."

"Did Pete find out anything about the kid who stabbed Holton?"

"Twenty-four. Grew up in the Excelsior. Father was a cop. He's been in and out of jail since he was sixteen. Did time for possession, shoplifting, and auto theft."

"Any chance he was connected to a bigger drug-dealing organization?"

"Not as far as I know."

"Has Pete made any progress connecting Holton to a bigger drug supplier?"

"Still looking."

Rosie took a moment to gather her thoughts. "Holton's death could help us. We can blame him for Blum's death, and he won't be able to deny it."

40
"I EXPECT YOU TO BE READY"

The Honorable Ignatius Tsang sat in a leather chair behind a government-issue desk in his musty chambers at two-thirty in the afternoon of Wednesday, July twenty-ninth. His floor-to-ceiling bookcases were packed with dusty legal tomes, and a bronze rendering of the scales of justice sat on his desk. A lithograph of the U.S. Supreme Court hung next to his law school diploma from UC-Berkeley. A framed photo of his wife, JoAnn, and his son, Nathan, a law professor at UCLA, sat on the credenza.

As always, he spoke with precision. "I expect you to be ready for trial on Thursday, August sixth, Mr. Daley."

"We will, Your Honor."

Judge Tsang was a slight man in his early sixties with a receding hairline and a subdued, but authoritative manner. The native of Taiwan had accompanied his mother and father to San Francisco when he was a baby. He grew up in Chinatown, where his parents held multiple low-paying jobs to allow him to focus on his studies. A brilliant student, he graduated at the top of his class at Lowell High School. He raced through UC-Berkeley in three years and placed first in his class at Berkeley Law. He clerked for Justice Byron White before he took an entry-level position at the San Francisco DA's office, where he labored for two decades while writing law review articles and teaching criminal procedure. He brought the same tenacity and intellectual rigor to the bench.

He stroked his chin as he pretended to study our pre-trial motions. Given his obsessive preparedness and photographic memory, I was confident that he could recite every word in our papers by heart. He took off his reading glasses and spoke to Nady, who was sitting next to me. "I've read your documents, Ms. Nikonova. Anything you'd like to add?"

"No, Your Honor."

He looked at Turner, who was sitting next to Erickson in front of the dirt-encrusted window overlooking the slow lane of I-80. "You?"

"Nothing, Your Honor."

He took a moment to gather his thoughts. "First, my gag order remains in place. I don't want you trying this case in the press."

We nodded.

"Second, I'm not going to allow television cameras in my courtroom."

Turner scowled. "It will give the public a chance to be informed about this case."

"The dynamics change when cameras are present."

"Many people don't have the time or wherewithal to come downtown."

"I've ruled, Ms. Turner." The judge put on his reading glasses and glanced at his computer. Then he spoke to Nady. "No request for a change of venue?"

"Correct."

He looked at Turner. "You're happy to stay here in San Francisco?"

"We are, Your Honor."

"Have you and the defense exchanged witness lists?"

"We have. No last-minute additions."

"Ms. Nikonova?"

"Not at this time, but we reserve the right to add additional names."

"I expect you and Ms. Turner to exchange final lists by close of business on Friday."

"We will."

We would load our list with the names of anybody we might remotely consider calling to testify. It would make Turner and Erickson prepare for more witnesses.

We spent forty-five minutes arguing about jury questionnaires, evidentiary issues, chain-of-custody disputes, and draft jury instructions. Turner said that the prosecution's case would be short—no more than two trial days after jury selection. Nady and I said that our defense would also be brief. Given the limited amount of physical evidence and the small number of witnesses, it was possible that it would take us longer to pick a jury than present the evidence.

Judge Tsang glanced at his watch. "Anything else, Ms. Nikonova?"

Nady shot a disdainful glance at Turner, then she addressed the judge. "Your Honor, we ask you to instruct Ms. Turner to provide any remaining evidence as soon as possible."

Turner feigned irritation. "We have, Your Honor."

"You provided us with more than a thousand hours of security videos, most of which were irrelevant. You were trying to take up our time."

"If we hadn't, you would be complaining that we had left something out. It's unfair to criticize us for being thorough. We were fulfilling our legal obligation to provide all evidence that would tend to exonerate your client."

The judge knew that prosecutors frequently dump mountains of irrelevant evidence on the defense. "If you have any additional evidence that should be shared with the defense, I want you to do so as soon as possible and, in any event, no later than Friday."

"Yes, Your Honor."

"Anything else?" the judge asked.

I spoke up. "Are you planning to give a manslaughter instruction?"

"I haven't decided, Mr. Daley."

By law, in a first-degree murder case, Judge Tsang was obligated to also instruct the jury that it may find Jaylen guilty of second-degree. He also had the discretion, but not the legal duty, to give a manslaughter instruction. The ramifications were significant. First-degree murder carries a minimum sentence of twenty-five years, second-degree, fifteen. Voluntary manslaughter has a minimum of three years, a maximum of eleven. For involuntary, the range is two to four.

He added, "I will make a final decision after the prosecution and the defense finish presenting their respective cases. Do you have a preference, Mr. Daley?"

"We're leaning in favor, Your Honor."

"Noted."

A manslaughter instruction is a mixed bag. It could lead to a shorter sentence, but it might also make it easier for a jury to reach a "compromise" guilty verdict.

Turner spoke up again. "We have no objection to a manslaughter instruction."

"Also noted."

Prosecutors are often willing to sacrifice longer sentences for a surer conviction.

Judge Tsang spoke in a somber tone. "I would like you to make a final effort to work out a deal so that we don't have to empanel a jury and take up resources for a trial."

"We've tried," Turner said. "Mr. Daley refused our very generous offer of a deal for second-degree murder with a relatively short sentence."

"It isn't a murder case," I said.

Judge Tsang's voice filled with impatience. "The charges are up to the D.A., Mr. Daley. Whether they can prove their case beyond a reasonable doubt is another matter. I would ask all of you to try once more to negotiate a plea bargain."

Turner wasn't buying. "Mr. Daley refuses to be reasonable, Your Honor."

"I have known Mr. Daley for many years. In my experience, he's always reasonable."

Nice to know.

The judge's eyes twinkled. "I know how persuasive you can be, Ms. Turner. I'm asking you to try to work your magic on Mr. Daley and Ms. Nikonova one more time."

* * *

"Do you think Turner knows something that we don't?" Nady asked.

"Probably," I said. "We won't find out until trial."

I was standing next to her desk at eight-thirty the same evening. The P.D.'s Office was quiet. Luna was sitting in the corner in anticipation of dinner. Pete was in the conference room studying video. We were a week from starting trial, and we were still trying to settle on a narrative and the best strategy to present our alternative suspects to the jury.

I pointed at Nady's laptop. "I want you to load up our witness list with as many names as possible. Include everyone who was in the clubhouse. And add the names of everybody Pete has talked to, including people who worked at the businesses near the ballpark. Turner gave us a lot of useless video to occupy our time. Let's make them prepare for more witnesses."

"You're as spiteful as I am."

"Spite is a harsh word."

"It's the right one."

Perhaps. "Rosie likes to say that I'm not as nice as I pretend to be."

"She's right. You think Turner will offer us a new deal?"

"Probably."

"One that Jaylen would be willing to accept?"

"Doubtful."

41
"LAST CHANCE"

The District Attorney of the City and County of San Francisco sat behind his city-issue metal desk. DeSean Harper adjusted his polka dot tie and spoke to me in a subdued tone. "Thank you for coming in to see us on short notice."

"You're welcome." Stay patient. Don't make the first move.

Our trial was scheduled to start in two days. I was sitting on the windowsill in his functional office on the second floor of a refurbished industrial building at the base of Potrero Hill. The space wasn't opulent, and the location wasn't as convenient as his old digs at the Hall, but the new plumbing and functioning air conditioner represented substantial upgrades. Nady was sitting in a chair near Harper's desk. Turner and Erickson were standing in front of the credenza, eyes on Harper.

"Water?" Harper asked.

"No, thank you," I said. Nady also declined.

He poured himself a glass of ice water and took a sip.

Wait for it. Let him talk first.

Harper looked at Turner.

"Any last-minute additions to your witness list?" she asked.

"No," I said. "You?"

"No."

"Any additional evidence that you'd like to provide?"

"None." Turner eyed me. "We're set to start on Thursday."

"So are we." I let my answer hang to see if she would feel compelled to fill the void. After an interminable pause, she did.

"Judge Tsang asked us to try once more to find a deal for Jaylen Jenkins." Her eyes turned to Harper.

His voice was even. "After lengthy debate, I have authorized Vanessa and Andy to make a final offer. We are prepared to go down to voluntary manslaughter."

Progress. "We're listening."

"Sentence would be at the higher end: ten years with credit for time served, possibility of parole after seven, and credit for good behavior. He could be out in seven. Maybe six."

Not bad.

"It's a good deal, Mike," he said. "Probably more generous than I should be offering."

You always say that. "He didn't kill Blum."

"The jury will be able to put the pieces together."

Let's see how much you're willing to deal. "Seven years with credit, possibility of parole, and time off for good behavior."

"Nine."

"Eight."

He took a deep breath. "I'll take heat for it, but I think we can go there."

"We'll take it to our client."

"Last chance, Mike. The offer will remain open until five o'clock tomorrow afternoon."

42
"I CAN TAKE CARE OF MYSELF"

Jaylen's answer was concise. "No."

"It's a good deal," I said.

"If I had killed Blum."

"It's the best that we're going to get."

"No, the best is that I'll be acquitted."

That deal isn't on the table. "With good behavior, you'd be out in six years, Jaylen. You would still be a young man with a long life ahead of you."

"A long life as a convicted murderer."

"Manslaughter."

"Doesn't matter. Nobody will hire me if I plead guilty."

"It gives you certainty."

"I want you to find the guy who did it."

"Then we should delay your trial to give us more time."

"If you're as good as everybody says, you don't need more time."

Yes, we do. "We're good, Jaylen, but we can't do miracles."

"Then do the best that you can. I'm not going to sit in this hellhole for another year."

I looked into the frustrated eyes of an exhausted young man who was being ground up by the system. "You're sure you want to start on Thursday?"

"Yes."

We go to war in two days. "If that's what you want, that's what we'll do."

Nady spoke to Jaylen in a calm voice. "We may need you to testify at trial. We'll need a forceful denial, and then we'll get you off the stand."

He hesitated. "I'll be ready."

"We'll protect you, but you'll need to be careful if the D.A. goes after you."

"I can take care of myself."

I'm not as confident as you are.

"Jaylen," she continued, "trials are about optics. It would look better to the jury if there are some people in court to support you. I talked to your mother earlier today and asked her again to come to trial. She said that she wasn't sure if she could handle it."

"Ask her again."

* * *

Nady and I were standing on the front steps of the Hall.

"Where to now?" she asked me.

"First to the office to drop off our laptops. Then to Oakland to talk LaTanya into coming to the trial."

"If we can find her. And if we do, she might not agree."

"We won't know unless we ask her." I pulled out my phone.

"Who are you calling?" Nady asked.

"Pete."

43
"SHE ISN'T HERE"

At eight-fifteen the same night, I heard the roar of a BART train on the elevated tracks behind us as Nady, Pete, and I approached the ramshackle lime-green Victorian across the street from the West Oakland BART station. The sun was setting as I tried the handle on the cast-iron grating blocking the weathered wooden door, but it was locked. I pressed the buzzer. No answer. I tried it again. Still no answer. I pressed it once more.

The inner door swung open, and a tattooed woman with two nose rings, a lip ring, and countless ear piercings looked at me through the grating. "What do you want?"

"My name is Michael Daley. We're looking for LaTanya Jenkins. We're her son's lawyers."

"Visiting hours are over."

"It's an emergency."

"Nobody in or out after eight. No exceptions."

"Jaylen's trial starts in two days. We need to talk to her."

"She isn't here."

Crap. "You let her leave?"

"This is a support house, Mr. Daley. If somebody wants to leave, we can't stop them."

"Do you know why she left?"

"She didn't tell me. Besides, it's none of my business."

"Is there somebody that we can talk to?"

"You can come back tomorrow before eight and talk to anybody you'd like."

Nady moved in front of me and spoke softly. "What's your name?"

"Priscilla."

"I'm Nady. Is there somebody staying here who was friends with LaTanya?"

"No. LaTanya kept to herself."

"We tried her phone, but she didn't answer."

"She didn't always keep it turned on."

Nady's lips turned down. "Did she ever talk about anybody? Family? Friends?"

"Just her son."

"Anybody else? Please, Priscilla."

She pointed down the street. "She knew some people living under the BART tracks."

* * *

The dirt-encrusted sleeping bag sprung to life, and a wild-eyed man with an unkempt beard poked his head out. "Watch where you're going!" he shouted.

"Sorry," I said.

He responded with a string of expletives as he pulled himself out of the sleeping bag and stood up. "You do that to somebody else, they'll cut you—or worse."

"Sorry," I repeated.

Nighttime had arrived in West Oakland. The tent city adjacent to the BART Station parking lot was a permanent encampment. The north side of Seventh Street had gentrified a little when they built the Mandela Gardens Apartments, a low-rise complex. On the south side, about fifty residents lived in tents and under tarps. The city provided a few porta-potties and a couple of sinks. Basic provisions were available at a gas station down the street.

Pete stepped around me, pulled out two twenties, and handed it to the guy. "Got a sec?"

He snatched the bills. "Maybe."

"We're looking for LaTanya."

The red-eyed man stroked his beard but didn't say anything.

Pete held up another twenty but pulled it back when the man reached for it. "Have you seen LaTanya?"

"Maybe."

"Where?"

Sensing that the negotiations and Pete's patience were coming to an end, the man pointed at the porta-potties. "Back there."

Pete handed him the twenty. "Thanks for your help."

Pete, Nady, and I made our way between the tents and sleeping bags and around the toilets until we found LaTanya and two other women sitting on lawn chairs and sharing a marijuana pipe.

LaTanya saw us, handed the bong to her neighbor, and frowned. "How did you find me?"

"That isn't important," I said. "We need to talk to you—in private."

"You can't make me go back to the house."

"We won't."

"You can't make me go anywhere with you."

"No, we can't."

Nady spoke up in a soothing tone. "Let us buy you something to eat, LaTanya. We need to talk to you about Jaylen."

* * *

Nady spoke softly. "You want to tell us why you left the house?"

LaTanya took a drink of the super-sized Coke Classic that we had purchased at the convenience store. "I got into an argument with Priscilla."

"About what?"

"I came back late. She didn't want to let me inside, so I took off."

"This wasn't the first time you and Priscilla had a disagreement, was it?"

"No."

"We can help you smooth things over."

"I'm not going back."

She meant it.

Nady and LaTanya were sitting in the back seat of Pete's car. Pete was behind the wheel. I was in the passenger seat. It wasn't an ideal location to discuss LaTanya's issues, but it was better than doing it in the homeless camp.

Nady touched LaTanya's hand. "Jaylen's trial starts on Thursday."

"I know."

"It's going to be okay."

"You're the lawyers."

"He's scared."

LaTanya frowned. "So am I."

"It would be nice if you could be at the trial to support him."

A long pause. "I can't."

"Yes, you can."

"I'm not in the right frame of mind. My oldest son never did well in court."

"You're strong, LaTanya."

"Jaylen doesn't want me there."

"Yes, he does."

"He's ashamed of me."

"No, he's not. He loves you."

"I haven't been a good mother."

"You're doing the best that you can."

"I can't go to court if I'm high."

"You'll stay straight."

"I have nothing to wear."

"We have clothes at the P.D.'s Office. I'll help you pick out something every day."

"I have no place to stay."

I turned around and spoke to her. "We have arrangements with a couple of hotels near the Hall of Justice. You can stay there."

"I can't afford it."

"We have a fund for circumstances like yours."

"I can stay for free?"

"As long as you stay straight."

She swallowed. "Thank you."

"You're welcome. We'll drive you over there and get you set up." I turned to Pete. "Let's take her over to America's Best. It's nicer than the Minna."

He turned on the ignition. "On our way."

I lowered my voice. "You'll stay in the lobby of the hotel to make sure that LaTanya has everything that she needs?"

"Of course." He understood that I was asking him to make sure that LaTanya didn't leave.

"You'll bring her over to the office in the morning so we can give her some clothes to wear to court?"

"Yes."

I looked at my brother. "Thanks, Pete."

44
"LET'S PICK A JURY"

At nine-fifteen on a foggy Thursday morning, Nady and I lugged our laptops, trial bags, and exhibits up the steps of the Hall and past the reporters who kept warm by shouting questions.

"Mr. Daley? Does your client plan to cut a deal?"

"Ms. Nikonova? Is it true that your client's mother has left rehab?"

"Mr. Daley? Ms. Nikonova? Mr. Daley?"

When we reached the top of the stairs, we stopped, turned around, and faced the cameras. I nodded at Nady, who dutifully recited the platitude that defense attorneys say before the start of every trial.

"We are pleased to have the opportunity to defend Jaylen Jenkins in court. We are confident that he will be exonerated."

* * *

"Good to go?" I asked.

LaTanya's voice was a hoarse whisper. "I think so."

Rosie spoke up for her. "We're all set, Mike. She's going to be fine."

Rosie and LaTanya were sitting in the front row of the gallery behind Nady and me. Pete was in the back row. He had spent the night in the lobby of the hotel where LaTanya was staying. He brought her over to the P.D.'s Office earlier this morning, where Nady and Rosie helped her select a navy pantsuit with a white blouse and a silk scarf. Rosie brought her over to Judge Tsang's courtroom. She was prepared to sit next to her for the entire trial, if necessary.

I touched LaTanya's hand. "They're going to bring Jaylen inside. This judge is a good person, but he's also a stickler about behavior. Rosie explained the rules, right?"

"No talking. Stay calm. Be respectful."

"Exactly. You'll be great. Jaylen is glad that you're here."

* * *

Two deputies escorted Jaylen into court, where he sat down at the defense table between Nady and me. Freshly shaved and wearing the charcoal suit and striped tie that I had picked out for him, his demeanor was calm—almost serene.

I whispered, "Don't be afraid to look the judge and the jurors in the eye."

"Right." He turned around and waved at his mother. He mouthed, "Thanks for coming."

She swallowed. "Everything's going to be fine."

Andy Erickson and Vanessa Turner were sitting at the prosecution table along with Inspector Lee. In a display of institutional support, DeSean Harper sat behind them in the gallery. Harvey Tate was alongside him, scribbling in his notebook. Reporters from the *Examiner*, the *Oakland Trib*, the *San Jose Mercury*, and Channel Two filled the second row. The remaining seats were taken by a ragtag assortment of courtroom junkies, retirees, law students, and homeless people.

I felt a rush of adrenaline as the bailiff recited the call to order. "All rise."

Here we go.

A standing fan pushed around the heavy air. Judge Tsang emerged from his chambers, surveyed his domain, and glided to his chair. He turned on his computer, put on his reading glasses, glanced at his docket, and removed the glasses. "Please be seated."

I had never seen him pick up his gavel.

He turned on his microphone and addressed the bailiff in an understated voice leaving no doubt that he was in command of his courtroom. "We are on the record. Please call our case."

"The People versus Jaylen DeMarcus Jenkins."

"Counsel will state their names for the record."

"Vanessa Turner and Andrew Erickson for the People."

"Nadezhda Nikonova and Michael Daley for the defense."

"Good to see all of you." He looked over Nady's shoulder. "I see that our Public Defender is with us today. Nice to see you, Ms. Fernandez."

"Thank you, Your Honor."

"Let's pick a jury."

* * *

Under Judge Tsang's expert direction, we selected twelve jurors and four alternates by the close of business on Friday. At ten o'clock on Monday morning, those who couldn't come up with a convincing sob story were seated in the jury box, feigning nonchalance, eyes revealing nervousness. We didn't have the resources to hire a jury consultant, so Nady and I went with our instincts. Most trial attorneys (including yours truly) believe cases are won and lost during jury selection. In all likelihood, Jaylen's fate would turn on whether we could convince at least one juror that the prosecutors didn't prove their case beyond a reasonable doubt. The legal issues weren't complicated, so we tried to seat people who were susceptible to persuasion.

Our lineup included eight women, seven of whom were college educated, and five of whom were people of color. We had five mothers (two single)—two African-Americans, two Latinas, and one Filipino. Two of the four alternates were female, and one of the male alternates was African-American. Three worked for tech firms, two worked for the City, one was a supervisor at PG&E, and two were retirees. Pete had a hunch that the woman who worked for PG&E would take a leadership role. His hunches were usually good.

Judge Tsang thanked the jurors for their service and invited them to notify the bailiff if they had concerns. Then he read the standard instructions. "Do not talk about this case to anyone or among yourselves until deliberations begin. Do not do any research on your own or as a group. You may take notes, but do not use a dictionary or other reference materials, investigate the facts or law, conduct any experiments, or visit the scene of the events to be described at this trial. Do not look at anything involving this case in the press, on TV, or online."

His voice was even, but he meant it.

He added the now-standard admonition that was unnecessary when I became a Deputy Public Defender a quarter of a century earlier. "Do not post anything on Facebook, Twitter, Instagram, Snapchat, WhatsApp, or other social media. If you tweet or text about this case, it will cost you."

The jurors nodded.

The judge looked at Turner. "Do you wish to make an opening statement?"

She wasn't required to do so, but I had never seen a prosecutor turn down the invitation.

"Yes, Your Honor." She stood to her full height, buttoned her charcoal jacket, strode to the lectern, placed a single sheet of paper in front of her, and spoke directly to the jury. "My name is Vanessa Turner. I am an Assistant District Attorney. I am grateful for your service, and I appreciate your time and attention."

Jaylen tensed.

Turner set up a poster-sized photo of a smiling Blum in front of the jury. "Robbie Blum was a gifted sports agent, businessman, attorney, counselor, confidante, and friend. He was also a dedicated father to a young son, a generous contributor to numerous charitable organizations, and a leader in various community causes. He was a respected and honorable man who was hardworking, dedicated, and loyal to his clients and friends."

Except for the cheating, spousal abuse, alcohol issues, drug use, and gambling.

She pushed out a melodramatic sigh. "And now he's dead. It is an unspeakable tragedy." She pointed at Jaylen. "We will demonstrate beyond a reasonable doubt that the defendant beat Robbie Blum to death behind the ballpark after a Giants game on June first of this year."

The first thing they teach every Assistant D.A. is to point at the defendant.

She lowered her arm. "Robbie was only fifty-five. His young son is devastated. So are his family and friends. We cannot bring him back, but we can bring his murderer to justice."

Nady interjected in a respectful tone. "Objection to the term 'murderer.' Argumentative."

"Sustained. The jury will disregard the use of that term."

Sure they will. It's generally bad form to interrupt during an opening statement, but Nady wanted to let the jury know that she was paying attention.

Turner ignored the objection. "I am asking you to listen carefully, weigh the evidence, and find justice for Robbie." She moved closer to the jury. "Robbie loved sports—especially baseball. He had transitioned from being a respected lawyer to being a successful agent. He represented several Giants, along with some Niners and Warriors. He was very good at his job."

"The sad irony is that Robbie knew the defendant and tried to help him. He hired the defendant to handle minor tasks for him. He gave the defendant Giants merchandise to sell outside the ballpark. Yet the defendant took advantage of this trust and killed Robbie after stealing from him. The police found fifteen hundred dollars in cash in the defendant's possession when he was arrested. Coincidence? I don't think so."

Her word choice was deliberate. She would always call Blum by his first name to humanize him. She would refer to Jaylen only as "the defendant."

"Robbie left the ballpark shortly before midnight. He provided some game jerseys and a bat to the defendant. Then Robbie headed to his car. The defendant followed him. We will show you a security video of the defendant running after Robbie while holding a bat. We will also show you a video taken a few minutes later showing the defendant running in the opposite direction without the bat. The autopsy concluded that Robbie died of blunt force trauma to his head. His body was found in the bay the next morning. A Louisville Slugger was floating next to him."

Turner gave the jury a moment to digest the information. "Coincidence? Not a chance." She shot a disdainful glance my way, then she faced the jury. "The defense is going to suggest that somebody other than the defendant hit Robbie. Or maybe they'll say that it was a misunderstanding or an accident. It's their job to distract you. That's why it is critical that you evaluate the evidence carefully."

Jaylen leaned over and whispered, "Can you do anything to stop this?"

"It'll be our turn in a minute."

Turner returned to the lectern. "During this trial, you are going to hear a lot about 'reasonable doubt.' It's an important legal concept. But common sense is even more important. It's your job to evaluate the evidence, deliberate carefully, and use your common sense. I am confident that you will do so. I will provide more than enough evidence for you to find the defendant guilty."

She returned to the prosecution table and sat down.

Judge Tsang looked at Nady. "Opening statement, Ms. Nikonova?"

"Yes, Your Honor."

We could have deferred until after Turner had completed her case, but it's better to connect with the jurors right away.

Nady walked to the lectern. She had a photographic memory, so she worked without notes. "My name is Nady Nikonova. I am a Deputy Public Defender. Jaylen Jenkins has been wrongly accused of a crime that he did not commit. It's your job to correct this error and see that justice is served."

I felt pride as I watched her work. She was in command of the courtroom. Her demeanor reminded me of Rolanda. Her tenacity reminded me of Rosie.

She moved in front of the jurors. "Jaylen Jenkins is a hardworking man who was doing everything he could to make ends meet and provide for his mother, who has health issues. He was a gifted baseball player at McClymonds High School in Oakland. Jaylen couldn't afford college, so he worked hard at several fast-food jobs. He also sold T-shirts outside the ballpark. He didn't get rich, but he paid the rent." She glanced at LaTanya. "He helped pay for his mother's treatments."

Nady made eye contact with the jurors in the first row. "I was born in Uzbekistan and came to the U.S. with my mom when I was seven. I know what it's like to live on ramen noodles and cereal. I know how it feels to be unemployed. I've worked as a waitress to pay for food. It makes you resilient. Jaylen is resilient. He isn't a murderer."

The juror who issued marriage licenses at City Hall was paying attention.

Nady kept talking. "Jaylen knew Robbie Blum, who was a regular customer. The decedent liked Giants memorabilia. And he liked Jaylen. To his credit, he gave Jaylen the opportunity to make some extra money. He gave Jaylen jerseys to sell. And he hired Jaylen to run errands for him." She frowned. "I generally prefer not to speak ill of the dead, but I also need to explain that the decedent had a dark side. Two failed marriages. Allegations of domestic abuse. A drinking problem. A drug problem. A serious gambling problem."

Turner made her presence felt. "Objection, Your Honor. Mr. Blum is not on trial."

Nady replied before Judge Tsang could answer. "It is no secret that the decedent had behavior issues and many enemies, Your Honor. He owed people money for drugs and gambling. We will provide evidence that several of the people to whom he owed substantial sums were angry at him and in the vicinity that night."

"The objection is overruled. You may continue, Ms. Nikonova."

"Ms. Turner and I agree that the decedent's death is a tragedy. On the other hand, it would be an even greater tragedy if an innocent man is convicted of a crime that he did not commit."

"Objection," Turner said. "Argumentative. I would ask you to instruct Ms. Nikonova to stick to the facts in her opening."

Judge Tsang turned to the jury. "An opening statement should not be treated as fact. It merely constitutes a roadmap of what the anticipated evidence will show."

He knew that the jurors weren't going to forget what they had just heard.

Nady flashed a caustic grin at Turner, smiled graciously at the judge, and picked up where she had left off. "Ms. Turner asked you to use your common sense. So will I. Bottom line: Ms. Turner cannot prove her case beyond a reasonable doubt. As a result, you cannot vote to convict Jaylen of murder."

There was no reaction from the jurors as Nady walked back to the defense table.

I subtly turned around and saw Rosie give LaTanya's hand a reassuring squeeze.

The judge spoke to Turner. "Please call your first witness."

"The People call Jesus Martinez."

45
"IT WAS FLOATING IN THE BAY"

Jesus Martinez poured himself a cup of water and tugged at the collar of his ill-fitting sports jacket. "I work at the South Beach Yacht Club."

Judge Tsang leaned over. "Please speak a little louder, Mr. Martinez."

"Yes, Your Honor. I work at the South Beach Yacht Club."

In a perfect world, Turner would have started with a more entertaining witness, but Martinez was the logical leadoff man. You need a decedent in a murder trial. Martinez had discovered Blum's body.

Turner stood a respectful distance from him. "The South Beach Yacht Club is located behind the left field bleachers of the ballpark?"

"Yes."

"You were working on the morning of Tuesday, June second of this year?"

"Yes."

"What time did you get to work?"

"Four-thirty a.m." In response to Turner's gentle questioning, Martinez confirmed that it was his job to make sure that the docks were clean, and the boats were fueled.

"How many piers are there?"

"Seven." Martinez said that there are about fifty berths on each side of each pier.

Turner set up a poster-sized aerial photo of the ballpark and the Yacht Club. "This is a photo of the Yacht Club?"

"Yes."

Turner pointed at a spot along the promenade behind the centerfield scoreboard. "You were walking here at approximately six-fifteen on the morning of June second?"

"Yes."

"You saw something in the water?"

"A body." Martinez took a sip of water. "It was floating in the bay."

"Male or female?"

"Male."

"Dead?"

"Objection," Nady said. "Mr. Martinez is not qualified to make that determination."

"Sustained."

Turner hadn't taken her eyes off Martinez. "Was the body moving?"

"No."

"Face up or down?" Turner asked.

"Down."

"Did it appear that the body had been in the water for a period of time?"

"Objection. Calls for speculation."

"Overruled."

Martinez shrugged. "It looked like it had been there for a while."

"What did you do next?" Turner asked.

"I called my boss and asked him to call nine-one-one. I threw a life preserver into the water. " He said that the police arrived five minutes later. "They pulled the man out of the water and gave him first aid."

"Were they able to help him?"

"No."

"No further questions, Your Honor."

"Cross-exam, Ms. Nikonova?"

"Yes, Your Honor. May we approach the witness?"

"You may."

Nady walked across the courtroom and stood in front of the box. "Mr. Martinez, the man was already in the water when you found him, right?"

"Right."

"You didn't see how he got there, did you?"

"No."

"So it's possible that he might have accidentally fallen into the water, right?"

A shrug. "I guess."

"Was anybody else around?"

"No."

"And you didn't see anybody hit him, did you?"

"No."

She pointed at Jaylen. "Just to be clear, Jaylen Jenkins wasn't there, was he?"

"No."

"It's possible that the decedent may have slipped and fallen into the water, right?"

A hesitation. "Right."

"No further questions."

* * *

The handsome young cop adjusted the star on his pressed patrol uniform. "I am Sergeant David Dito. San Francisco Police Department. I work out of Southern Station."

When my dad was working there, Southern Station was housed on the ground floor of the Hall of Justice. In 2015, it moved to the new headquarters between the ballpark and the Warriors arena. The state-of-the-art facility and the adjoining fire station had cost the taxpayers almost a quarter of a billion dollars. If you asked the cops who worked there, it was worth every penny.

Turner was at the lectern. "How long have you been a police officer?"

"Five years. I was promoted to sergeant about six months ago."

"You've received multiple commendations and you train younger officers?"

"I have and I do."

Nady spoke from her chair. "Your Honor, we will stipulate as to Sergeant Dito's resume and qualifications."

"Thank you, Ms. Nikonova."

Dito was, in fact, a good cop. Now approaching thirty, the native of the Sunset was born into a multi-generational SFPD family. His uncle, Phil Dito, was my classmate at S.I. and a fellow back-up on the football team. Phil had worked with Pete at Mission Station.

The judge granted Turner permission to approach the box. She took her position a short distance from Dito. "You were on duty at six a.m. on Tuesday, June second?"

"Yes." He confirmed that he had just started his shift. "My partner and I were preparing to go out on patrol when we received a nine-one-one call about a body in the bay at the South Beach Yacht Club. We drove to the scene immediately."

"Could you please describe what you found?"

With an experienced witness like Dito, Turner would ask open-ended questions and let him tell his story to the jury.

On cue, Dito turned and addressed the jury. "We were met by Mr. Jesus Martinez, who had discovered the body, and his boss, Mr. Christopher Neils, the on-site manager. An ambulance was on its way, so my partner and I began removing the body from the water. The EMTs arrived a few minutes later. The victim never regained consciousness."

"Was Mr. Blum pronounced dead at the scene?"

"Yes."

"Could you tell how long the victim had been in the water?"

"At least several hours."

"Did you observe any visible injuries?"

"There was a serious injury to the decedent's skull."

"Did you find anything else of any significance in the water?"

"A Louisville Slugger baseball bat which we later determined was of the same model used by the Giants left fielder, David Archer."

Turner walked over to the evidence cart, picked up the bat, which was encased in a clear plastic evidence bag, walked back to the box, and handed it to Dito. "Is this the bat?"

"Yes, ma'am."

"No further questions, Your Honor."

"Cross-exam, Ms. Nikonova?"

"Mr. Daley will be handling Sergeant Dito's cross, Your Honor."

"Fine."

Nady and I had agreed that I would play the role of the heavy for certain witnesses so that she could maintain empathy with the jurors.

I stood and buttoned my jacket. "May we approach the witness, Your Honor?"

"Yes, Mr. Daley."

I marched to the front of the courtroom and spoke to Dito. "You didn't see Jaylen hit the decedent, did you?"

"No."

"Mr. Martinez didn't see Jaylen hit the decedent either, did he?"

"No."

"And you were unable to find any witnesses who saw Jaylen hit the decedent?"

"Correct."

"And I'm sure that you canvassed the area extensively in search of witnesses, right?"

"Right."

"So you have no personal knowledge and no eyewitness accounts as to how the decedent died, do you?"

"No.

"In fact, for all that you know, the decedent could have slipped and fallen into the bay."

"That doesn't account for the decedent's head injury, Mr. Daley."

"Which could have been caused when the decedent fell and accidentally banged his head on the railing, right?"

"Seems unlikely."

"But it's possible, right?"

"That doesn't take into account the fact that we found the bat in the water."

"But you have no personal knowledge as to how that bat got into the bay, do you? It might have been there for days or weeks, right?"

"It seems unlikely."

"In fact, you just don't know. No further questions, Your Honor."

"Redirect, Ms. Turner?"

"No, Your Honor."

"Please call your next witness."

"The People call Dr. Joy Siu."

46
"A BLOW TO THE HEAD"

Dr. Siu sat in the witness box, makeup subtle, hair coiffed. She had eschewed her white lab coat in favor of a navy pantsuit. "I have been the Chief Medical Examiner of the City and County of San Francisco for five years. Before that, I was a full professor and Chair of the Ph.D. Program in anatomic pathology at UCSF."

Nady and I didn't want to give Siu the chance to read her C.V. into the record. "Your Honor," Nady said, "we will stipulate that Dr. Siu is a recognized expert in anatomic pathology."

"Thank you, Ms. Nikonova."

Turner introduced the autopsy report into evidence and presented it to Siu. "You determined Robbie Blum's cause of death?"

"A blow to the head from a hard object."

Turner handed her the Louisville Slugger. "You're familiar with this weapon?"

"Objection," Nady said. "Foundation. There is no evidence that it's a weapon."

"Sustained."

Turner rolled her eyes. "You've seen this bat, Dr. Siu?"

"Yes, Ms. Turner. Sergeant Dito pulled it out of the water beside the decedent's body."

"Was Mr. Blum's fatal injury consistent with a blow caused by this bat?"

"Yes."

"No further questions."

"Cross-exam, Ms. Nikonova?"

"Yes, Your Honor." She walked to the box. "Dr. Siu, did you find the decedent's blood on the bat?"

"No."

"My client's fingerprints?"

"No."

"And unlike a gunshot wound where you can match the spent shells to a particular firearm, you cannot determine that Mr. Blum's injury was caused by this bat, can you?"

"The bat was in the water next to the decedent."

"It could have been there weeks before Mr. Blum died. You have no way of determining for certain that the injury was caused by this bat, do you?"

"No."

"No further questions."

* * *

Turner stood a few feet from the box. "Mr. Kawakami, how long have you been the Giants clubhouse manager?"

Yosh's leathery face transformed into a proud smile. "Forty-five years."

The jury was entranced by the team's longest-tenured employee. With a fresh haircut and sporting a stylish double-breasted suit, he drew nods suitable for a San Francisco icon.

Turner's tone was conversational. "Do you enjoy your job, Mr. Kawakami?"

"It's the best job in the world." His manner was relaxed, his tone engaging. "I go to the ballpark every day, interact with players and fans, and watch baseball for free."

The juror who worked at PG&E smiled.

"How did you come to work for the Giants?"

"You might say that I inherited my job. My dad was the clubhouse manager. I started helping him when I was in high school. When he retired, I took over the position."

"You knew guys like Willie Mays, Willie McCovey, and Juan Marichal?"

Turner was milking it.

"Yes," Yosh said. "Good guys. They always treated me well—even when I was a kid. Nowadays, players make more money, but they treat me nicely, too."

"What was the most fun that you've ever had during your

career?"

The question was irrelevant, but Nady and I couldn't object.

Yosh smiled. "The World Series years."

Turner asked him to describe his responsibilities.

"It's like being a concierge at a fine hotel. I make sure that the players have plenty to eat and that their equipment is ready." He flashed a conspiratorial grin. "Of course, most guests at the Ritz don't curse and spit the way baseball players do."

Chuckles in the gallery. I'd heard Yosh use this line during interviews on TV.

Turner asked him what time he arrives at work.

"Seven a.m. for day games. Noon for night games. I'm always the first one in and the last one out the door."

Turner moved a half-step closer to him. "Mr. Kawakami, were you at the ballpark during the Giants-Cubs game on the night of June first of this year?"

"Of course. The Giants won four to three on a walk-off homer by David Archer."

"I trust that you were in the clubhouse after the game?"

"Of course."

"Was it crowded?"

"Always. Players. Coaches. Media. Some family and friends."

"Agents?"

"Sometimes."

Turner pointed at the enlarged photo of Blum. "You knew the decedent?"

"I'd met him a few times. He was David Archer's agent." He confirmed that Blum was in the clubhouse that night.

"Was he a good agent?"

"Objection," Nady said. "Foundation. With all due respect, Mr. Kawakami's qualifications to opine on this question have not been established."

"Sustained."

She was trying to break up their rhythm, but I probably would have let that one go.

Turner ignored the objection. "Mr. Kawakami, did Mr. Archer ever talk to you about his relationship with the decedent?"

"Objection. Hearsay."

"Sustained."

Nady was getting jumpy. I subtly held up a hand to signal to ease up.

Turner didn't fluster. "Mr. Kawakami, as far as you know, was Mr. Archer satisfied with the services being provided by Mr. Blum?"

"Yes."

"Did you see them interact that night?"

"Briefly. Mr. Blum congratulated David on his homer. They chatted for a few minutes."

"Did they argue?"

"I believe that they exchanged a few sharp words. I don't know what they were talking about. Mr. Blum also asked David if he could take a bat home for his son. David asked me to provide one of his older batting practice bats to Mr. Blum, which I did."

"A David Archer model Louisville Slugger?"

"Yes."

Turner walked over to the evidence cart, retrieved the bat, and handed it to Kawakami. "Is this the type of bat that Mr. Blum took?"

"Yes. The bats are custom made for each player. They cost about a hundred and eighty dollars each. Mr. Blum left the clubhouse with the bat. He also took a couple of jerseys."

"No further questions."

"Cross-exam, Ms. Nikonova?"

"Yes, Your Honor." Nady moved in front of Kawakami and spoke in a deferential tone. "You didn't see where Mr. Blum went after he left the clubhouse, did you?"

"I presume that he headed to his car in the players' parking lot. The attendants usually allowed him to park there when they had space."

Especially since he represented the cleanup hitter.

"But you didn't actually see Mr. Blum after he left the clubhouse, did you?"

"No."

"Which means that you didn't see anybody hit him, right?"

"Right."

"And it's possible that nobody hit him, right?"

"Objection," Turner said. "Calls for speculation."

"Sustained."

It was Nady's turn to walk to the evidence cart, pick up the bat, and hand it to Kawakami. "You said this is one of David Archer's bats??"

"Yes."

"But you can't tell us for sure that this is the same bat that Mr. Blum took from the clubhouse, can you?"

"It's the same model."

"But you have no way of knowing whether it's the very same bat, right?"

"Right."

"No further questions."

* * *

Tom Eisenmann sat in the box. The water cup next to him was empty. His charcoal suit, stoic expression, and unblinking eyes evoked the appearance of an FBI agent.

Turner was at the lectern. "How long have you been the Giants Director of Security?"

"Fifteen years. Prior to the Giants, I was in private security for ten years. Before that, I was in law enforcement."

"Could you please be more specific?"

"FBI Special Agent dealing with surveillance to stop potential terrorist activities."

Two of the jurors looked at each other as if to say, "Impressive."

Turner spent five minutes walking Eisenmann through his achievements with the Bureau. Eisenmann had, in fact, been an exemplary agent who had put a bunch of bad guys away.

Turner finally asked for permission to approach, which the judge granted. On her way to the front of the courtroom, she activated the flat-screen TV next to the box. "In your capacity as

Director of Security, you oversee the positioning and use of security cameras at the ballpark?"

"Correct."

"How many cameras?"

"Including those outside the ballpark and in the parking areas, more than a hundred. They're located throughout the concourses, seating areas, luxury suites, concession stands, press facilities, restrooms, stairways, and ramps. In addition, we surveil the players' areas: clubhouses, weight rooms, batting cages, and workout areas, all of which have key-only access. Outside the park, cameras are positioned every fifty feet or so along walkways and in parking lots. It's almost impossible to walk more than a few feet without being filmed."

Turner nodded with approval. "You were working on the night of June first?"

"Yes." Eisenmann said that he was in his usual spot in the surveillance center.

"On the morning of June second, were you contacted by San Francisco police regarding a body discovered in the bay behind the center field fence?"

"Yes. Inspector Kenneth Lee requested our assistance. I informed him that the Giants organization—including myself— would cooperate fully. He requested copies of all security videos taken inside and outside the ballpark from the previous night, which I provided."

"Did that include video taken from a camera mounted on the outside of the left field wall and showing the players' parking lot?"

"It did."

Turner ran a video on the TV. Against a black backdrop with a Giants logo, the white-block lettering read, "San Francisco Giants. Official Security Video. Left Field Corner Exterior Camera 88. Authorized Use Only." The date and time were stamped in the upper left corner.

Turner pointed at the screen. "When was this was taken?"

"The evening of July first of this year. Eleven forty-five p.m."

"You provided this video to Inspector Lee?"

"I did." He confirmed that the video had not been altered.

"Thank you, Mr. Eisenmann. No further questions."

"Cross-exam, Ms. Nikonova?"

"Not at this time."

Jaylen turned to me and whispered, "Aren't they going to show the video?"

"Later," I said. "Eisenmann is here to verify that it's an official video. Turner will let Lee describe what's on it."

Judge Tsang looked at the clock. "We'll recess for lunch and resume at two p.m."

It gave the jury two hours to think about what was coming next.

47
"YOU CAN SEE IT RIGHT HERE"

Inspector Lee was standing next to the flat-screen TV and using a silver Cross pen to gesture. "As Mr. Eisenmann explained, this video was taken from a camera mounted on the exterior wall of the ballpark overlooking the entrance to the players' parking lot."

Turner spoke to him from the lectern. "At what time?"

"Eleven-forty-five p.m. on the night of Monday, June first."

The gallery was full at three-fifteen on Monday afternoon. The media contingent expanded after Turner leaked word that Lee would be the prosecution's last witness. Our side had a couple of new guests, too. Roosevelt Johnson was sitting next to Rosie. He wanted to watch his protégé testify. Nick "the Dick" was next to Pete. He had been swarmed by reporters when he sauntered into court, and he worked the room like a politician.

"You obtained this video from Mr. Eisenmann?" Turner asked.

"Correct," Lee said.

He had been on the stand for an hour. He was answering Turner's softballs with authority and patience. Although he looked nothing like Roosevelt, his cadence was similar to my father's longtime partner's. The jury was dialed in as Lee described his years of undercover work and more recent experience in homicide. Turner then shifted to the matters at hand. Lee described his arrival at the scene. He assured the jurors that he had collected the evidence in accordance with SFPD practice, and that there had been no lapses in chain-of-custody. Turner introduced crime scene photos with just enough gore to support her narrative that Jaylen had beaten Blum. Finally, Turner fed Lee a series of open-ended questions about the discovery of the Louisville Slugger which he repeatedly referred to as the "murder weapon." Nady objected at appropriate times with little impact on the jury.

Turner gave the jury a final reassuring glance before she turned back to Lee. "Inspector, as I run the video, I would like you to describe what's happening."

"Of course."

Lee narrated as Turner ran the video in slow motion. "That's the decedent, Robert Blum, walking from King Street toward his car. The defendant runs after him." Lee looked at Turner, who paused the video. "The defendant is holding a bat." Lee pointed. "You can see it right here."

Yes, we could.

Turner nodded at the jury. The woman who worked at City Hall nodded back. The other jurors' eyes were focused on the TV. It was a reminder that trial work is theater. The best lawyers tell compelling stories with easy-to-understand narratives and quality visual effects.

Turner started the video again. The screen remained empty for a moment. Then Jaylen reappeared, this time running in the opposite direction.

Lee sounded like Jon Miller, the Giants Hall of Fame broadcaster, as he continued the play-by-play. "There's the defendant again." He nodded at Turner. "Could you rewind slightly?"

She did as he asked. Then she started the video and stopped it as Jaylen crossed the screen.

Lee pointed with his pen. "The defendant is no longer holding the bat. I therefore concluded that the defendant hit Mr. Blum with the bat, thereby causing his death. I believe that the defendant tossed the bat into the bay next to the body."

"No further questions."

"Cross-exam, Ms. Nikonova?"

"Yes, Your Honor." Nady strode to the front of the courtroom, where Lee had returned to the box. "You heard Mr. Kawakami testify that Mr. Blum had requested a bat from David Archer that Mr. Blum planned to give to his son, right?"

"Right."

"You're aware that Mr. Blum occasionally provided bats, balls, jerseys, and other collectibles to Jaylen?"

"Yes."

"Mr. Blum had texted Jaylen that he wanted to meet him after the game, right?"

"Right."

"Mr. Blum wasn't holding the bat when he was filmed, was he?"

"No."

"If he wanted the bat for his son, why wasn't he holding it when he walked to his car?"

"Objection. Speculation."

"Sustained."

"Mr. Blum must have changed his mind and decided to give the bat to your client."

"You think Mr. Blum lied to his client, David Archer, about why he wanted the bat?"

"I don't know, Ms. Nikonova."

"It's more likely that Mr. Blum intended to do exactly what he said: give the bat to his son, right?"

"I don't know, Ms. Nikonova."

"It's far more likely that he accidentally left the bat with Jaylen, isn't it?"

"I don't know, Ms. Nikonova."

"And the likely reason we saw Jaylen running with the bat was because he was returning it to Mr. Blum?"

"Objection. Calls for speculation."

"Overruled."

Lee folded his arms. "Highly unlikely, Ms. Nikonova."

"But highly possible, right?"

"Objection. Calls for speculation."

"Sustained."

Nady moved a step closer. "You have no video of the area where Mr. Blum's body was found, do you?"

"No."

"That's because the cameras on the exterior of the park are blocked by a row of trees between the ballpark and the marina, right?"

"Right."

"And the video cameras at the marina didn't show Jaylen hitting Mr. Blum, right?"

"Right."

"So, you have no video showing Jaylen hitting Mr. Blum, right?"

"Right."

"Or anybody else hitting Mr. Blum, right?"

"Right."

"And you have no witnesses who saw Jaylen hit Mr. Blum, do you?"

"No."

"So it's possible that somebody else hit Mr. Blum, isn't it?"

"Anything's possible, Ms. Nikonova, but it's highly unlikely."

"And it's also possible that Mr. Blum slipped and banged his head against a railing and fell into the bay, isn't it, Inspector?"

"That's even less likely, Ms. Nikonova."

"There were forty thousand people at the game that night, weren't there?"

"Yes."

"So there were forty thousand potential suspects other than Jaylen who could have hit Mr. Blum, right, Inspector? And that doesn't even consider the possibility that somebody who wasn't at the game could have hit Mr. Blum, right?"

"Objection. Speculation."

"Overruled."

Lee shook his head with disdain. "That isn't what happened, Ms. Nikonova."

"You didn't seriously consider any other potential suspects, did you?"

"We didn't have any evidence, Ms. Nikonova."

"And it wouldn't have fit within your narrative that Jaylen was guilty, right Inspector?"

"Objection. Foundation."

"Sustained."

"No further questions, Your Honor."

"Redirect, Ms. Turner?"

"No, Your Honor. The prosecution rests."

The judge shifted his eyes to Nady. "I take it that you'd like to make a motion?"

"Yes, Your Honor. The defense moves that the charges be dropped as a matter of law because the prosecution has failed to meet its burden of proof."

"Denied." Judge Tsang looked at his computer. "I'm going to recess for the day. We'll resume at nine-thirty tomorrow morning."

48
"WE MAY NEED YOU TO TESTIFY"

Jaylen was agitated when Nady and I met with him in the consultation room at the Glamour Slammer. "What the hell just happened?" he asked.

I kept my voice even. "We explained to you that the prosecution has an advantage when they present their case."

His eyes shifted to Nady. "Why didn't you go after Lee?"

"We will when we put on our defense."

"You didn't mention any of the other suspects."

"It's better to introduce them to the jury in person rather than just mention their names. Tomorrow, we'll put them on the stand. Then we'll bring back Lee and ask him why he didn't seriously consider anybody else."

"What if it isn't enough?"

"We may need you to testify, Jaylen."

* * *

The Terminator was sitting at his desk when Nady and I returned to the office. "I heard you had a rough day in court."

"It happens, T."

"Not to you."

"It happens to all of us. We start our defense in the morning."

He pointed at Rosie's closed door. "The boss wants to see you." He pointed a crooked index finger at Nady. "You, too."

"Is she by herself?"

"She's with Jaylen's mother."

* * *

Nady and I had taken seats on either side of Jaylen's mother. Rosie eyed us. "LaTanya and I were talking about you."

I nodded at LaTanya. "Thank you for coming to court. It meant a lot to Jaylen."

"I got the impression that things didn't go well."

Nady answered her. "The prosecution always has an advantage at first. We'll go after them tomorrow morning."

"You're going to be able to get Jaylen off, right?"

"Right."

"I don't know what I'll do if you're wrong."

Rosie spoke up. "Pete is waiting for you in Mike's office. He'll get you something to eat and take you back to the hotel. You should get a good night's sleep."

I stood up. "I'll let him know that you're ready to go."

* * *

I walked into my office, where Pete was sitting in my chair, feet on my desk. He looked up from his phone. "You okay, Mick?" he asked.

"LaTanya is ready to go back to the hotel."

"I'll be ready in a minute."

"You'll stay at the hotel again?"

"Of course."

"Thanks." I looked at the table in the corner, where Nick "the Dick" Hanson was sipping bourbon from a glass with the Giants logo. "I didn't expect to see you this evening, Nick."

"I didn't expect to see you, either."

"I work here."

"You gotta sleep."

He operated on four hours a night. "You of all people know that sleep is overrated."

"Indeed I do."

I smiled. "You're taking the night off?"

"Founder's privilege. I have more than a hundred employees at the agency. Nobody will miss me if I take the night off."

"How do you think it went in court?"

He arched an eyebrow. "You still have a lot of work to do."

True. "What brings you here tonight?"

"Pete invited me to drink your bourbon. You've upgraded your liquor since you worked in that little office on Mission Street."

"Rosie and I get regular paychecks nowadays." I grinned at my brother. "The bourbon is for special occasions, Pete."

"A visit from Nick qualifies."

"Indeed it does." I turned to Nick. "You got any time in the next few days? We could use a little extra help. I can't pay you much."

He held up his glass in a friendly salute. "We go back a long way, Mike. I'll do some poking around. No promises, but if I find anything that helps, you can buy me a bottle of bourbon—the *really* good stuff."

* * *

Rosie poked her head inside Nady's office at ten-thirty that night. "You're still here."

I was sitting on the corner of Nady's desk. "So are you."

"I just got back from a community outreach meeting in the Tenderloin with the mayor."

"Lucky you."

"Nicole sends her best."

"Was she civil?"

"Of course. There were TV cameras. I'm heading home. You want a ride?"

"Ten minutes."

"Fine." She looked over at Nady, who was sitting at her desk, a sleeping Luna at her feet. "You should take Luna home."

"Soon."

"You ready to rock and roll tomorrow?"

"Absolutely."

"You're going to have to throw some punches."

"Trials aren't like Little League where everybody gets a participation trophy."

"At the risk of using yet another baseball metaphor, who's in our lineup?"

"We'll start with Archer. He'll get the jury's attention and confirm that he told Yosh to give a bat to Blum. Then we'll call the Giants GM to say that Blum was a miserable guy."

"It's risky to put the decedent on trial."

"We need to show that he pissed off a lot of people. Then we'll put up Jeff Franklin to confirm that Blum was a dishonest business partner."

"Are you planning to accuse him of murder?"

"I'm planning to accuse *everybody* of murder. We'll call Bryant to say that Blum screwed him on a business deal, too. Next, we'll get Jen Foster to testify that Blum had a serious gambling problem. Then we'll call Logan and Killian and see if I can get anything useful from them."

Rosie remained skeptical. "And then?"

"I'll get Darlene Green to say that Blum owed Brian Holton money for drugs. Then we'll show the footage of Holton outside the ballpark that night."

"You're planning to blame the dead guy?"

"Holton can't defend himself. We need to give the jury options. Then we'll put Lee back on the stand and ask him why he didn't consider any other suspects."

"You think it'll muddy the waters enough to get one juror to reasonable doubt?"

"Hopefully."

"It's unlikely to play out exactly as you've planned it."

"It never does. The first thing you and Mike taught me is that trial work is improvisational theater."

"It is. What's Plan B?"

"We'll put Jaylen on the stand to make a forceful denial."

"If it reaches that point, the jury will know that you're desperate."

* * *

"You awake?" Rosie asked.

I opened my eyes. "Yes."

"You and Nady going to be able to get Jaylen off?"

I answered her honestly. "I don't know."

She was at the wheel of her Prius and I was in the passenger seat as we drove north on 101 above Sausalito. Rosie had turned on her wipers to see through what natives would describe as summer fog, and tourists would more accurately call heavy drizzle. It was almost midnight, and traffic was light.

She gripped the wheel tightly. "You don't sound wildly confident."

"I'm at the point in my career where I no longer feel compelled to BS my boss."

"I don't recall any point where you felt compelled to BS anybody, Mike."

"I might have been a more successful priest and lawyer if I had been more diplomatic."

"You wouldn't have been as effective. Are you and Nady going to get an acquittal?"

"When I was a baby Public Defender, a very smart attorney once told me that if the facts and the law aren't on your side, you should try to muddy the waters enough to get one juror to reasonable doubt."

She smiled. "I remember that conversation."

"It's still good advice."

"I know. Are you going to be able to turn one juror?"

"The same attorney told me that it was a bad idea to make predictions while you're in trial."

"Come on, Mike."

"I think so, but it's going to be very close."

49
"HE WAS MY AGENT"

Judge Tsang looked up from his computer at nine-thirty the following morning. "Are you prepared to call your first witness, Ms. Nikonova?"

"We are, Your Honor. The defense calls David Archer."

The full gallery murmured in anticipation as a sheriff's deputy went outside to find the Giants slugger. Through the open door, I saw Archer standing in the hallway. He handed an autographed baseball to a police officer who shook his hand and thanked him.

Just another day in the life of a cleanup hitter.

Sporting a pin-striped suit with a maroon tie and matching pocket square, Archer's wide body filled the aisle as he strode to the front of the courtroom with the same swagger that he displayed when he walked from the on-deck circle to the batter's box. The only things missing were the roaring crowd and his blaring walk-up music of Warren Zevon's "Send Lawyers, Guns, and Money."

Judge Tsang's usually stoic bailiff smiled as he swore Archer in. Archer squeezed into his seat in the box, poured himself a cup of water, smiled at the jury, and nodded at Nady, as if to say, "Show me your best fastball."

The judge granted Nady's request to approach Archer. She positioned herself about three feet in front of him. She was a foot shorter and a hundred and twenty pounds lighter than the slugger, but she carried herself in a confident manner making it clear to the jury that she was in charge.

"What is your occupation, Mr. Archer?" she asked.

He responded with a smirk. "I think everybody knows, Ms. Nikonova."

"For the record."

"For the record, I'm the Giants left fielder."

"And for the record, I'm a Giants fan. You lead the National

League in homers?"

"And RBIs. I was also named the MVP of the All-Star game."

"Good for you. You knew the decedent, Robert Blum?"

"He was my agent."

"How long did you know him?"

"About five years."

"You must have known him very well."

"Pretty well. It was strictly a business relationship."

"Were you aware of his alcohol, drug, and gambling issues?"

The smirk disappeared. "I wasn't involved in any of that stuff."

"I didn't say that you were. I asked you if you knew about it."

"I'd heard rumors."

"Did it bother you that he was an alcoholic, a chronic drug user, and a compulsive gambler?"

"Yes."

"Was he a good agent?"

"Yes."

"How much of a commission did he earn?"

"Five percent of my baseball salary. Ten percent of my endorsement money."

"That must have added up to millions."

"It did."

"Have you hired a new agent?"

"Not yet."

"Your contract is up at the end of the season, isn't it?"

"Yes."

"So it would behoove you to hire a new agent in the near future, wouldn't it?"

"Probably."

"Have you interviewed any other agents?"

"Not yet. I'm putting together a list. I don't like to deal with contract matters during the season."

"Have you talked with Mr. Blum's former partner, Jeff Franklin, about representing you?"

"He's on the list."

"The *Chronicle* reported that you and Mr. Blum didn't see eye to eye about his strategy for negotiating a new contract."

"Just business."

"Harvey Tate wrote that you thought Mr. Blum was slow-walking negotiations on your deal to gain leverage for some of his other clients."

"Not true."

"Mr. Tate is a Pulitzer Prize-winning journalist. You're saying that he made it up?"

Archer shot a glance at Tate, who was in the gallery. "He was misinformed."

"So you were happy with the way that Mr. Blum was working on your new deal?"

"It was just business, Ms. Nikonova."

Good answer. Says nothing.

Nady smiled. "Speaking as a Giants fan, I hope that you re-sign with the team."

"Thank you, Ms. Nikonova. So do I."

Nady moved a step closer. "You were in the clubhouse after the Giants beat the Cubs on June first?"

"Yes."

"You hit the game-winning homer?"

"First-pitch fastball. Up and in."

"Mr. Blum was also in the clubhouse?"

"We let family and friends come inside from time to time."

"And agents, evidently. You and Mr. Blum chatted?"

"Briefly."

"Yosh Kawakami said that you and Mr. Blum argued that night."

"I don't recall."

Sure you do.

Nady didn't fluster. She walked over to the cart, picked up the bat, returned to the box, and handed it to Archer. "Do you recognize this bat?"

"It's one of mine."

"How many do you have?"

"Dozens. I keep the best for games. I use the others for batting practice."

"Is this a game bat or a practice bat?"

"Practice." Archer said that he put more pine tar on game bats.

"Did you instruct Mr. Kawakami to give this bat to Mr. Blum?"

"I asked Yosh to give a bat to Robbie for his son. I don't know if it's the same bat."

Nady nodded at the jury as if Archer had just revealed something significant. "What time did you leave the clubhouse?"

"Around eleven-thirty." He said that he drove home.

"Did you see Mr. Blum after he left the clubhouse?"

"No."

"Just so we're clear, you didn't see anyone hit Mr. Blum, did you?"

"No."

"And, in particular, you didn't see Jaylen Jenkins hit Mr. Blum, right?"

"Right."

"So it's possible that any number of people—including the forty thousand or so who were at the game that night—could have killed Mr. Blum, right?"

"Objection. Speculation."

"Sustained."

"No further questions."

"Cross-exam, Ms. Turner?"

"No, Your Honor."

"Please call your next witness, Ms. Nikonova."

"The defense calls Eric Chen."

50
"HE NEVER LEFT A PENNY ON THE TABLE"

Eric Chen was in the box, eyes locked onto Nady's. The Giants GM approached his testimony in the same manner that he reviewed scouting reports—with numerical precision. "I am the Vice President of Baseball Operations and General Manager of the Giants."

"You know David Archer?" Nady asked.

"Of course. He's our left fielder."

"And you knew Robert Blum?"

"Yes. He was Mr. Archer's agent."

"Was he a good agent?"

"He was effective."

"How so?"

"He never left a penny on the table."

Nady nodded. "You must have known him very well."

"We met about a dozen times."

"We've heard testimony that he wasn't easy to deal with."

"He took very aggressive positions on behalf of his clients. I realize that this was part of his job, but his 'scorched-earth' strategy was frequently counterproductive."

"Was he taking unreasonable positions regarding Mr. Archer's contract extension?"

"I am not at liberty to discuss ongoing contract negotiations."

"But you were negotiating a new deal for Mr. Archer at the time of Mr. Blum's death?"

"We had some preliminary discussions. It's a process."

"Was Mr. Archer unhappy with Mr. Blum's representation?"

"I don't know."

"Did he ever mention the possibility of changing agents?"

"Not to me."

"We've heard testimony that Mr. Blum had alcohol and drug

issues."

"I heard rumors."

"Did you ever see any evidence?"

"On a couple of occasions, his eyes were red, and his speech was slurred."

"Did you mention this to anybody?"

"It wasn't my place."

"He also had a gambling issue."

"I heard rumors about that, too."

"Did you report it to the commissioner's office?"

"They were already aware of it. It is my understanding that they conducted an investigation and did not find sufficient evidence to take any action."

"Did they rule out the possibility that Mr. Blum had substantial gambling debts?"

"I don't know."

Nady returned to the lectern. "Mr. Blum once had a business partner named Jeff Franklin, didn't he?"

"Yes. They terminated their partnership a few years ago."

"Mr. Franklin alleged that Mr. Blum had misappropriated funds and attempted to steal Mr. Franklin's clients, didn't he?"

"I read about those allegations in the news."

"There were hard feelings, weren't there?"

"Yes."

"I understand that Mr. Franklin may become Mr. Archer's new agent."

"That's up to Mr. Archer."

"Mr. Blum wasn't well-liked around baseball, was he?"

"He was difficult at times."

"Did you know that he owed money to several known drug dealers?"

"I wouldn't know."

"And several gamblers?"

Turner spoke up in a respectful voice. "Objection, Your Honor. Ms. Nikonova is asking Mr. Chen to comment upon matters for which there is no foundation, and which are clearly outside the scope of his knowledge."

"Sustained."

"Mr. Chen," Nady continued, "a lot of people disliked Mr. Blum, didn't they?"

"Objection. Ms. Nikonova is asking Mr. Chen to speculate as to the internal workings of the minds of individuals whom she hasn't even identified.

Yes, she is.

"Sustained."

"No further questions."

* * *

Jeff Franklin adjusted the Rolex on his left wrist. "I met Robbie Blum when we were in college. We were business partners for five years."

Nady was at the lectern. "Were you still friends at the time of Mr. Blum's death?"

"No. We had a falling out after a business dispute."

"Money?"

"Yes."

"And he stole some of your clients from you, didn't he?"

"Yes."

"And he stole money from your clients, didn't he?"

"Yes."

"And from you?"

"Yes."

Nady nodded. "Is that why you decided to terminate your partnership?"

"Yes."

Nady moved to the front of the box. "You were at the Giants game on the night that Mr. Blum died, weren't you?"

"I was entertaining clients in my firm's luxury suite."

"You went down to the clubhouse after the game?"

"Yes. I talked to a couple of my clients."

"Did you talk to David Archer?"

"Briefly. I congratulated him on his walk-off home run."

"Did you mention the possibility of switching agents from Mr. Blum to yourself?"

"I did not."

"But you would have been happy if he had chosen to do so, right?"

"Of course, but that's up to him."

"You know that Mr. Archer's contract terminates at the end of the season?"

"Yes."

"And if he decides to switch agents, you would stand to collect a substantial commission, right?"

"Right."

"Have you talked to Mr. Archer about representing him now that Mr. Blum has died?"

"Given the circumstances, I didn't think it was appropriate. If he contacts me, I would, of course, be interested."

"Your usual commission is five percent of a player's salary?"

"Correct."

"If you were Mr. Archer's agent, how big a contract could you get for him?"

"Objection. Speculation."

Nady feigned irritation. "Your Honor, this is within Mr. Franklin's area of expertise."

"Overruled."

Franklin glanced at his Rolex. "It's hard to say, Ms. Nikonova. The market changes year to year, and there are many factors impacting a player's market value."

"There's been speculation that Mr. Archer will command 'Mookie money.' Could you please explain what that means?"

"Mookie Betts is an outfielder for the Dodgers. He recently signed a twelve-year contract for three hundred and sixty-five million dollars."

Nady nodded at the woman from PG&E, then she turned back to Franklin. "On behalf of Giants fans, we hope that you'll be able to get a similar deal for Mr. Archer—if he hires you."

"Mookie Betts is a unique talent, Ms. Nikonova."

"So is Mr. Archer. And you're an even better agent than Mr. Betts's agent, right?"

"I'd like to think so."

Faux modesty wasn't a convincing look for a high-end sports agent.

Nady inched closer to Franklin. "If you negotiate a three-hundred-million-dollar contract for Mr. Archer, your commission would be fifteen million dollars, right?"

"Right."

"That's a lot of money."

Turner stood up to object, then reconsidered.

"Yes," Franklin said.

"After you congratulated Mr. Archer on his game-winner, you left the clubhouse?"

"Yes."

"And you went out to get your car, which was parked near the players' parking lot?"

"Yes."

"A short time later, you saw Mr. Blum come out to the same area, didn't you?"

"No."

"You had words with him, didn't you?"

"No."

"He walked away, but you followed him, didn't you? You ended up by the marina where you continued your argument, right?"

"No."

"You lost your temper and you hit him, didn't you? And he fell into the bay, right?"

"No."

"You'll feel better if you come clean, Mr. Franklin."

"Objection," Turner said. "There is no foundation for any of these questions."

"Sustained."

Nady moved right to the front of the box. "You and Mr. Blum went through an acrimonious business breakup that led to litigation, right?"

"Yes."

"You saw him behind the ballpark, and you snapped. In addition to the fact that you had hard feelings based on your prior history, you saw a business opportunity—one that could make up for the money you'd lost from Mr. Blum's shady dealings, right? I'd say that you had about fifteen million reasons to want Mr. Blum dead, Mr. Franklin."

"Objection. There isn't a shred of evidence supporting Ms. Nikonova's contention."

No, there isn't.

"Sustained."

"No further questions."

"Cross-exam, Ms. Turner?"

"Just one question, Your Honor. Mr. Franklin, did you kill Robert Blum?"

"No, Ms. Turner."

"No further questions."

"Please call your next witness, Ms. Nikonova."

"The defense calls Adam Bryant."

51
"WE WERE TEAMMATES"

The bailiff stood at the front of the courtroom. "Please state your name and occupation for the record."

"Adam Bryant. People call me 'AB.' I'm an entrepreneur, investor, and athletic trainer."

Not necessarily in that order.

Bryant squeezed his sculpted torso into the wooden chair. Clean-shaven and sporting a five-thousand-dollar Bruno Cucinelli suit, he looked more like a Silicon Valley venture capitalist than a retired minor-league ballplayer. He adjusted his silk tie and grinned.

I glared at him from the lectern. Nady and I had decided that I would have the opportunity to wipe away the smirk.

"Nice to see you again, Mr. Bryant," I lied.

"Nice to see you, too, Mr. Daley."

"You run a gym near the new Warriors arena, don't you?"

"It's a state-of-the-art facility where we offer personalized workouts for elite athletes."

"So it's an expensive gym?"

That got a smile from the juror from PG&E.

Bryant wasn't amused. "Many of our clients are professional or Olympic-level athletes. As a result, we employ only the most qualified trainers."

"I take it that you must have an advanced degree in kinesiology or a related field?"

"Actually, I have a B.A. from Stanford."

"In what subject?"

"English."

"Stanford is a world-class university, but an English degree hardly qualifies you as an expert in athletic training."

"I was also a professional athlete."

"You played minor league baseball for a couple of years, right?"

"Yes. And I played college ball at Stanford."

"Which qualifies you to teach people how to hit a curveball, but it doesn't give you any particular expertise in athletic training."

"Move to strike," Turner said. "Mr. Daley is testifying."

Yes, I am.

"Sustained."

"Mr. Bryant," I continued, "you know David Archer, don't you?"

"We were teammates at Stanford and remain good friends."

"He works out at your gym?"

"Yes. I also provide personalized stretching and training for him at the ballpark."

"He pays you a lot of money?"

"Yes."

"You socialize?"

"From time to time. He's very busy—especially during the baseball season."

"You talk business?"

"Sometimes."

"You know that Mr. Archer's contract expires at the end of the season, right?"

"Yes."

"He wants to stay in San Francisco, doesn't he?"

"I hope so."

"So does every Giants fan in this courtroom, including me. Is he close to a new deal?"

"Objection. Relevance."

"Your Honor," I said, "I promise to show relevance soon."

"Make it very soon, Mr. Daley."

"Yes, Your Honor." Judge Tsang was a Giants season-ticket holder and was probably curious, too. I turned back to Bryant. "Is Mr. Archer close to a new deal?"

"He said that things were moving more slowly than he had hoped."

"Was that because of his agent, Mr. Blum?"

"Yes."

"Mr. Archer was unhappy with Mr. Blum?"

"Frustrated."

"Why?"

"He thought that Mr. Blum was slow-walking his deal and using him as a bargaining chip to get better deals for some of his other clients."

"Wasn't that unethical?"

"You're the lawyer."

Yes, I am. "He had other concerns with Mr. Blum, didn't he?"

"I'm not sure what you're talking about."

Yes, you are. "Mr. Blum had alcohol, drug, and gambling issues, didn't he?"

Bryant tensed. "I've heard rumors."

Everybody's heard rumors. "Mr. Archer was thinking about changing agents, wasn't he?"

"He mentioned the possibility."

Here we go. "You also knew Mr. Blum through business dealings, didn't you?"

"He invested in our facility."

"You're planning a second location in Silicon Valley, aren't you?"

"Yes."

"You asked Mr. Blum to invest in that location, didn't you?"

"Yes."

"And after agreeing to do so, he reneged on his promise, didn't he?"

A hesitation. "Just business."

"You must have been very disappointed."

"I was."

"And angry."

His tone became more emphatic. "Just business, Mr. Daley. We are looking into other sources of financing."

So far, so good. "You're at the ballpark for every game to help Mr. Archer stretch and work out, right?"

"Yes."

"Were you at the game on the night of Monday, June first?"

"Yes."

"You went down to the clubhouse after the game?"

"Yes. I congratulated David on his game-winning homer and helped him stretch."

"You also spoke to Mr. Blum?"

"I said hello."

"In fact, you got into an argument with him, didn't you?"

"No."

I pointed at Nady, who pressed a button on her laptop and turned on the TV. I handed a legal document to the judge and a copy to Turner. "Your Honor, we would like to introduce an affidavit from Ms. Jennifer Foster, the Giants broadcaster, in which she affirms that the video we're about to see was taken in the Giants clubhouse on the night of June first of this year. She provided a copy of this video to the D.A."

Turner speed read the papers. "No objection."

Nady ran the footage showing Blum and Bryant standing behind Archer. It was impossible to hear what they were saying, but they looked angry as they exchanged words.

On my signal, Nady paused the video, and I turned back to Bryant. "You and Mr. Blum got into an argument that night, didn't you?"

"No."

I pointed at Nady again, who advanced the video in slow motion. Bryant and Blum shoved each other. "You were angry at Mr. Blum for pulling out of your deal, weren't you?"

"No."

"So you pushed him."

"Not true."

I pointed at the TV. "You're saying that we shouldn't believe what we just saw?"

"It was a misunderstanding."

"There were witnesses, Mr. Bryant." I pointed at the screen.

"That's Mr. Kawakami, the Giants clubhouse manager. We can call him to testify that you and Mr. Blum were arguing and that you shoved him."

Bryant folded his arms tightly. "It was just business."

"Adults don't hit each other over business deals."

"I didn't hit him."

"You definitely shoved him."

"He shoved me first."

It generally isn't a good idea to try a fifth-grade excuse in a grown-up courtroom. "You're saying that it was okay for you to shove him because he started it?"

"No."

"You're a foot taller than he was and you outweighed him by a hundred pounds. You told him that he was a liar, didn't you?"

"He was."

"And he mocked you, didn't he? So you hit him."

"I defended myself."

Changing your story mid-testimony is also a bad idea. "A moment ago, you said that you shoved him because he shoved you first. Now you're claiming that you acted in self-defense?"

"I did. He started it."

I shot an incredulous look at the jury. "Mr. Bryant, you were angry at him, right?"

"Frustrated."

"Frustrated enough to hit him."

"Shove him."

I'd made my point. "You left shortly thereafter?"

"Yes."

"You saw him outside the ballpark, didn't you?"

"No."

"He was standing next to the South Beach Marina behind the left field wall, where you continued your argument, didn't you?"

"No."

"You lost your temper, and instead of walking away, you picked up the bat that he had taken from the clubhouse and you hit him, didn't you?"

"No."

"And you pushed him into the bay and tossed the bat in after him, didn't you?"

"Absolutely not, Mr. Daley."

"Maybe he taunted you. Maybe you lost control. Or maybe it was just an accident. But you lost your composure and you hit him, didn't you?"

"No, Mr. Daley."

"Just like you hit him in the clubhouse."

"No, Mr. Daley."

"Because he started it, right?"

"Objection."

"Withdrawn. No further questions."

"Cross-exam, Ms. Turner?"

"No, Your Honor."

"Please call your next witness, Mr. Daley."

"The defense calls Jennifer Foster."

52
"HE HAD A SERIOUS GAMBLING PROBLEM"

Jen Foster looked like an anchor on SportsCenter as she sat in the box. In lieu of her customary black polo shirt with a Giants logo, she wore a gray pantsuit with an orange scarf—Giants colors.

Nady stood at the lectern. "What is your occupation, Ms. Foster?"

"I am a journalist and sportscaster for the Giants. I handle in-game and post-game interviews."

Nady smiled. "I enjoy your work, and I would give anything to have your job."

Foster returned her smile. "Thank you, Ms. Nikonova. A lot of people would."

Nady walked her onetime housemate through her C.V. Undergrad degree from UCLA. Two-time All-American softball player. Sportscaster in Modesto, Sacramento, and, finally, the Bay Area. For the last five years, Giants ballpark reporter. The jury was charmed by the charismatic woman whom they recognized from TV.

Nady moved to the front of the box. "You work all the Giants home games?"

"Except for a few games on national TV."

"You were working the Giants game on the night of Monday, June first?"

"Yes. The Giants won on a walk-off homer by David Archer."

"What time did you arrive at the ballpark?"

"Two o'clock."

"The game didn't start until seven. It takes you five hours to get ready?"

"There's a lot of preparation."

"Could you walk us through your responsibilities on the day of a game?"

"Of course." Foster spoke in easy-to-understand sound bites. She arrived at the park at two. She spent an hour reading scouting reports and watching video highlights. She talked to the manager, coaches, and, to the extent available, players. She spent another hour with the director and the other members of the broadcast team preparing for the game. Thirty minutes before game time, she put on her Giants windbreaker and cap, got together with her cameraman, and began working her way through the crowd.

"And after the game?" Nady asked.

"I spend the ninth inning next to the dugout so that I can interview one or two players when the game ends. On June first, I interviewed David Archer. During the commercial break, I went down to the clubhouse, where I did more interviews for the post-game show."

"What time did you go home?"

"About eleven-thirty."

Nady moved in closer. "You knew Robert Blum?"

"Yes."

"Did you know him well?"

"Pretty well. I interviewed him several times regarding player contracts."

"You also had a personal relationship with him, didn't you?"

"For a short time. We weren't a good fit."

"He was hard to get along with, wasn't he?"

"At times."

"He had a temper?"

"Yes."

"And a drinking problem?"

"Yes."

"And he used illegal drugs?"

Foster frowned. "He used a high-end version of Ecstasy called Molly."

"Anything else?"

"He had a serious gambling problem. He placed bets online constantly. He went to Las Vegas two or three times a month."

"Did he go by himself?"

"Most of the time."

"Did he also place private bets?"

"I think so."

"Was he in debt for his gambling?"

"I think so."

"Do you know the names of the individuals with whom he placed those bets?"

"I'm afraid not."

53
"YOU SPENT A LOT OF TIME TOGETHER"

Benjamin Logan glared at me from the box, silver hair flowing, goatee trimmed. His tailored suit made him look thinner than he did when we'd met at his office.

"You're the President and CEO of Bayshore Moving and Storage?" I asked.

"Correct. My grandfather started the business in 1944 with one moving van and a couple of employees. Now we have almost a hundred trucks and hundreds of employees."

"Impressive," I lied.

"Thank you."

The judge granted my request to approach Logan. I moved directly in front of him and worked without notes. "You were friends with the decedent, Mr. Blum?"

"Acquaintances."

"You spent a lot of time together, didn't you?"

"Some."

"You went to baseball and basketball games together?"

"From time to time."

"You had adjoining suites at the ballpark?"

"We did."

"You traveled to Las Vegas with him on several occasions to gamble, didn't you?"

"A few."

"You like to gamble?"

"Yes. So did Mr. Blum."

"He liked to gamble a lot, didn't he?"

"Yes."

"He had a gambling problem, didn't he?"

A hesitation. "I don't know."

"You saw him lose thousands of dollars at blackjack and craps, didn't you?"

"I also saw him win a lot of money."

"And you saw him lose thousands on sports bets, didn't you?"

"He won sometimes, too."

"But you didn't think he had a problem?"

"I thought that he liked to gamble."

Come on. "You knew him well enough to join him on several trips to Las Vegas, but you didn't know that he was a compulsive gambler?"

"I saw him place large bets at the sports books and the tables."

"You never noticed it even though you were gambling buddies?"

"Acquaintances."

I feigned disbelief. "You talked to Mr. Blum regularly, didn't you?"

"From time to time."

"About gambling?"

"About business. I was trying to persuade him to recommend our company to his clients."

"Did any of his clients hire you?"

"No."

"When was the last time that you saw him?"

"On the night that he died."

"Where?"

"In the concourse on the suite level at the ballpark. We exchanged greetings. I asked him if David Archer was going to re-sign with the team. He said that he couldn't talk about it."

"You were at the game on the night that Mr. Blum died?"

"I go to all of the games, Mr. Daley."

"Did you stay until the end?"

"I always do. I was entertaining some of our customers in our luxury suite." He said that he returned to his office after the game. "I picked up my car and went home."

I moved in closer. "Mr. Blum placed bets outside of Vegas, didn't he?"

"I don't know."

"You and Mr. Blum were both serious gamblers and you didn't know whether he placed bets outside of the casinos?"

"No."

I looked at the juror from PG&E and shook my head. "Mr. Blum had placed bets with you, didn't he?"

"No."

"He owed you a substantial amount of money, didn't he?"

"No."

"And you got tired of waiting to be paid, didn't you?"

"No."

"You saw him at the game that night, didn't you? And you told him that you wanted to clear the air, so you arranged to meet him afterward, didn't you?"

"No."

"You agreed to meet on the path near the South Beach Marina, didn't you?"

"No."

"When he refused to pay you, you lost your temper and you hit him, didn't you?"

"No."

"Or perhaps you had somebody else do it for you? Maybe your employee, Mr. Killian?"

"That's absurd, Mr. Daley."

"Maybe it was an accident. Or maybe you hit him with a bat that David Archer gave him earlier that night. Either way, Mr. Blum suffered a severe head injury and died."

"Objection," Turner said. "There isn't a shred of foundation as to any of this."

"Overruled."

Logan eyed me with unvarnished contempt. "Nothing that you just said is true, Mr. Daley. Mr. Blum didn't owe me money. I didn't see him after the game. Most important, I didn't hit him—intentionally, by accident, or otherwise. And I certainly didn't kill him. And neither did Mr. Killian."

"No further questions, Your Honor."

Turner declined cross exam."

Judge Tsang's chin was resting in his palm. "Please call your next witness, Mr. Daley."

"The defense calls Kevin Killian."

54
"HE'S MY BOSS"

Killian's eyes darted over my shoulder as he sweated through his navy suit. The hasty dye job of his red hair looked like a hasty dye job.

I planted myself in the front of the box. "You know Benjamin Logan?"

"He's my boss. I'm a supervisor for Bayshore Moving and Storage."

"In addition to your regular duties, you also handle personal matters for Mr. Logan?"

"I run errands and do deliveries for him."

"He pays you for doing this?"

"Yes."

"He asks you to be discreet because they're personal matters, right?"

"Right."

"You deliver sensitive documents like contracts?"

"Yes."

"And money?"

"I don't know." He took a drink of water. "I never look inside the envelopes."

"They're big envelopes, right?"

"Sometimes."

I glanced at the juror from PG&E. "Over the years, Mr. Logan asked you to deliver packages to the decedent, Robbie Blum, right?"

"Yes."

"You also picked up packages from Mr. Blum?"

"On occasion."

"There was money inside those packages, wasn't there?"

"Like I said, I don't know."

"Come on, Mr. Killian. Mr. Logan didn't ask you to hand-deliver items of no value to an important sports agent like Robbie Blum, did he?"

"Objection. Asked and answered."

"Sustained."

Fine. "Mr. Logan likes to gamble, doesn't he?"

"Yes."

"He testified earlier that he made several trips to Las Vegas with the decedent."

"I'll take your word for it."

"Because both of them liked to gamble, right?"

"That's the usual reason that people go to Vegas."

"Mr. Logan also likes to take bets from his friends, doesn't he?"

"So do I."

"So did Mr. Blum." *Here goes.* "Mr. Blum placed bets with Mr. Logan, didn't he?"

"I don't know."

"Those bets were for thousands of dollars, weren't they?"

"I don't know."

"When Mr. Logan won, he asked you to collect the money from Mr. Blum, didn't he?"

"I don't know."

One more try. "You were Mr. Logan's collector, weren't you?"

"No."

"In the vernacular, you were his 'muscle,' right?"

"No."

"Come on, Mr. Killian."

"Objection. There wasn't a question."

"Withdrawn." I moved closer to Killian. "Mr. Logan sent you to the ballpark on the night that Mr. Blum died, didn't he?"

"No."

"Because Mr. Blum owed Mr. Logan a substantial gambling debt, didn't he?"

"I don't know."

"Mr. Logan instructed you to tell Mr. Blum to pay up, didn't he?"

"No."

"And if Mr. Blum refused, your boss told you to rough him up, didn't he?"

"No."

"You met Mr. Blum behind the ballpark, and you demanded money, didn't you?"

"No."

"You got into an argument. And you threatened him. And then you hit him, didn't you?"

"No."

"And whether it was on purpose or it was an accident, you killed him, didn't you?"

"That's ridiculous, Mr. Daley."

"Come on, Mr. Killian."

"Objection. Mr. Daley is living in a fantasy world. There isn't a shred of evidence that Mr. Killian was anywhere near the ballpark that night. Given the opportunity, Mr. Daley would accuse the forty thousand people at the game that night of killing Mr. Blum."

Except for Jaylen.

"Sustained."

"No further questions."

* * *

Jaylen's expression was grim as Nady and I met with him in the consultation room during the mid-afternoon break. "The jury isn't buying what you're selling," he said.

Nady answered him. "We're giving them options. We've saved our best for last: Brian Holton."

"He's dead."

"Which means that he can't defend himself."

55
"YOU DON'T HAVE A SHRED OF EVIDENCE"

Nady stood at the lectern. "You're still under oath, Mr. Eisenmann."

The Giants Director of Security nodded. "Yes, Ms. Nikonova."

Nady walked purposefully to the front of the box. "You gave the police copies of all security videos taken at the ballpark on the night of June first of this year, didn't you?"

"I did."

"So, if I show you a video from that night, you would be able to confirm that it's an official Giants video?"

"I would."

Nady activated the TV. Against a plain black backdrop with a Giants logo in the middle, the white-block lettering read, "San Francisco Giants. Official Security Video. Right Field Promenade. Exterior. Authorized Use Only." The date and time were stamped in the corner.

Nady paused the video. "When and where was this taken?"

"June first. Eleven forty p.m. The camera is mounted on the exterior wall overlooking the pedestrian walkway in right field next to McCovey Cove."

The illuminated path was empty.

Nady ran the video at normal speed. A few seconds later, a pedestrian walked across the screen. She stopped it. "This is an official Giants video that you provided to Inspector Lee?"

"Yes."

"You can confirm that it shows what was happening behind the right field wall at eleven-forty p.m. on Monday, June first?"

"Yes."

"Were you able to identify this pedestrian?"

"No."

"No further questions."

* * *

The bailiff cleared his throat. "Please state your name and occupation for the record."

"Darlene Green. I am a cocktail server at the Gold Club on Howard Street."

She took her seat in the box. Darlene could have passed for an accountant in her powder-blue blouse with a navy skirt. Her hair was pulled back, makeup muted.

I turned around and scanned the gallery. LaTanya and Rosie were sitting behind us, expressions impassive. Pete gave me a subtle nod. He was in the back row next to Nick Hanson.

Nady moved forward and stopped an arm's length from Darlene. "How long have you worked at the Gold Club, Ms. Green?"

"About a year."

"I understand that you use your earnings to pay for college."

"I do. I'm a junior at State. I'm studying to become a dental hygienist."

"That's great."

"Thank you."

"A man named Brian Holton also worked there, didn't he?"

"Yes. He was our doorman."

"You knew him pretty well?"

"Yes."

"Sadly, Mr. Holton recently passed away, didn't he?"

"He was stabbed to death in the alley behind our club. The man who stabbed him also died in the encounter."

"I'm so sorry. Do you know anything about the circumstances of Mr. Holton's death?"

Darlene took a sip of water. "I wouldn't be surprised if it involved a drug deal."

"Mr. Holton bought illegal narcotics?"

"He sold them."

"Did he ever offer drugs to you?"

"Yes. I turned him down."

"Did you ever see him provide drugs to others?"

"Objection," Turner said. "I fail to see the relevance."

Nady responded with an icy glare. "Your Honor, I will show a direct connection to the matters at hand in the next minute."

"Please proceed, Ms. Nikonova."

"Thank you." She repeated her question, and Darlene confirmed that she had, in fact, seen Holton sell illegal drugs to several customers. "You knew Robert Blum?"

"I met him several times at the club. He came in once or twice a month."

"Did he partake in services offered by the hostesses at the club?"

"Yes." Darlene's expression didn't change. "I am told that he was an excellent tipper."

"Did he know Mr. Holton?"

"Yes."

"Did Mr. Blum ever buy drugs from Mr. Holton?"

"I don't know for sure, but I saw Mr. Blum give Brian money on several occasions."

"Did you ever see them argue?"

"Several times."

Nady backed up a step. "Ms. Green, was Mr. Holton at work on June first of this year?"

"Yes. He arrived around the same time that I did: four p.m. We both went home a few minutes after two a.m."

"Was he at the club the entire time?"

"I don't know. I work inside. He spent most of his time outside."

Nady pulled a remote from her pocket and activated the TV. She re-ran the video that she had just shown to Eisenmann, first at regular speed, and then in slow motion. In the latter case, she paused it when the pedestrian appeared.

She pointed at the screen. "This video was taken at eleven-forty p.m. on June first on the promenade behind the right field wall at the ballpark. Do you recognize the person?"

"Yes. It's Brian Holton."

"How far is the ballpark from the Gold Club?"

"About a fifteen-minute walk."

"Given the fact that Mr. Holton had a relationship with Mr. Blum, it's possible that Mr. Holton met Mr. Blum that night, isn't it?"

"Objection. Speculation."

"Sustained."

"And given their history, it's likely that Mr. Blum owed Mr. Holton a substantial amount of money for drugs, isn't it?"

"Objection. Speculation."

"Sustained."

Nady tried once more. "In an attempt to collect the money, isn't it likely that Mr. Holton and Mr. Blum got into an argument? And Mr. Holton struck Mr. Blum and killed him?"

"Objection. Speculation."

"Sustained."

Nady looked at the jury as if to say, "You can put the pieces together." Then she turned back to the judge. "No further questions, Your Honor."

"Ms. Turner?"

"Just a couple of questions." She addressed Darlene from the prosecution table. "Did Mr. Holton appear nervous or agitated that night?"

"Not that I recall."

"Did you see any blood on his hands or clothing?"

"Not that I recall."

"I presume that he didn't confess to you that he had killed Robbie Blum, did he?"

"No."

"You don't have a shred of evidence proving that Mr. Holton killed Mr. Blum, do you?"

"No."

"Ms. Nikonova is trying to impress the jury with unsubstantiated inuendo, isn't she?"

"Objection. Ms. Turner should save such speculation for her closing."

"Sustained."

"No further questions, Your Honor."

Judge Tsang glanced at the clock. "Any more witnesses, Ms. Nikonova?"

"Just one, Your Honor. The defense calls Inspector Kenneth Lee."

56
"WE FOUND NO EVIDENCE"

Nady had positioned herself three feet in front of the box. "Water, Inspector Lee?"

"No, thank you, Ms. Nikonova."

"You're the inspector in charge of the investigation of the death of Robbie Blum?"

"Yes."

"You were called to the scene behind the ballpark on Tuesday, June second?"

"Yes."

"The decedent had already been pronounced dead?"

"Yes."

It was the proper strategy for questioning an uncooperative witness. You formulate your questions as statements and try to get the witness to agree with you.

"You are aware that Dr. Siu concluded that the decedent died of a head injury?"

"Yes."

"You supervised the collection of evidence at the scene?"

"In accordance with standard procedure. I observed chain of custody protocols."

"I didn't expect you to tell us otherwise, Inspector. You arrested Jaylen Jenkins the following day?"

"Yes."

"You acted very quickly."

"It was a righteous arrest. We had placed the defendant at the scene. We found fifteen hundred dollars of cash in his wallet. There was a David Archer model Louisville Slugger floating in the bay next to the decedent's body."

"So you immediately jumped to the conclusion that Jaylen hit the decedent, didn't you?"

"Dr. Siu determined that the fatal injury was inflicted by a blunt object like a bat."

Nady raised an eyebrow. "You didn't find the decedent's blood on the bat, did you?"

"No."

"You didn't find Jaylen's fingerprints, either?"

"We had a video showing the defendant carrying a bat."

"But you didn't find his fingerprints on the bat, did you?"

"No."

"So you have no direct evidence connecting Jaylen to this bat, do you?"

"We had video."

"The bat floating in the water could have been there for weeks. You have no physical evidence that it was the same bat that you found in the water, do you?"

"You can put the pieces together, Ms. Nikonova."

"No, I can't, Inspector. And it isn't my job to prove your case for you."

"Move to strike."

"Withdrawn." Nady waited a beat. "Notwithstanding the fact that you had no physical evidence connecting this bat to my client, you arrested him?"

"I disagree with your premise. We arrested the defendant based upon visual evidence that he was holding a bat within a hundred feet of Mr. Blum's body."

"You didn't find any video showing Jaylen striking the decedent, did you?"

"No."

"You didn't find any witnesses who saw Jaylen strike the decedent, did you?"

"No."

"You didn't find any witnesses who saw anybody strike the decedent, did you?"

"No."

"It's possible that the decedent could have tripped, hit his head, and fallen into the bay, right?"

"It's highly unlikely, Ms. Nikonova."

"You jumped to the conclusion that Jaylen struck Mr. Blum, didn't you?"

"Objection. Argumentative."

"Sustained."

Nady shot a glance my way. I nodded. Time to start tossing people under the bus.

She turned back to Lee. "Inspector, you didn't seriously consider other suspects, did you?"

"We found no evidence that anybody else was involved in Mr. Blum's death."

"Seriously?"

Turner started to stand but reconsidered.

Lee folded his arms. "Seriously."

Nady glanced at the juror from PG&E, then she spoke to Lee. "The bat was a David Archer model Louisville Slugger, wasn't it?"

"Yes."

"Mr. Archer was at the ballpark that night, wasn't he?"

"Yes. He hit the game-winning homerun."

"Yet you didn't consider Mr. Archer as a suspect?"

"You really think the team's best hitter used his own bat to hit his own agent?"

"You ruled him out because he's hit a lot of homeruns?"

"I ruled him out because I found no evidence that he was involved in Mr. Blum's death."

"Mr. Archer testified that he and Mr. Blum were having disagreements about Mr. Archer's contract extension."

"He said that it was just business."

"It was hundreds of millions of dollars of business. Mr. Archer had parked his car in the players' lot behind the left field bleachers, right?"

"Right."

"Which was very close to the decedent's body, right?"

Lee feigned exasperation. "We found no evidence that Mr.

Archer was closer than a hundred feet to the spot where Mr. Blum's body was found."

"So, you didn't consider the possibility that Mr. Archer hit Mr. Blum?"

"We found no evidence."

"Especially since you arrested my client less than a day later, right?"

"Objection. Argumentative."

"Sustained."

Nady moved on. "The decedent also had an argument with Adam Bryant in the clubhouse that night, didn't he?"

"Yes."

"Mr. Bryant was very upset that the decedent had reneged on his promise to provide funding for Mr. Bryant's new exercise facility, wasn't he?"

"Yes."

"Yet you didn't consider Mr. Bryant as a suspect, either?"

"We found no evidence."

"We saw video of Mr. Bryant shoving Mr. Blum. Yet you didn't consider the possibility that he waited for Mr. Blum behind the players' parking lot and hit him?"

"We found no evidence that he did so."

"And it wouldn't have fit within your theory of the case, right?"

"Objection. Argumentative."

"Sustained."

Nady kept going. "You are also aware Mr. Blum's former business partner, Jeff Franklin, was at the game that night?"

"Yes."

"Mr. Blum and Mr. Franklin had terminated their business relationship on acrimonious terms, hadn't they?"

"Yes."

"Mr. Franklin believed that Mr. Blum had stolen clients and money from him, didn't he?"

"So I've read."

"Mr. Franklin was also in the clubhouse after the game, wasn't he?"

"Yes."

"Did you consider the possibility that Mr. Franklin ran into Mr. Blum after the game? And that they argued? And that Mr. Franklin lost his temper and hit Mr. Blum?"

"We found no evidence."

"Because you had already decided to arrest Jaylen, right?"

"Objection."

"Sustained."

Turner got to her feet. "With respect, Your Honor, it appears that Ms. Nikonova's defense consists of accusing everybody at the Giants game of killing Mr. Blum."

That's the whole idea of a SODDI defense.

Judge Tsang kept his voice even. "The jury will disregard Ms. Turner's comment, which is neither a question of a witness nor testimony. You may continue, Ms. Nikonova."

"Thank you. Inspector, you also interviewed a man named Benjamin Logan, the owner of Bayshore Moving and Storage, right?"

"Right."

"Mr. Logan and Mr. Blum were gambling buddies who traveled to Las Vegas, right?"

"Yes."

"Mr. Blum also placed thousands of dollars of bets with Mr. Logan, for which Mr. Blum owed him a substantial amount of money, didn't he?"

"Mr. Logan has denied those allegations."

"You took his word for it?"

"I had no reason to disbelieve him."

"Because you had already arrested Jaylen, right?"

"Objection. Argumentative."

"Sustained."

Nady shook her head. "Mr. Logan was at the game that night, wasn't he?"

"Yes."

"Yet you didn't consider him as a suspect in connection with Mr. Blum's death?"

"We found no evidence of any gambling debt or confirmation that he was anywhere near the spot where Mr. Blum's body was found."

"Mr. Logan employs a man named Kevin Killian, doesn't he?"

"Yes."

"In addition to his regular job, he handles personal matters for Mr. Logan, doesn't he?"

"Yes."

"Among other items, Mr. Killian collects bets for Mr. Logan, doesn't he?"

"Mr. Killian denied it."

"And you took his word for it, too?"

"I had no reason to disbelieve him."

"Did you consider the possibility that Mr. Logan sent Mr. Killian to collect his gambling winnings from Mr. Blum? And that Mr. Blum refused to pay?"

"We found no evidence."

"Did you consider the possibility that Mr. Killian hit him? And whether it was intentional or an accident, that Mr. Killian killed him?"

"We found no evidence that Mr. Killian was anywhere near the ballpark that night."

"It seems to me that you didn't look very hard."

"Objection. Argumentative."

"Sustained."

Just one more reputation to trash.

Nady locked eyes with Lee. "Inspector, you interviewed a man named Brian Holton in connection with Mr. Blum's death, didn't you?"

"Yes."

"Mr. Holton isn't available to testify, is he?"

"He was stabbed to death by a man with whom he had a dispute over a drug deal."

"Mr. Blum bought drugs from Mr. Holton, didn't he?"

"We believe so."

"Mr. Blum owed Mr. Holton a substantial sum, didn't he? And Mr. Holton was upset about not being paid, wasn't he?"

"We found no evidence."

"You were here when we saw Mr. Holton appear in a security video taken outside the ballpark at eleven-forty that night, weren't you?"

"Yes."

"So you would acknowledge that Mr. Holton was within a few hundred feet of where Mr. Blum's body was found just a few minutes before Mr. Blum died?"

"Yes."

"Did you consider the possibility that Mr. Holton came looking for Mr. Blum? And that he and Mr. Blum argued over money? And that Mr. Holton lost his temper and killed him?"

"We found no evidence."

"You think he was just out for a walk that night?"

"I don't know."

"And we can't ask Mr. Holton about it because he died a few weeks later, right?"

"Right."

"Looks to me that you didn't look very hard for other suspects."

"Objection."

"Withdrawn," Nady said. "No further questions."

"Cross-exam, Ms. Turner?"

"No questions, Your Honor."

Judge Tsang glanced at his watch. "It's almost four o'clock. I am going to adjourn until tomorrow morning. How many more witnesses do you anticipate calling, Ms. Nikonova?"

"Just one, Your Honor."

57
"IT ISN'T ENOUGH"

"Are you going to have Jaylen testify?" Rosie asked.

I looked up from my laptop. "No."

"It isn't enough," she said.

"I disagree."

"I thought you were going to put him on the stand to issue a forceful denial."

"We were," I said. "We've reconsidered. He isn't in the right frame of mind."

"Then you'll need to get him into the right frame of mind."

Rosie, Nady, and I were sitting in Rosie's office after court. The heat was oppressive. The mood was glum.

Rosie wasn't finished. "It will impress the jury if Jaylen stands up for himself."

Nady shook her head. "Turner will rip him to shreds."

"You got anything else?"

"Pete is looking at more video."

"It's too late for new evidence. Are our jury instructions ready?"

"Yes. We're going to ask the judge to instruct for manslaughter in addition to murder."

"I would ask for the same thing. Are you ready to deliver your closing argument tomorrow?"

"All set."

"What's the narrative?"

"The prosecution hasn't proved its case beyond a reasonable doubt. Blum had a lot of enemies and owed a lot of people money. One of them got mad and killed him."

* * *

I walked into Nady's office at ten-forty-five the same night. "You want to go through your closing again?" I asked.

"Yes. I'll come down to your office in a minute."

"You okay?"

"Fine."

I pointed at Luna, who was sleeping in the corner. "She okay?"

"Couldn't be happier."

"Great." I inhaled the stale air and looked over at the desk in the corner, where Pete was staring at security videos on his laptop. An uneaten slice of pizza was on the desk next to an empty Coke can. "You need anything?"

He didn't look up. "I'm fine, Mick."

"You want another Coke?"

"Sounds good."

"You still looking at video?"

"Yeah."

"You got anything?"

He finally looked at me. "I might."

58
"BUILDING SECURITY"

Nady stood at the lectern at nine-thirty the next morning, a Wednesday. Our trial had started a week earlier, but it felt as if we'd been going much longer. "Would you please state your name for the record?"

"Heather Stewart."

I glanced at Turner and Erickson, who were frantically trying to figure out who she was. Nady and I had included Heather's name among dozens on our witness list.

"What is your occupation, Ms. Stewart?" Nady asked.

"Building security. Eighty-eight King Street condominium complex."

"That's across the street from the Giants ballpark?"

"Yes, ma'am. Near the Gaylord Perry statue."

We had asked Heather to wear her uniform: maroon blazer, white dress shirt, black necktie.

Nady remained at the lectern. "How long have you worked at your current position?"

"Twelve years."

"What did you do previously?"

"I was in law enforcement."

Well, sort of. She had mastered clipped cop dialect, but she had never been a police officer. Pete had explained that Heather wanted to follow in the footsteps of her father, a Daly City police sergeant, but she couldn't pass the Academy's physical test. She took a job cataloguing evidence and eventually became the executive assistant to the Daly City Police Chief until she was laid off during the Great Recession.

Nady addressed the judge. "May we approach the witness, Your Honor?"

"You may.'

I stole a glance at Rosie, whose expression betrayed no emotion. Pete was sitting in the back row. He gave me a reassuring nod.

Nady's voice was even. "Ms. Stewart, what does your job entail?"

"I am stationed at the security console at the King Street entrance to our building. I greet residents as they enter and exit, sign in visitors, monitor our security cameras, accept deliveries, and deal with service and maintenance personnel. I am trained to provide first aid and respond to emergencies. I handle other issues as they arise and summon assistance if necessary."

"Do you enjoy your work?"

"I do. I find it rewarding to provide a secure environment for our residents."

"If somebody needs medical attention, they would contact you first?"

"Yes, ma'am. Safety is our first priority."

She struck me as the type who had memorized the safety posters in her break room.

"Ms. Stewart," Nady continued, "you get to know the residents pretty well, don't you?"

"Yes, ma'am. We memorize their names so that we can greet them individually."

"Your building has multiple security cameras inside and out?"

"Dozens. Every entrance and exit, including the garage doors."

"Were you working on the night of Monday, June first, of this year?"

"Yes, ma'am. I arrived at ten p.m. My shift lasted until eight o'clock the following morning. Ordinarily, I don't work nights, but I picked up an extra shift to cover for a colleague."

"Was it busy?"

"Not especially. There's more activity in the vicinity when the Giants are playing."

Turner stood and spoke in a respectful tone. "Your Honor, with all due respect to Ms. Stewart, we fail to see any relevance to her testimony."

Nady waved her off. "I'm getting to that right now, Your Honor."

"You may proceed, Ms. Nikonova."

Nady activated the TV next to the box. "Ms. Stewart, were you at your post at eleven-fifty-nine p.m. on Monday, June first?"

"Yes, ma'am."

"You provided us with this security video from that night, didn't you?"

"Yes, ma'am."

Nady introduced the video into evidence. Then she started the video and stopped it an instant later. Unlike the grainy black-and-white footage from cameras in convenience stores, the HD video was in color. "Would you please confirm that this was taken by the camera in the lobby next to your security console?"

"Yes, ma'am."

The jurors focused on the TV. It was a reminder that trials are theater where it is better to give them something to watch than to have somebody describe it.

Nady kept her tone conversational. "You were present when it was taken?"

"Yes, ma'am."

Nady ran the video for a few seconds, then stopped it again. "Someone left the building at eleven-fifty-nine, right?"

"Right."

"Do you recognize that person?"

"Yes, ma'am." Heather pointed at the screen. "It's Ms. Foster."

"Jennifer Foster, the Giants broadcaster?"

"Yes, ma'am. She's very nice. When she isn't in a hurry, we talk about sports. She said that she was going out for a few minutes."

"Was it unusual for someone to leave the building at midnight?"

"Not really. People come and go at all hours."

"Did you see her image on any of your exterior cameras?"

"No, ma'am."

"Did she appear angry or upset?"

"Objection," Turner said. "Calls for the witness to read Ms. Foster's mind."

"No, it doesn't," Nady snapped. "I asked Ms. Stewart to describe Ms. Foster's demeanor."

"Overruled."

Heather shrugged. "She didn't appear angry or upset to me."

"Did you see her return?"

"Yes, ma'am. At twelve-twenty a.m."

Nady fast-forwarded the video to the point where Foster came back into the lobby. We saw her wave to Heather and head to the elevator. "This is where Ms. Foster returned?"

"Yes, ma'am."

"Did she say anything to you?"

"'Good night.'"

"No further questions, Your Honor."

"Cross-exam, Ms. Turner?"

"Just a couple of questions." Turner walked to the front of the box. "Ms. Stewart, you didn't see where Ms. Foster went, did you?"

"No, ma'am."

"And your security cameras didn't show her outside the building?"

"No, ma'am."

"So, all you know is that she went outside and returned twenty minutes later, right?"

"Right."

Turner glanced at the jury, then turned back to Heather. "I don't know what the defense is trying to show, Ms. Stewart, but just to be clear, the only thing you saw was Ms. Foster leaving the building and returning about twenty minutes later, right?"

"Right."

"You have no evidence that she was involved with the death of Robert Blum, do you?"

"No, ma'am."

"No further questions."

"Redirect, Ms. Nikonova?"

"No, Your Honor."

Judge Tsang looked at his watch. "I need to call a brief recess to deal with an administrative matter. Are you planning to call any additional witnesses?"

"Just one, Your Honor. We'd like to recall Jennifer Foster."

59
"YOU SURE YOU WANT TO DO THIS?"

Rosie sat at the table in the consultation room down the hall from Judge Tsang's courtroom, hands clasped. "You think it's a good idea to call Foster?"

Nady looked up from her laptop. "Yes."

Rosie looked my way. "You?"

I nodded. "It'll give the jurors another viable option. You've always said that if you can't give the jury a direct route to acquittal, then you should muddy the waters."

"I agree with myself, but there's a risk that we'll look desperate and piss them off."

"I'd rather take the offensive."

Rosie looked at Nady, who didn't hesitate.

"I agree with Mike. We probably won't get a Perry Mason moment, but it'll give the jury somebody else to think about." Nady closed her laptop. "What would you do?"

Rosie thought about it for a moment. "Exactly what you're doing."

"Good to hear." Nady stood up, but I stopped her before she reached the door.

"You sure you want to do this?" I asked.

"Yes."

"You may lose a friend."

"Being a Public Defender isn't a popularity contest."

"I can do her direct exam."

"It will be better for our client if I do it. Jen may look sympathetic if we have an older guy go after her."

I decided not to challenge her description that I was an "older guy." "I agree."

60
"I WENT OUT FOR SOME AIR"

Judge Tsang spoke to Foster, who had taken her seat in the box. "I remind you that you're still under oath."

"Yes, Your Honor." She adjusted the microphone like a professional announcer and looked up at Nady, who was standing at the lectern.

"Would you care for some water, Ms. Foster?"

"No, thank you, Ms. Nikonova."

"May we approach the witness, Your Honor?"

"You may."

Nady moved to the front of the box. "You conducted post-game interviews from the Giants clubhouse on the night of June first of this year?"

"Yes."

"Was it crowded?"

"Yes."

"Just players and coaches?"

"Mostly. There were also broadcasters, camera people, print reporters, management people, and a few others."

Nady moved a little closer. "Did you see the decedent, Robert Blum?"

"Yes."

"Did you talk to him?"

"Briefly."

"You testified earlier that you knew him both professionally and personally."

"Correct."

"You ended your brief relationship with Mr. Blum, didn't you?"

A hesitation. "As I mentioned in my earlier testimony, it wasn't a good fit."

"He mistreated you, didn't he?"

"It wasn't a good fit," Foster repeated.

"He was abusive, wasn't he?"

Foster's eyes narrowed. "At times."

Nady took a deep breath. "He hit you, didn't he?"

Foster froze. "He tried once."

"That's why you terminated your relationship, isn't it?"

Foster nodded.

Nady lowered her voice. "But that wasn't the end of it, was it?"

No answer.

"He kept calling and texting, didn't he?"

Still no answer.

Nady looked at the judge, who spoke in a gentle voice. "You'll need to answer Ms. Nikonova's questions."

"Yes."

Nady's voice was calm. "He wouldn't leave you alone, would he?"

Turner started to stand, but she reconsidered.

"No," Foster said.

Nady gave her old housemate a moment to get her bearings. "The harassment continued for months, didn't it?"

"Yes."

"He was stalking you, wasn't he?"

Foster's lips turned down. "Yes."

"He spoke to you in the clubhouse that night, didn't he?"

"Yes."

"He asked to see you, didn't he?"

"Yes."

"And you refused?"

"Of course."

"He insisted that you meet him outside the ballpark to clear the air, didn't he?"

"No."

"And you agreed to meet him to tell him once more to leave you alone, didn't you?"

"No."

Nady responded with an inquisitive expression. "You're saying that you never left your apartment that night?"

Another hesitation. "I went out for some air."

Nady cued the security video from Foster's building and narrated as Foster watched in silence. "Here's where you left your building at one minute before midnight."

"I went out for some air," Foster repeated.

Nady played more of the video. "Here we see you returning at twelve-twenty-two a.m. You went across the street and saw Robbie Blum, didn't you?"

"No."

"And you told him to leave you alone, didn't you?"

"No."

"And you told him that if he refused, you would get a restraining order, right?"

"No."

Nady let her answer hang.

Foster's voice cracked. "I told him several weeks earlier that I would get a restraining order, sue him for harassment, and call the police." She swallowed. "He told me that I wouldn't have the guts to do it—that he was 'untouchable.'"

"He mocked you."

A nod.

"He demeaned you. He humiliated you."

Another nod.

"And that night, he put his hands on you, didn't he?"

Foster swallowed but didn't answer.

"And you reacted, didn't you?"

"No."

"You grabbed the bat that he had taken for his son. And you hit him. Maybe you didn't mean to hurt him, but you acted in self-defense, right?"

"No."

"And he fell into the water. And you tossed the bat into the water, too."

"No."

Nady looked my way and I closed my eyes. She turned around and said, "No further questions, Your Honor."

"Cross-exam, Ms. Turner?"

"Just one question, Your Honor. Ms. Foster, did you kill Robbie Blum?"

"No."

"No further questions."

"Any additional witnesses, Ms. Nikonova?"

"No, Your Honor. The defense rests."

"We will begin closing arguments after lunch. Hopefully, we'll be in a position to instruct the jury later this afternoon."

61
"HARD TO SAY"

"Your closing was excellent," I said.

Nady looked up from her computer. "I did what I had to do."

Rosie spoke up. "You did very well."

Nady, Rosie, Pete, and I were in the conference room at the P.D.'s Office at four-thirty on Wednesday afternoon. The adrenaline rush of trial had transitioned into exhaustion. Turner and Nady had delivered passionate closing arguments. It was compelling theater to watch two up-and-coming lawyers go toe-to-toe. I gave the edge to Nady. The jurors were dialed in, but it was impossible to discern if they were leaning either way. The judge gave them our carefully negotiated instructions and sent them off to deliberate. In addition to first- and second-degree murder instructions, Judge Tsang elected to give manslaughter instructions. We returned to the office and spent the rest of the day second-guessing ourselves—a fruitless and utterly unproductive exercise. In reality, the only thing that we could do was wait.

Rosie touched Nady's forearm. "Your direct exam of Foster was very good."

"Thanks."

"It's hard to examine a friend."

"Ex-friend," Nady said.

"You did the right thing."

"Did I?"

"Yes. You provided a zealous defense for our client and acted within the bounds of the California Rules of Professional Conduct. That's what we do."

"I feel like crap."

Rosie pushed out a sigh. "I've been doing this a lot longer than you have. For what it's worth, I've never handled a more difficult direct exam."

"I accused her of murder."

"Unfortunately, the road to reasonable doubt for Jaylen ran through her."

"Do you think she killed Blum?"

"I don't know. And for our purposes, my opinion doesn't matter."

"What if they arrest her?"

"That's out of our hands. We have to let the system play out."

"The system sucks."

"Sometimes. We can only deal with things that we can control. Unfortunately, this isn't one of them."

We sat in silence for a long moment. Nady checked her e-mails. Rosie and I exchanged a glance. Pete took a sip of coffee as he looked at his phone.

Nady finally spoke up again. "How is LaTanya holding up?"

"She's worried," I said. "Terrence is keeping her company in my office."

"How long do you think the jury will be out?"

"Hard to say. You know that I never make predictions. It could be a few hours or a few days. I couldn't read them."

"Neither could I," Rosie said.

We turned to face Pete, who looked up from his phone.

"What?" he asked.

"What do you think?" I asked.

He responded with a shrug.

"Come on, Pete. You're the jury whisperer."

"They won't be out long."

"Which way do you think they're going to go?"

"Acquittal."

"Any particular reason why?"

"Never question the jury whisperer."

Rosie gave him a knowing smile. "How did you know to check the video from Foster's building?"

"I'm very thorough."

"Did Heather tip you off?"

"No."

"You played a hunch?"

"I played Nick the Dick's hunch. His instincts are still excellent. We aren't out of the woods. We proved that Foster went out for a walk around the time that Blum was killed. We didn't prove that she killed him."

"It may get the jury to reasonable doubt on Jaylen."

"Then it's a good result."

"How did you know that Heather would be willing to testify?"

The corner of Pete's mouth turned up. "That was my hunch."

I smiled at my perceptive kid brother. "I'll give you some extra twenties to put in her box of See's Candy at Christmas."

* * *

"You holding up okay?" I asked.

"Not so good," LaTanya said. "I went through this with my oldest son. The result wasn't good."

"It'll be better this time."

We were sitting in my office at five-thirty on Thursday afternoon. The jury had been out for twenty-four hours. LaTanya was nervous—legitimately so.

"Pete will take you back to the hotel," I said.

"Thank you."

"Do you have a place to stay after trial?"

"My sister said that I can stay with her for a few days. Hopefully, Jaylen will be with me."

"He will," I said, trying to sound confident.

Terrence knocked on the open door. "I just got a text from Judge Tsang's clerk. The jury reached a verdict. They want everybody back in court at ten o'clock tomorrow morning."

62
"WHAT SAY YOU?"

Judge Tsang's courtroom was silent except for the buzz of the fluorescent lights, the hum of the standing fan, and the sound of Harvey Tate flipping through his notebook. The gallery was full. People always show up for the ninth inning.

Jaylen was sitting between Nady and me. He appeared resigned to his fate—whichever way the jury went. He just wanted it to be over.

I glanced at his mother, who was sitting behind us, hands clasped, eyes shut, lips moving in silent prayer. I tried to give her a reassuring look, but her eyes remained closed. Rosie was next to her. Rosie never showed emotion in court. Pete was in his usual spot in the back row.

Judge Tsang tapped his microphone. "The defendant will please rise."

Jaylen lifted himself to his feet. Nady and I stood up with him. Attorneys are not required to stand during the reading of the verdict, but I've always done so in a show of solidarity.

The judge spoke to the foreperson. "Have you reached a verdict?"

The woman from PG&E answered him. "We have, Your Honor."

Time moved slowly as she handed the verdict to the bailiff, who delivered it to the judge, who studied it for a moment, nodded, and handed the slip of paper to the clerk.

"Please read the verdict."

"On the charge of murder in the first degree, the jury finds the defendant not guilty. On the charge of murder in the second degree, the jury also finds the defendant not guilty."

So far, so good.

"On the charge of voluntary manslaughter, the jury finds the defendant not guilty. On the charge of involuntary manslaughter, the jury finds the defendant not guilty.”

Yes!

Jaylen slid back into his chair, eyes filled with relief. Then he stood up, turned around, and hugged his mother, who was sobbing.

When your client is acquitted, the attorneys become bystanders. I looked over at a beaming Nady and nodded with admiration. I turned around and looked at Rosie—beautiful Rosie—whose expression hadn’t changed except for the triumphant glow in her eyes. She allowed herself a satisfied smile, then she turned to Nady and mouthed the words, “Nice work.”

I looked past Rosie to Pete, whose stoic expression hadn’t changed. It was his way of saying, “Nice work, I told you so, and you owe me dinner.”

The judge gave us a moment to settle back into our seats. Then he asked the foreperson the obligatory question of whether the verdict was unanimous.

“Yes, Your Honor.”

“Thank you for your service.” After he excused the jurors, he spoke to Jaylen. “You are free to go, Mr. Jenkins. We wish you and your mother well.”

“Thank you, Your Honor.”

Everybody stood as Judge Tsang left the courtroom.

Jaylen took a moment to get his bearings. Finally, he spoke to Nady and me. “Thank you.”

Nady answered him. “You’re welcome.”

I motioned to his mother to join us. She came around and hugged her son.

After they separated, I said, “You have some catching up to do.”

Jaylen nodded. “We have no place to live.”

His mother smiled through her tears. “My sister said that we can stay with her for a few days. Then we’ll figure out what happens next.”

It’s a start. “We’ll take you downstairs to get Jaylen’s belongings,” I said. “Pete will give you a ride to your sister’s house.”

“Can we buy you a celebratory lunch?” LaTanya asked.

"After you get settled. I want to get you and Jaylen out of here right away."

Nady and I collected our briefcases. Rosie joined us as we escorted Jaylen and LaTanya out of the courtroom, where Pete was waiting for us in the hallway.

"Nice work," I said to him. "Thanks for everything."

"You're welcome, Mick."

I felt a tap on my shoulder. I turned around and looked into the eyes of Andy Erickson.

"Congratulations," he said. "You and Nady did a nice job."

"Thank you."

"Can I talk to you for a minute?"

"I'm usually the one who accosts you in the corridor."

His expression didn't change. "In private?"

"Sure."

* * *

Erickson and I were sitting in the back row of the gallery in Judge Tsang's otherwise empty courtroom. "Confidentially," he said, "we've asked Jennifer Foster to come in and talk to us. We've also pulled a warrant to search her condo."

"It would have been nice if you had done so before you arrested Jaylen."

He ignored the dig. "We'll see if there's enough evidence to file charges."

"Thanks for letting me know, Andy. Good luck."

63
"WELCOME TO PLANET EARTH"

The back room at Dunleavy's was quiet at eight o'clock the same night. A couple of off-duty cops were playing pool. The Giants game was on TV. The Daley and Fernandez clans were well represented.

Big John tossed his dish towel over his shoulder. "No Pete?"

"We gave him the night off," I said.

"What'll it be, lad?"

"Guinness."

"Good man." He turned to Rosie. "Same?"

"Yes, please."

His eyes turned to Nady. "And you?"

"In this fine establishment, I can't order anything but a Guinness."

"Good call, darlin'." Big John nodded at Nady's husband. "Max?"

"Same, Big John."

"Coming up." He pointed at Luna, who was sleeping under the table. "Anything for her?"

Nady answered him. "She's fine. Thanks for letting us bring her inside."

"She's always welcome. When you were a kid in Uzbekistan, did you ever think you'd be drinking Irish beer in a homely pub in a foggy place called San Francisco?"

"No, Big John."

"As of tonight, you're an honorary Daughter of the Emerald Isle."

"I'm honored. I'll bet I'm the first Jewish woman from Uzbekistan who's ever received that title."

"I suspect you're right. I heard you got a good result today. Congratulations."

"Thank you."

He addressed Roosevelt, who was nursing a cup of coffee. "Let me heat that up for you."

"Thanks, John. That would be nice."

He turned to Rolanda, who was sitting between Rosie and Sylvia. "You and Zach getting any sleep?"

"Not much."

"Little ones mess with your minds for a few months. Then they take pity on you and let you sleep. Can I bring you anything?"

"Just water."

"Coming up." He spoke to Sylvia, who was rocking her sleeping great-granddaughter in her arms. "What can I get you?"

"Club soda, please."

"Thanks for coming over tonight, Sylvia."

"Happy to be here, John. We wanted you to meet the baby."

"Lovely to make her acquaintance."

"I wanted to be here for her first visit to Dunleavy's."

"I'm delighted, although I'm not sure that it's a great idea to bring a baby into a bar."

"You need to teach the little ones about the important things in life while they're still young." Sylvia's eyes gleamed. "Besides, this isn't just any bar. This is our family's bar. We've also decided to make you her honorary great-great-uncle."

"I'm honored." Big John's wide face transformed into a broad smile. "Tell me her full name again?"

"Maria Sylvia Teresa Fernandez Epstein."

He reached over and lightly touched the sleeping baby on the nose. "Hello, darlin'. Welcome to Planet Earth, Maria Sylvia Teresa Fernandez Epstein. Be kind to your mommy and daddy and let them sleep. And be extra kind to your Great-Grandma Sylvia. And drinks are on the house for the rest of your life."

* * *

Pete's name appeared on my phone as Rosie and I were pulling into Rosie's driveway at ten-thirty the same night. "I hope you aren't working," I said.

"Nope. I took Donna and Margaret out for dinner at the

Buckeye."

"Good. Send me the bill."

"I will. And you still owe me another dinner—a fancy one."

"You name the time and the place. Did you get Jaylen and LaTanya settled in at LaTanya's sister's house?"

"Yes. It's going to be an uphill climb, but they're in a better place than they were this morning."

"Thanks to you."

"In part."

"In *large* part." I waited a beat. "Andy Erickson told me that he asked Jen Foster to come in for questioning."

"I heard. Any word?"

"Not yet."

"You think she killed Blum?"

"I'm not sure, Pete."

"You think Erickson will file charges?"

"Hard to say. If he does, it's going to be a tough case to prove. And even if Foster admits to killing Blum, she may claim self-defense. It will be difficult to disprove unless he finds another witness."

My ever-practical brother chuckled. "The only other witness was Blum. As far as I know, he's still dead, Mick."

64
"IT'S AWFULLY QUIET"

Three days later, Rosie took a sip of Pride Mountain Cab Franc—her favorite. "It's awfully quiet."

"It is," I said. "I liked Tommy's roommate."

"So did I." She grinned. "Did it make you feel old seeing Tommy living in the same dorm where you lived forty years ago?"

"Nostalgic."

"Were you always this diplomatic when you were a priest?"

"No. It's a big reason why I'm no longer a priest."

The flickering light from a candle on the coffee table in her living room reflected in her eyes. "I'll bet you were a better priest than you let on. Still glad you became a lawyer?"

"Absolutely. For one, I'm pretty sure that I'm a better lawyer than a priest. And for two, if I hadn't, I wouldn't have met you, and Grace and Tommy never would have been born."

She raised her glass. "I'd say things worked out pretty well."

I tapped her glass. "So would I."

At ten p.m. on Monday, August seventeenth, Rosie and I were sitting on opposite ends of her sofa. We had spent the day moving Tommy into his dorm at Cal, getting his computer set up, and buying him books. We took him out for dinner along with Grace and her boyfriend, Chuck. We offered to take them someplace fancy, but Tommy insisted on Juan's Place, an earthy restaurant in West Berkeley that was my go-to stop for cheap burritos when I was an undergrad. In those days, Juan's was in an industrial neighborhood where Dobermans patrolled the fenced parking lots of the surrounding buildings after dark. Over the years, the area gentrified, but Juan's didn't. Fancy lofts and trendy restaurants were now interspersed among the remaining auto body shops. The Dobermans were long gone, but the fajitas at Juan's were as good as ever.

Rosie took another sip of wine. "How do you feel about Tommy studying biology?"

"It's great. We already have two lawyers in the family, and Grace has a film degree. Now we'll have a doctor, so we'll have all of our needs covered."

"Mama is very pleased. She always wanted me to go to medical school."

"You would have been a fine doctor, but I think you found the right calling."

"So do I. It was nice of Grace and Chuck to join us. They seem good together."

"Agreed. More important, he treats her like royalty."

"As he should."

"Are you okay with him moving into her place?"

She nodded. "You?"

"Yes. I trust that he'll be making a contribution toward her mortgage?"

"Absolutely." She chuckled. "Grace wouldn't have let him move in otherwise."

True. Our entrepreneurial daughter developed a wildly successful relationship advice app when she was in college. She used the profits for a down payment on a condo a few blocks from the Pixar campus in Emeryville. When it came to business acumen and money, she was light years ahead of me.

I refilled my glass. "You think they'll get married?"

"Could be. This is the first time that Grace has moved in with a boyfriend."

Hmm. "Did she say anything to you?"

"No, but you saw the way that they looked at each other."

"I did. You up for planning a wedding?"

"Absolutely. She's our only daughter. Her wedding is going to be a lot nicer than ours. You understand that your role will be limited to writing checks, smiling, and agreeing with everything that Grace and I decide."

As always. "I do."

Rosie and I got married in an immediate-family-only ceremony at St. Peter's Catholic Church, around the corner from Sylvia's house. The rehearsal dinner was at Dunleavy's and featured a plentiful supply of Big John's fish and chips and copious amounts of Guinness and Jameson's. The reception was at the Brava Theater down the street from St. Peter's and across from the St. Francis Fountain, a century-old ice cream shop where my mom and dad took us to celebrate good report cards. Dinner was catered by La Taqueria on Mission Street. Tony's garage band provided the entertainment.

"Do you have a place in mind?" I asked.

"We'll do the ceremony at St. Peter's, but the reception is going to be someplace fancier than the Brava."

"I'll be there."

"Yes, you will." She got a faraway look in her eyes—I could tell that she was pondering all of the delicious possibilities. She refilled her glass and her expression turned serious. "Did you talk to Jaylen?"

"Briefly. He and LaTanya found a basement apartment in West Oakland. It'll be tight, but it'll work for now. Jaylen got a job at the Amazon distribution center in Richmond. He's also going to start taking classes at Laney College. LaTanya promised to go back into rehab."

"Is Jaylen going to continue selling T-shirts by the ballpark?"

"He's moving his business online."

"Sounds like a good plan." Her expression turned serious. "You and Nady got a good result for him."

"With a lot of help from Pete."

"As always." She put her glass down. "Any word about Jen Foster?"

"I talked to Andy Erickson. He isn't going to press charges. Foster and her lawyer came in and laid it out. She confessed to hitting Blum, but she said it was self-defense. Blum was stalking her. He asked her to meet him after the game to talk it out. She claimed that he took a swing at her. She grabbed the bat and hit him to protect herself. Andy believed her."

"That's a good result for her."

"It is. She's taking a little break from the Giants games."

"Have you told Nady?"

"Yes."

"How is she dealing with the fact that her former housemate killed Blum?"

"She's pretty shaken up. I told her to take some time off. Surprisingly, she agreed."

"It's out of character."

"She's learning to pace herself a little better."

"That's good. She's an excellent lawyer."

"She's ahead of where I was when I was her age."

"Maybe a little." Rosie's eyes narrowed. "I knew that you were the real deal when I met you. You were smart. And relentless. And creative. And you cared. Most important, I've never seen anybody better at connecting with juries."

"Good to hear."

"Nady will make an excellent co-head of the Felony Division if you ever retire."

"It isn't going to happen anytime soon. Besides, Rolanda is doing an excellent job."

"I have bigger plans for her."

I'm not surprised. "Are you going to talk to her about running for P.D. when you retire?"

"Possibly."

"You still have three years remaining on your term."

She flashed a sly grin. "It's better to start planning a few years in advance."

"You aren't going to retire, are you?"

"I'm going to finish my term. Then I'll find something else to do."

"Working as a lawyer?"

"Unless I come up with something better. Are you ever going to retire?"

"We still need to get Tommy through college. And I was just informed that we may be paying for a very expensive wedding in the not-too-distant future. Besides, I would go crazy at home. And I would drive you crazy."

She chuckled. "Probably true."

I looked at the latest photo of Rolanda's baby, which was sitting on the mantle. The picture was between Grace's college graduation photo from USC and Tommy's high school graduation photo from Redwood. "Everybody okay?"

"Fine. Maria gained a half pound last week. She slept three straight hours last night."

"How are their housing arrangements working out?"

"It's getting a little cramped."

Rolanda, Zach, and Maria had moved out of their one-bedroom apartment in the Mission and were staying at Sylvia's house for a few weeks until they could move into their new house around the corner from us. We had offered to let them stay with us, but Sylvia convinced them to stay with her.

I smiled. "I'm looking forward to hanging out with our new neighbors and babysitting our great-niece."

"Just like old times. You sure you're up for it?"

"If we stay with Maria on Saturday nights, we'll have all day Sunday to recover."

"I'll set up a schedule with Rolanda."

"Sounds great. How's your mother holding up with a newborn in the house?"

"She'll never admit that she's exhausted. And she couldn't be happier. She's ordering Rolanda and Zach around like they're her own kids."

"Old habits."

"Indeed. As much as they love Mama, they're ready to move into the new place." She grinned. "So?"

"So what?"

"Here we are again, Mike. Just the two of us. Back to where we started, except the house is a little bigger, we have a few more dollars in the bank, and we're a little older."

"I'd like to think that we're a little wiser, too."

"Hopefully." Her tone turned thoughtful. "Are you going to be able to deal with being an empty-nester?"

"I think so. You?"

"I think so. It will be nice to go out for dinner without having to worry about making Tommy do his homework."

"You think we'll be bored?"

"We'll find ways to fill the extra time. Are you planning to keep your apartment?"

"For now."

"You spend all of your time over here."

"Wilma the cat will miss me."

"She'll be fine, Mike. Why do you really want to keep the apartment?"

"I'm superstitious." I reached over and took her hand. "We started getting along better when I moved into the apartment. I don't want to jinx anything."

"After all these years, you're still worried about us?"

"I never take anything for granted—especially you."

"You're sweet. And you have nothing to worry about." She finished her wine and flashed the smile that still made my heart beat faster. "We'll have more time to travel. Maybe we can finally take Big John over to Ireland."

"I'd like that."

"And we'll have time for other recreational activities here at home."

"I'm available."

"Good." She stood up, grasped my hand, and looked down the hall at the bedroom. "I love you, Mike."

"I love you, too, Rosie."

ACKNOWLEDGMENTS

It takes a village to write a novel. Over the course of writing twelve Mike Daley/Rosie Fernandez stories, I have been fortunate to have an extraordinarily generous "board of advisors" who have graciously provided their time and expertise. I can't thank everybody, but I'm going to try!

Thanks to my beautiful wife, Linda, who reads my manuscripts, designs the covers, is my online marketing guru, and takes care of all things technological. I couldn't imagine trying to navigate the chaos of the publishing world without you.

Thanks to our son, Alan, for your endless support, editorial suggestions, thoughtful observations, and excellent cover art and formatting work. I will look forward to seeing your first novel on the shelves in bookstores in the near future.

Thanks to our son, Stephen, and our daughter-in-law, Lauren, for being kind, generous, and immensely talented people.

Thanks to my teachers, Katherine Forrest and Michael Nava, who encouraged me to finish my first book. Thanks to the Every Other Thursday Night Writers Group: Bonnie DeClark, Meg Stiefvater, Anne Maczulak, Liz Hartka, Janet Wallace, and Priscilla Royal. Thanks to Bill and Elaine Petrocelli, Kathryn Petrocelli, and Karen West at Book Passage.

A huge thanks to Jane Gorsi for your excellent editing skills.

A huge thanks to Linda Hall for your excellent editing skills, too.

Another huge thanks to Vilaska Nguyen of the San Francisco Public Defender's Office for your thoughtful comments and terrific support. If I ever get into serious trouble, you're my guy.

Thanks to Joan Lubamersky for providing the invaluable "Lubamersky Comments" for the twelfth time.

Thanks to Tim Campbell for your stellar narration of the audio version of this book (and many others in the series). You bring these stories to life!

Thanks to my friends and colleagues at Sheppard, Mullin,

Richter & Hampton (and your spouses and significant others). I can't mention everybody, but I'd like to note those of you with whom I've worked the longest: Randy and Mary Short, Chris and Debbie Neils, Joan Story and Robert Kidd, Donna Andrews, Phil and Wendy Atkins-Pattenson, Julie and Jim Ebert, Geri Freeman and David Nickerson, Bill and Barbara Manierre, Betsy McDaniel, Ron and Rita Ryland, Bob Stumpf, Mike Wilmar, Mathilde Kapuano, Susan Sabath, Guy Halgren, Ed Graziani, Julie Penney, Christa Carter, Doug Bacon, Lorna Tanner, Larry Braun, Nady Nikonova, Joy Siu, and DeAnna Ouderkirk.

Thanks to Jerry and Dena Wald, Gary and Marla Goldstein, Ron and Betsy Rooth, Jay Flaherty, Debbie and Seth Tanenbaum, Jill Hutchinson and Chuck Odenthal, Tom Bearrows and Holly Hirst, Julie Hart, Burt Rosenberg, Ted George, Phil Dito, Sister Karen Marie Franks, Chuck and Nora Koslosky, Jack Goldthorpe, Peter and Cathy Busch, Steve Murphy, Bob Dugoni, and John Lescroart. Thanks to Lloyd and Joni Russell and Rich and Leslie Kramer. Thanks to Gary and Debbie Fields. Thanks to the wonderful Mercedes Crosskill.

Thanks to Tim and Kandi Durst, Bob and Cheryl Easter, and Larry DeBrock at the University of Illinois. Thanks to Kathleen Vanden Heuvel, Bob and Leslie Berring, Jesse Choper, and Mel Eisenberg at Berkeley Law.

Thanks to the incomparable Zvi Danenberg, who motivates me to walk the Larkspur steps.

Thanks as always to Ben, Michelle, Margie, and Andy Siegel, Joe, Jan, and Julia Garber, Roger and Sharon Fineberg, Scott, Michelle, Kim, and Sophie Harris, Stephanie, Stanley, and Will Coventry, Cathy and Richard Falco, Matthew Falco and Sofia Arnell, and Julie Harris and Matthew, Aiden, and Ari Stewart. A huge thanks once again to our mothers, Charlotte Siegel (1928-2016) and Jan Harris (1934-2018), whom we miss every day.

A NOTE TO THE READER

I have been a baseball fan my whole life. When I was growing up in Chicago, my goal was to be the starting centerfielder for the White Sox. When that didn't work out, I went to Plan B: writing stories. The best job that I ever had (other than writing novels) was working as a security guard at Wrigley Field during the summer when I was in college. I got paid three dollars and sixty cents an hour to watch baseball. Not bad, eh?

I hope you liked **FINAL OUT**. I enjoy spending time with Mike & Rosie, and I hope that you do too. If you like my stories, please consider posting an honest review on Amazon or Goodreads. Your words matter and are a great guide to help my stories find future readers.

If you have a chance and would like to chat, please feel free to e-mail me at **sheldon@sheldonsiegel.com**. We lawyers don't get a lot of fan mail, but it's always nice to hear from my readers. Please bear with me if I don't respond immediately. I answer all of my e-mail myself, so sometimes it takes a little extra time.

Many people have asked to know more about Mike and Rosie's early history. As a thank you to my readers, I wrote **FIRST TRIAL.** It's a short story describing how they met years ago when they were just starting out at the P.D.'s Office. I've included the first chapter below and the full story is available at: **www.sheldonsiegel.com**.

Also on the website, you can read more about how I came to write my stories, excerpts and behind-the-scenes from the other Mike & Rosie novels and a few other goodies! Let's stay connected. Thanks for reading my story!

Regards,
Sheldon

FIRST TRIAL

A Mike Daley/Rosie Fernandez Story

1

"DO EXACTLY WHAT I DO"

The woman with the striking cobalt eyes walked up to me and stopped abruptly. "Are you the new file clerk?"

"Uh, no." My lungs filled with the stale air in the musty file room of the San Francisco Public Defender's Office on the third floor of the Stalinesque Hall of Justice on Bryant Street. "I'm the new lawyer."

The corner of her mouth turned up. "The priest?"

"Ex-priest."

"I thought you'd be older."

"I was a priest for only three years."

"You understand that we aren't in the business of saving souls here, right?"

"Right."

Her full lips transformed into a radiant smile as she extended a hand. "Rosie Fernandez."

"Mike Daley."

"You haven't been working here for six months, have you?"

"This is my second day."

"Welcome aboard. You passed the bar, right?"

"Right."

"That's expected."

I met Rosita Carmela Fernandez on the Wednesday after Thanksgiving in 1983. The Summer of Love was a fading memory, and we were five years removed from the Jonestown massacre and the assassinations of Mayor George Moscone and Supervisor Harvey Milk. Dianne Feinstein became the mayor and was governing with a steady hand in Room 200 at City Hall. The biggest movie of the year was *Return of the Jedi,* and the highest-rated TV show was *M*A*S*H.* People still communicated by phone and U.S. mail because e-mail wouldn't become widespread for another decade. We listened to music on LPs and cassettes, but CD players were starting to gain traction. It was still unclear whether VHS or Beta would be the predominant video platform. The Internet was a localized technology used for academic purposes on a few college campuses. Amazon and Google wouldn't be formed for another decade. Mark Zuckerberg hadn't been born.

Rosie's hoop-style earrings sparkled as she leaned against the metal bookcases crammed with dusty case files for long-forgotten defendants. "You local?"

"St. Ignatius, Cal, and Boalt. You?"

"Mercy, State, and Hastings." She tugged at her denim work shirt, which seemed out-of-place in a button-down era where men still wore suits and ties and women wore dresses to the office. "When I was at Mercy, the sisters taught us to beware of boys from S.I."

"When I was at S.I., the brothers taught us to beware of girls from Mercy."

"Did you follow their advice?"

"Most of the time."

The Bay Area was transitioning from the chaos of the sixties and the malaise of the seventies into the early stages of the tech boom. Apple had recently gone public and was still being run by Steve Jobs and Steve Wozniak. George Lucas was making Star Wars movies in a new state-of-the-art facility in Marin County. Construction cranes dotted downtown as new office towers were changing the skyline. Union Square was beginning a makeover after Nieman-Marcus bought out the City of Paris and built a flashy new store at the corner of Geary and Stockton, across from I. Magnin. The upstart 49ers had won their first Super Bowl behind a charismatic quarterback named Joe Montana and an innovative coach named Bill Walsh.

Her straight black hair shimmered as she let out a throaty laugh.

"What parish?"

"Originally St. Peter's. We moved to St. Anne's when I was a kid. You?"

"St. Peter's. My parents still live on Garfield Square."

"Mine grew up on the same block."

St. Peter's Catholic Church had been the anchor of the Mission District since 1867. In the fifties and sixties, the working-class Irish and Italian families had relocated to the outer reaches of the City and to the suburbs. When they moved out, the Latino community moved in. St. Peter's was still filled every Sunday morning, but four of the five masses were celebrated in Spanish.

"I was baptized at St. Peter's," I said. "My parents were married there."

"Small world."

"How long have you worked here?" I asked.

"Two years. I was just promoted to the Felony Division."

"Congratulations."

"Thank you. I need to transition about six dozen active misdemeanor cases to somebody else. I trust that you have time?"

"I do."

"Where do you sit?"

"In the corner of the library near the bathrooms."

"I'll find you."

* * *

Twenty minutes later, I was sitting in my metal cubicle when I was startled by the voice from the file room. "Ever tried a case?" Rosie asked.

"It's only my second day."

"I'm going to take that as a no. Ever been inside a courtroom?"

"Once or twice."

"To work?"

"To watch."

"You took Criminal Law at Boalt, right?"

"Right."

"And you've watched Perry Mason on TV?"

"Yes."

"Then you know the basics. The courtrooms are upstairs." She handed me a file. "Your first client is Terrence Love."

"The boxer?"

"The retired boxer.'

Terrence "The Terminator" Love was a six-foot-six-inch, three-hundred-pound small-time prizefighter who had grown up in the projects near Candlestick Park. His lifetime record was two wins and nine losses. The highlight of his career was when he was hired to be a sparring partner for George Foreman, who was training to fight Muhammad Ali at the time. Foreman knocked out The Terminator with the first punch that he threw—effectively ending The Terminator's careers as a boxer and a sparring partner.

"What's he doing these days?" I asked.

"He takes stuff that doesn't belong to him."

"Last time I checked, stealing was against the law."

"Your Criminal Law professor would be proud."

"What does he do when he isn't stealing?"

"He drinks copious amounts of King Cobra."

It was cheap malt liquor.

She added, "He's one of our most reliable customers."

Got it. "How often does he get arrested?"

"At least once or twice a month."

"How often does he get convicted?"

"Usually once or twice a month." She flashed a knowing smile. "You and Terrence are going to get to know each other very well."

I got the impression that it was a rite of passage for baby P.D.'s to cut their teeth representing The Terminator. "What did he do this time?"

She held up a finger. "Rule number one: a client hasn't 'done' anything unless he admits it as part of a plea bargain, or he's convicted by a jury. Until then, all charges are 'alleged.'"

"What is the D.A. *alleging* that Terrence did?"

"He *allegedly* broke into a car that didn't belong to him."

"Did he *allegedly* take anything?"

"He didn't have time. A police officer was standing next to him when he *allegedly* broke into the car. The cop arrested him on the spot."

"Sounds like Terrence isn't the sharpest instrument in the operating room."

"We don't ask our clients to pass an intelligence test before we represent them. For a guy who used to make a living trying to beat the daylights out of his opponents, Terrence is reasonably intelligent and a nice person who has never hurt anybody. The D.A. charged him with auto burglary."

"Can we plead it out?"

"*We* aren't going to do anything. *You* are going to handle this case. And contrary to what you've seen on TV, our job is to try cases, not to cut quick deals. Understood?"

"Yes."

"I had a brief discussion about a plea bargain with Bill McNulty, who is the Deputy D.A. handling this case. No deal unless Terrence pleads guilty to a felony."

"Seems a bit harsh."

"It is. That's why McNulty's nickname is 'McNasty.' You'll be seeing a lot of him, too. He's a hardass who is trying to impress his boss. He's also very smart and tired of seeing Terrence every couple of weeks. In fairness, I can't blame him."

"So you want me to take this case to trial?"

"That's what we do. Trial starts Monday at nine a.m. before Judge Stumpf." She handed me a manila case file. "Rule number two: know the record. You need to memorize everything inside. Then you should go upstairs to the jail and introduce yourself to your new client."

I could feel my heart pounding. "Could I buy you a cup of coffee and pick your brain about how you think it's best for me to prepare?"

"I haven't decided whether you're coffee-worthy yet."

"Excuse me?"

"I'm dealing with six dozen active cases. By the end of the week, so will you. If you want to be successful, you need to figure stuff out on your own."

I liked her directness. "Any initial hints that you might be willing to pass along?"

"Yes. Watch me. Do exactly what I do."

"Sounds like good advice."

She grinned. "It is."

There's more to this story and it's yours for FREE!

Get the rest of **FIRST TRIAL** at:

www.sheldonsiegel.com/first-trial

ABOUT THE AUTHOR

Sheldon Siegel is the New York Times best-selling author of twelve critically acclaimed legal thrillers featuring San Francisco criminal defense attorneys Mike Daley and Rosie Fernandez, two of the most beloved characters in contemporary crime fiction. He is also the author of the thriller novel The Terrorist Next Door featuring Chicago homicide detectives David Gold and A.C. Battle. His books have been translated into a dozen languages and sold millions of copies. A native of Chicago, Sheldon earned his undergraduate degree from the University of Illinois in Champaign in 1980, and his law degree from Berkeley Law in 1983. He specializes in corporate law with the San Francisco office of the international law firm of Sheppard, Mullin, Richter & Hampton.

Sheldon began writing his first book, Special Circumstances, on a laptop computer during his daily commute on the ferry from Marin County to San Francisco. A frequent speaker and sought-after teacher, Sheldon is a San Francisco Library Literary Laureate, a former member of the Board of Directors and former President of the Northern California chapter of the Mystery Writers of America, and an active member of the International Thriller Writers and Sisters in Crime. His work has been displayed at the Bancroft Library at the University of California at Berkeley, and he has been recognized as a Distinguished Alumnus of the University of Illinois and a Northern California Super Lawyer.

Sheldon lives in the San Francisco area with his wife, Linda. Sheldon and Linda are the proud parents of twin sons named Alan and Stephen. Sheldon is a lifelong fan of the Chicago Bears, White Sox, Bulls and Blackhawks. He is currently working on his next novel.

Sheldon welcomes your comments and feedback. Please email him at sheldon@sheldonsiegel.com. For more information on Sheldon, book signings, the "making of" his books, and more, please visit his website at www.sheldonsiegel.com.

ACCLAIM FOR
SHELDON SIEGEL'S NOVELS

Featuring Mike Daley and Rosie Fernandez

SPECIAL CIRCUMSTANCES

"An A+ first novel." *Philadelphia Inquirer*.

"A poignant, feisty tale. Characters so finely drawn you can almost smell their fear and desperation." *USA Today*.

"By the time the whole circus ends up in the courtroom, the hurtling plot threatens to rip paper cuts into the readers' hands." *San Francisco Chronicle*.

INCRIMINATING EVIDENCE

"Charm and strength. Mike Daley is an original and very appealing character in the overcrowded legal arena—a gentle soul who can fight hard when he has to, and a moral man who is repelled by the greed of many of his colleagues." *Publishers Weekly*.

"The story culminates with an outstanding courtroom sequence. Daley narrates with a kind of genial irony, the pace never slows, and every description of the city is as brightly burnished as the San Francisco sky when the fog lifts." *Newark Star-Ledger*.

"For those who love San Francisco, this is a dream of a novel that capitalizes on the city's festive and festering neighborhoods of old-line money and struggling immigrants. Siegel is an astute observer of the city and takes wry and witty jabs at lawyers and politicians." *USA Today*.

CRIMINAL INTENT

"Ingenious. A surprise ending that will keep readers yearning for more." *Booklist.*

"Siegel writes with style and humor. The people who populate his books are interesting. He's a guy who needs to keep that laptop popping." *Houston Chronicle.*

"Siegel does a nice job of blending humor and human interest. Daley and Fernandez are competent lawyers, not superhuman crime fighters featured in more commonplace legal thrillers. With great characters and realistic dialogue, this book provides enough intrigue and courtroom drama to please any fan of the genre." *Library Journal.*

FINAL VERDICT

"Daley's careful deliberations and ethical considerations are a refreshing contrast to the slapdash morality and breakneck speed of most legal thrillers. The detailed courtroom scenes are instructive and authentic, the resolution fair, dramatic and satisfying. Michael, Rosie, Grace and friends are characters worth rooting for. The verdict is clear: another win for Siegel." *Publishers Weekly.*

"An outstanding entry in an always reliable series. An ending that's full of surprises—both professional and personal—provides the perfect finale to a supremely entertaining legal thriller." *Booklist.*

"San Francisco law partners Mike Daley and Rosie Fernandez spar like Tracy and Hepburn. Final Verdict maintains a brisk pace, and there's genuine satisfaction when the bad guy gets his comeuppance." *San Francisco Chronicle.*

THE CONFESSION

"As Daley moves from the drug and prostitute-ridden underbelly of San Francisco, where auto parts and offers of legal aid are exchanged for cooperation, to the tension-filled courtroom and the hushed offices of the church, it gradually becomes apparent that Father Ramon isn't the only character with a lot at stake in this intelligent, timely thriller." *Publishers Weekly*.

"This enthralling novel keeps reader attention with one surprise after another. The relationship between Mike and Rosie adds an exotic dimension to this exciting courtroom drama in which the defense and the prosecutor interrogation of witnesses make for an authentic, terrific tale." *The Best Reviews*.

"Sheldon Siegel is to legal thrillers as Robin Cook is to medical thrillers." *Midwest Book Review*.

JUDGMENT DAY

"Drug dealers, wily lawyers, crooked businessmen, and conflicted cops populate the pages of this latest in a best-selling series from Sheldon Siegel. A compelling cast and plenty of suspense put this one right up there with the best of Lescroart and Turow." *Booklist Starred Review*.

"An exciting and suspenseful read—a thriller that succeeds both as a provocative courtroom drama and as a personal tale of courage and justice. With spine-tingling thrills and a mind-blowing finish, this novel is a must, must read." *New Mystery Reader*.

"It's a good year when Sheldon Siegel produces a novel. Siegel has written an adrenaline rush of a book. The usual fine mix from a top-notch author." *Shelf Awareness*.

PERFECT ALIBI

"Siegel, an attorney-author who deserves to be much more well-known than he is, has produced another tightly plotted, fluidly written legal thriller. Daley and Fernandez are as engaging as when we first met them in Special Circumstances, and the story is typically intricate and suspenseful. Siegel is a very talented writer, stylistically closer to Turow than Grisham, and this novel should be eagerly snapped up by fans of those giants (and also by readers of San Francisco-set legal thrillers of John Lescroart)." *Booklist*.

"Sheldon Siegel is a practicing attorney and the married father of twin sons. He knows the law and he knows the inner workings of a family. This knowledge has given him a great insight in the writing of Perfect Alibi, which for Siegel fans is his almost perfect book." *Huffington Post.*

FELONY MURDER RULE

"Outstanding! Siegel's talent shines in characters who are sharp, witty, and satirical, and in the intimate details of a San Francisco insider. Nobody writes dialogue better. The lightning quick pace is reminiscent of Elmore Leonard—Siegel only writes the good parts." *Robert Dugoni, New York Times and Amazon best-selling author of MY SISTER'S GRAVE.*

SERVE AND PROTECT

An Amazon rating of 4.5/5. Readers say: "A strong, thought-provoking novel. It is a page-turner and well worth the time and effort." "His stories are believable and entertaining. The main characters are written with human foibles. With everyday problems they reflect real life." "Sheldon keeps the reader involved, wondering and anxious to read the next line... And the real magic is the ability of the author to keep the reader involved up to and including the very last page."

HOT SHOT

With over 300 amazon reviews and an average of 4.6/5 stars. "The reader gets an inside view of Silicon Valley and is allowed us to see its very dark side. What a hornet's nest of cutthroat people only concerned for two things - themselves and money!"

"Sheldon Siegel is a great storyteller... One of my favourite parts of this series is reading what Mike thinks — I love his sense of humour!"

THE DREAMER

An average of 4.5/5 stars Amazon rating. "Celebration is in order when a new Mike Daley and Rosie Fernandez legal thrillers is released. Sheldon Siegel's San Francisco-based series always fits the times. In THE DREAMER, the brisk, whip-smart dialogue, the familiar cast of characters (including nonagenarian Nick the Dick), and Siegel's masterful portrayal of The City are hallmarks of the series.

Featuring Detective Gold and Detective A.C. Battle

THE TERRORIST NEXT DOOR

"Chicago Detectives David Gold and A.C. Battle are strong entries in the police-thriller sweepstakes, with Sheldon Siegel's THE TERRORIST NEXT DOOR, a smart, surprising and bloody take on the world of Islamic terror. As a crazed bomber threatens to shut down American's third-largest city, the Chicago cops, the FBI, Homeland Security and even the military sift through every available clue to the bomber's identity, reaching for a climax that is both shocking and credible." *New York Times* best-selling author Sheldon Siegel tells a story that is fast and furious and authentic." *John Sandford. New York Times Best Selling author of the Lucas Davenport Prey series.*

"Sheldon Siegel blows the doors off with his excellent new thriller, THE TERRORIST NEXT DOOR. Bombs, car chases, the shutdown of Chicago, plus Siegel's winning touch with character makes this one not to be missed!" *John Lescroart. New York Times Best Selling Author of the Dismas Hardy novels.*

"Sheldon Siegel knows how to make us root for the good guys in this heart-stopping terrorist thriller, and David Gold and A.C. Battle are a pair of very good guys." *Thomas Perry. New York Times Best Selling Author of POISON FLOWER.*

ALSO BY SHELDON SIEGEL

Connect with Sheldon

Email:	sheldon@sheldonsiegel.com
Website:	www.sheldonsiegel.com
Amazon:	amazon.com/author/sheldonsiegel
Facebook:	www.facebook.com/SheldonSiegelAuthor
Goodreads:	goodreads.com/author/show/69191.Sheldon_Siegel
Bookbub:	bookbub.com/authors/sheldon-siegel
Twitter:	@SheldonSiegel

Made in the USA
Coppell, TX
01 February 2021

49418750R00174